MISTER
MONEYBAGS

VI KEELAND
PENELOPE WARD

MISTER MONEYBAGS

Edited by: Elaine York, Allusion Graphics, LLC/
Publishing & Book Formatting
Cover model: Richeli Murari
Cover designer: Letitia Hasser, r.b.a. designs
Formatted by: Elaine York, Allusion Graphics, LLC/
Publishing & Book Formatting

The truth is rarely pure and never simple.

– Oscar Wilde

CHAPTER 1

Bianca

It figures the asshole's company would occupy the entire top floor.

I pushed the button on the elevator panel and finished typing a half-ass list of interview questions into my phone. Sylvia, my editor, wasn't going to be happy, especially since they were due two days ago, and now she wouldn't have any time to suggest changes. She *lived* to suggest changes.

I was already five minutes late for my appointment, and the damn elevator was crawling. Jabbing my finger at floor number thirty-four a few times, I mumbled something about taking the stairs next time. But who was I kidding? In these shoes? With this tight skirt on? It was a miracle I could even make it up the curb when the cab dropped me off out front.

I sighed audibly. *Are we even moving?* It was seriously the slowest elevator I'd ever taken. Frustrated, and maybe a bit anxious to get the interview over with, I took another shot at the elevator panel. Again, pressing the button repeatedly, I groaned, "Come on. I'm already freakin' late."

I breathed a sigh of relief when the car seemed to finally pick up speed. But then, it jolted to an abrupt stop, and the elevator went pitch black.

"Well now you've gone and broken the damn thing," a deep voice said from behind me. Startled, I jumped and bobbled my cell phone in the dark, which resulted in it falling. From the sound of it smashing against the floor, I knew it had broken.

"Shit! Look what you made me do." I bent over and patted the floor, but I couldn't find it. "Can you at least give me some light so I can find my phone?"

"It would be my pleasure."

"Thank you," I huffed.

"If I had a cell phone on me."

"Are you kidding? You don't have a cell phone on you? Who walks around without their cell phone?"

"Maybe you should try it. If you weren't so obsessed with yours, we wouldn't be in this predicament."

I stood, and my hands went to my hips. "How so?"

"Well, you were so busy typing away on your phone, you didn't even notice another passenger was in the car with you."

"And?"

"Had you seen me, you wouldn't have jumped hearing my voice and broken your phone. Then we would have had light, and you would be able to see that elevator panel well enough to push that button another twenty or thirty times. I'm sure that would've helped."

I felt the man moving around behind me.

"What are you doing?"

When he answered, his voice came from a different place. It was to my left and beneath me. "I'm on the floor looking for your cell phone."

It really was pitch dark. I couldn't see a thing, but I felt the air move, and I knew he must have stood back up.

"Put your hand out."

"You're going to put my phone in it, right?"

"No, I've taken down my pants and I'm going to stick my dick in it. Christ, you're really a bitch, aren't you?"

Thinking he couldn't see me, I smiled at his sarcasm and put out my hand. "Just give me my phone."

One of his hands brushed along mine, and then he held it while the other one placed the phone into my palm and closed it into my hand. "You have a nice smile. You should try using it more often."

"It's pitch black in here. How would you know my smile is nice?"

"I can see your teeth."

He let go of my hand, and I immediately started to feel a panic attack come on. *Shit. Not here. Not now.*

I reached and grabbed for his hand back before he could fully pull away. "I'm sorry...I...um...can you just keep your hand wrapped around mine for a minute?"

He did as I asked without question. Oddly, the man just stood there and held my hand, squeezing a few times as if he knew I needed reassurance. Eventually, I felt the wave start to pass, and I loosened my grip on the stranger. "You can let go now. I'm sorry. I had a little panic attack."

"It's over?"

"They come and go like that sometimes. I have a feeling the longer we're in here, the more of a chance another one will develop. Just keep talking to me. It will distract me."

"Okay, what's your name?"

The urge to let out a scream was overwhelming. "Aaaaaaaaaaaaaaaaaaaaaaaagh!!!!"

"What the fuck was that?" he growled.

I let out another scream that was even louder.

"Why are you doing that?"

Without answering his question, I panted and simply said, "Oh, that felt good."

"You scared the shit out of me."

"Sorry. It's a technique I use to fend off the panic—screaming at the top of my lungs."

"That's the best technique you have?"

"I have a few different techniques. I can also massage my balls."

"Excuse me?"

"I have balls. Massaging them really helps."

"Your...*balls*? You looked like a woman to me, pretty damn shapely from the back, at least."

"They're *Baoding* balls. Metal meditation balls. I massage them against each other in a circular motion in my palm. It helps calm me down." I began to frantically search through my purse.

"What's all that rustling?" he asked.

"I'm trying to find them. They're somewhere in my bag." Without light, I wasn't able to easily locate them. "Shit, where are they?"

He chuckled. "I have some balls you could massage if you're in a pickle."

"You're disgusting. Keep your balls and your pickle away from me, please."

"Oh, come on. I'm not serious. Lighten up. You're the one who brought up massaging balls. We're stuck in a dark elevator. I was trying to make a joke, for fuck's sake."

Finally able to locate the Baoding balls, I said, "Okay, here they are." I took a deep breath and began to rotate them in my hand, focusing on the soothing sounds of the metal rubbing together.

"They chime. How nice," he said in a seemingly sarcastic manner. "What exactly are you doing with them?"

"Rotating them."

"This actually does something for you?"

"Yes." After a few minutes, I turned to him. "Open your hand." I placed the balls in his palm. "Keep them separated with the use of your index finger." When I could feel him using the wrong finger to position the balls, I said, "No, I said index finger, not middle finger."

"Ah, good. Better rest my middle finger anyway. I may need to lift it repeatedly if this elevator doesn't move anytime soon."

"You're not taking this seriously. Give them back to me." I took them from his hand.

"I once went on a date with a woman who leaned over the table to tell me that she had some metal balls stuck up her hoo-ha."

"Ben Wa balls."

"Ah. So, you know of them?"

"Yes."

"Well, aren't you the balls expert. Ever use the Ben Wa balls?"

"No. I don't need balls to have an orgasm."

"Is that right?"

I couldn't see it, but I could feel him smiling at me.

Shaking my head, I said, "Okay, this conversation is just getting weird."

"Just *now* getting weird? I believe this encounter started getting weird the moment you broke my eardrum."

This whole situation was so ridiculous. Suddenly, I started to laugh. The metal balls slipped out of my hand onto the elevator floor and rolled away.

"You dropped your balls."

The deadpan way he said it caused me to laugh even harder. He joined me, and we were both officially laughing hysterically. This situation was making us both delirious.

Eventually, we were sitting on the ground with our backs against the wall. A few moments of silence passed. It hit me that he smelled really freaking good. It was like a mix of cologne and a manly scent that was all his own. I wondered if he was even attractive. I had to admit, his voice alone was sexy as hell.

I finally asked, "What do you look like?"

"You'll find out soon enough."

"I'm just trying to make conversation."

I could feel his words vibrating against me when he leaned in. "What do you think I look like?" His voice really was very arousing.

I cleared my throat. "You actually have a really nice voice, very mature. I kind of picture you as an older, distinguished man. Maybe you look like James Brolin."

"I'll accept that."

"What about me?" I asked.

"Well, see, I got a look at you—from behind. So all I really know is that you have an amazing ass and nice teeth, since they're practically glowing in the dark."

My breathing was starting to become a bit labored.

He must have sensed my nerves acting up again when he chided, "If you're about to yell like a hyena again, why don't you at least yell for some help. Put that shit to good use."

I got up suddenly and began to bang on the elevator doors. "Help! Help!"

My cries for help were to no avail.

"Okay, you can stop now."

Rejoining him on the ground, I felt another wave of panic coming on. It was really hard to fight these feelings without any visual distractions. I had never had to deal with this in the pitch dark before.

"Can you hold my hand again?"

"Sure," he simply said.

He tightly enveloped my hand in his. Without visual stimuli, I focused on the other senses, particularly smell and touch. Relishing the feel of his big, warm hand and breathing in his scent, I closed my eyes and tried to calm down.

He suddenly jumped and let go of me. "Light!"

My eyes flashed open to find that the lights in the elevator car had turned back on.

"Light!" I screamed.

When I turned to instinctively hug him, I stopped short, and my heart nearly skipped a beat. I took him in for several seconds. This guy was far more handsome than I could ever have imagined—to the point where I was now painfully embarrassed by everything that had ensued in the darkness.

He looked nothing like James Brolin. He was younger, hotter, more rugged. I'd put him in his early thirties.

My elevator mate had dark, inky-colored hair, long around the ears and buried under a baseball cap that was turned backwards. His eyes were a striking steel blue, and he was sporting just the right amount of chin scruff over his beautifully defined jaw.

The words wouldn't come to me. I simply said, "Hi," as if it were the first moment we'd actually met.

He flashed a dangerously sexy smile and winked. "Hi."

CHAPTER 2

Dex

Wow. My little ball player was quite the fox.

I'd only seen her from the back before the lights went out. Now, I was staring into her beautiful, big brown eyes, feeling like this elevator mishap wasn't such a bad thing after all.

She cleared her throat. "The lights came back, but we're still stuck."

I clicked on some of the buttons. "Seems that way. But this is a step in the right direction. I bet this thing will be moving in no time."

And by this thing moving, I do not mean my dick, although I could have sworn I felt it twitch when she just licked her beautiful full lips.

Do that again.

Fuck.

She is beautiful.

My eyes travelled down the length of her body then back up again, loving how the small buttons on her conservative

8

blouse formed a path up to her delicate neck. I wouldn't have minded sucking on that skin.

Maybe I could entice her to play hooky with me.

"Where are you headed once we get out of here?" I asked.

"The thirty-fourth floor," she said.

What?

What is she doing going up to my floor?

I know she doesn't work for me. I would have remembered that face, those eyes.

"What kind of business you have going on up there?"

"I actually have the pleasure of interviewing Mister Moneybags himself."

My stomach sank.

Ohhhh.

This didn't bode well for me.

I swallowed then cocked my head to the side and played dumb. "Who?"

"The elusive Dexter Truitt. He's the CEO of Montague Enterprises. They occupy the entire top floor."

Trying to seem like I was not seriously about to lose my shit, I asked, "Why do you call him Mister Moneybags?"

"I just picture him to be this crabby, money-hungry asshole, I guess. Sounds like a fitting name. Of course, I don't actually know him."

"Why do you think that way about him, then?"

"I have my reasons."

"Maybe you shouldn't assume the worst about people until you get to know them." Even though I knew the answer, I asked, "Why are you interviewing him anyway?"

"I work for a business magazine, *Finance Times*. I was assigned to cover an exclusive we snagged. It's about Truitt's 'coming out' of sorts. He's always kept very private after taking over the company from his father, not wanting to be photographed or interviewed. His ability to keep himself pretty much a mystery has been impeccable. When I found out that we would be granted his first interview, I jumped at the opportunity to volunteer."

"Why is that? I mean, if you don't like the guy..."

"I think it will be fun to grill him."

"You don't strike me as someone who typically gets off on making other people sweat, especially considering your panic issues."

"Well, believe me when I say I *will* get my shit together for this. I am not letting this opportunity pass me by."

"You know you really shouldn't judge a book by its cover. You've already determined that you think this guy is an asshole, and you've never even met him. Just because someone is rich and powerful doesn't make them a bad person."

"It's not just that."

"What is it, then?"

"Let's just say, I've done my homework for this interview, and I have first-hand knowledge the guy's an asshole. It's too much to get into."

Fuck. My pulse was starting to race. I needed to know why she had such preconceived notions about me. She definitely couldn't have suspected that I was Dexter Truitt, given the casual clothes I was wearing after the gym. I looked like a fucking bike messenger instead of the CEO of a multi-million-dollar empire.

My office had its own shower and closet, and I'd planned to change as soon as I got upstairs. I guess I would've been late for the interview.

"What's your name?" I asked.

"Bianca."

"Bianca what?"

"Bianca George."

That was the name of the reporter I was meeting with.

"Nice to meet you, Bianca."

"And you are?"

What was my name?

Do I tell her that the interview with Mister Moneybags actually started from the moment she got into the elevator, or do I play along and pretend to be the down-to-earth guy she's beginning to open up to? The latter sounded like a hell of a lot more fun.

My name.

My name.

I stared down at the piece of mail I'd picked up after the gym this morning. It was laying on the elevator floor next to her metal balls.

Envelope.

Brand of envelopes.

Mead.

Reed.

I looked over at the elevator doors.

The Doors.

Jim Morrison.

Jim.

James.

Jay.

Reed. Jay Reed.

"Jay Reed."

"Nice to meet you, Jay."

"Likewise, Bianca."

A voice rang over the intercom. "This is Chuck Sansone from building maintenance. Is someone there?"

"Yes!" Bianca answered. "We're in here! We're stuck!"

"We just wanted to let you know that we should have you out of there in no time. You're in no danger, and we have a crew working on it."

She looked extremely relieved when she shouted, "Thank you. Thank you so much! Please keep us posted."

"Will do."

I, on the other hand, wanted nothing more than to stay in this confined space with her. I needed to get to the bottom of why she hated me, but a part of me was also really enjoying playing Jay, the everyday guy whom she likely had no fucked-up, preconceived notions about.

"What do you do, Jay?"

It was the only thing I could think of based on my attire. "I own my own bike messenger service. I'm headed to the twenty-sixth floor."

"Oh, that explains the package."

"Because I'm well-endowed?"

She blushed a little. "No, the envelope there." It pleased me that she was finally going along with my sense of humor.

"I know. Just messing with that pretty little head again."

Bianca was still blushing. The lights coming on seemed to have been a game changer. She was definitely attracted to me. Sometimes, you just know. When she caught me staring at her, she batted her eyelashes and looked down at the ground.

Oh, yeah. I was definitely having an effect on her.

"How did you get into this field? Interviewing men you hate?"

"Well, I used to work as a trader on Wall Street."

"How does that lead to reporting?"

"It doesn't. It leads to a near nervous breakdown, which, therefore, leads to reporting. I figure, at least I'm still utilizing my degree somewhat, working for a business magazine."

"How long do you think your interview will take?"

"Well, I'm already late. So, who knows if it's still happening."

"I'm sure he'll understand, given the circumstances."

"For all I know, he knew I was coming up and rigged this whole mechanical issue. Maybe he got cold feet about doing his first interview."

"I think that's a bit of a stretch. He would've just called and cancelled rather than tampering with elevator wires. I think you're a bit paranoid, Georgy Girl. But lucky for you, I think I have the cure for that."

"Does it involve your package?"

I bent my head back and chuckled. "It involves neither my package nor your balls."

"What's the cure for my paranoia?"

"Cronuts."

"Whose nuts?"

"Cronuts." I laughed. "They're these half-donut, half-croissant thingies."

"Oh, I think I saw them on the news, from that bakery on Spring Street?"

"Yup. They're so friggin' good. Want to get some for breakfast after your interview?"

Bianca nodded. "I'd like that."

Fuck yeah.

She added, "If we ever get out of here."

Almost as soon as she'd said it, the floor swayed a bit before building maintenance came on the intercom to let us know the elevator had been fixed.

I pressed the buttons for our respective floors and, lo and behold, we were moving. It was bittersweet.

When we arrived at my fake destination, I stood in between the doors to keep them from shutting. "How do I get in touch with you when you're done?"

Bianca squinted her eyes at me. "Why don't you carry a phone, anyway?"

"Long story. Maybe when you tell me your Mister Moneybags dirt, I'll let you know why I don't carry one."

The truth was, I'd stupidly left my phone at Caroline's last night. I wasn't going to tell Bianca that my phone was at the apartment of my long-time, casual fuck buddy.

"I'll meet you out front," I said.

"How will you know when I'm finished?"

"I'll just wait for you."

"Are you sure?"

"Yeah. I can browse some of the magazines in the stand out there. Maybe I'll see what Bianca George has to say in the latest issue of *Finance Times*." I winked.

"Okay." She smiled. "See you soon."

When the elevator closed, my heart was pumping. I immediately made my way to the front desk of this random company and flirted with the receptionist just so she would let me borrow her phone.

I used it to ring my secretary.

"Hi, Josephine. As you know, there's a Bianca George from *Finance Times* coming to interview me this morning. I need you to keep her waiting initially for about forty-five minutes. When the time is up, then and only then, please inform her that I will no longer be able to make today's interview. Let her know I'll be in touch via email to reschedule."

"Why have her wait at all? I don't understand."

"You don't need to understand, okay? You just need to do it."

"Yes, sir."

Despite the fact that I'd left my personal cell at Caroline's, I had a business phone I kept in my office.

"Can you also have someone run my phone down to the twenty-sixth floor right away? I'll be waiting outside of the elevator. It's charging on my desk."

"I'll take care of it."

Needing to make the most of those forty-five minutes, I first had to find me a fucking bike. What good was a bike messenger without one?

"One more thing, Josephine. Can you please Google the nearest Manhattan bike shop located closest to our building?"

She gave me the name of a place about ten minutes away. My driver wasn't in range, so after my phone was delivered, I cabbed it over there and purchased a bike that the salesperson swore would befit a bike messenger, except I doubted a messenger would need the tandem version I'd purchased. I'd figure out how to explain *that* to her when the time came.

Wearing my newly purchased helmet, I anxiously waited outside my building. When I saw her emerge, she looked downright pissed.

"What happened?"

"The asshole stood me up."

"He didn't give a reason?"

"Nope. They made me wait only to tell me he had to cancel. He's supposedly going to reschedule, but I don't buy it."

Handing her the second helmet I'd bought, I said, "You know what? Fuck him."

And I do mean that literally and figuratively.

"You're right. Fuck him."

"Do you have to be back to work?"

"No, I'm blowing off the rest of the day after this crap," she said.

I nudged my head. "Get on the back."

She examined the bike. "Why do you drive a double-seated one?"

"I have multiple bikes. This is for when I need a helper. Luck just had it that my normal bike blew a tire, so I happened to be using this one today. Seems like fate to me. Because today *you're* my helper, Bianca George. Now put that helmet on."

She positioned herself on the back, and we began to pedal away in unison.

I spoke behind my shoulder. "First stop, Cronuts."

She spoke through the wind, "What's the second stop?"

"Wherever the day takes us, Georgy Girl."

CHAPTER 3

Dex

"Did you see that?"

"What?" I was having difficulty focusing on anything but the erect nipples peeking out of her thin shirt, if I was being honest.

"Those two guys," Bianca pointed to two suits sitting on a park bench along the paved walkway about forty feet from where we were sitting on the grass. It was the first time I'd stepped foot on the Great Lawn in Central Park since I was a kid. Although I had a spectacular view of it from my apartment, on most days I didn't find the time to look out at it.

"What about them?"

She lifted her chin in the direction of an old lady who was several feet on the walk past the two men. "That lady almost tripped and fell on her face."

"And it's their fault?"

"The one on the left has his legs stretched so far out, there's barely room to pass. That walk is only about three feet wide, and his legs are taking up thirty inches of it."

"He's tall. I doubt it was his intention to trip an old lady."

"Maybe not. But that's the trouble with that type of guy. He doesn't have common courtesy for the people around him. He's only aware of things that have a direct impact on him. I bet if a woman with tight yoga pants and a big rack walked by, he would've moved his legs because he was interested in the view."

"I think you might be a bit pessimistic of the entire suit-wearing population."

"Nope." Bianca unwrapped her lunch as she spoke. We'd picked up burgers and fries at some deli I'd passed a million times and never stepped foot into before today. "There is a direct correlation between the net worth of a man and his manners. The higher the tax bracket, the worse his etiquette."

"I think you're exaggerating. Where's your research to support such a bold conclusion, Ms. *Finance Times*?"

She reached into her cardboard cup of fries inside a small white bag and pulled one out. Waving it at me, she said, "I'll show you my research. You up for a bet?"

"That depends on what I stand to lose?"

She took a bite of her fry and smirked. "You already know you're going to lose, huh?"

"I didn't say that. But I like to know all the facts before I jump into anything."

"Sure you do, *chicken*."

I laughed. "What's the wager, smart ass?"

"I bet I can make that suit move his legs without even asking."

"And how do you propose to do that?"

"Is it a bet?"

I was intrigued. "Tell me the prize."

She thought for a moment. "If I win, you have to drive me back to my apartment on the back of your tandem bike with my feet up."

"And what happens if you lose?"

"I'll pedal, and you can sit in the back and relax."

I was six foot one and a hundred and ninety-five pounds. She couldn't have been more than one-ten soaking wet. There was no way I was going to let this woman pedal me around town. "I'll tell you what, if you win, I'll drive you wherever you want to go with your feet up. But if you lose, you have dinner with me. And I'm taking you to a nice restaurant filled with men in expensive suits."

She seemed to like that bet. Holding out her hand, she said, "You're on. Be prepared for a good workout this afternoon."

I wanted to give her a good workout, but it had nothing to do with a damn bicycle.

She stood and dusted off the grass from her hands. "Can I borrow your sweatshirt?"

I'd had a hoodie with me when I went to the gym. Since it was beautiful out, I tucked it into one of the two carrying bags on the back of my new messenger bike. Her purse and heels were in the other one. She'd exchanged her sexy sandals for a pair of flip flops that were in her bag before she'd hopped onto the back of the bike.

Bianca pulled a ponytail holder from her purse and tied her long hair back into a knot. Then she proceeded to slip on my sweatshirt and zip it all the way to the top before pulling up the hood.

"What are you doing?"

"I'm going to walk past those suits and show you they won't even notice that I almost trip."

"And you need to be incognito for that?"

She pulled the sweatshirt all the way down so it covered her ass. The thing hung to her knees. "I'm covering up my assets."

"You do have some pretty distracting assets."

With a dark sweatshirt four sizes too big covering her body and a hoodie pulled tightly over her head to hide her beautiful face, she took off, jogging back a bit and then entering the concrete path. When she reached the two suits, she pretended to trip. One guy looked up for a brief second and then kept right on talking. Damn if they weren't making the rest of us look bad.

Smiling like she'd already won, Bianca strutted back to where we were sitting. She immediately began to take off the sweatshirt as she spoke. "See. Rude. No manners. The one who didn't even look up, probably has a view of the park from his living room."

It probably wasn't the time to mention I lived on Central Park West and had a view from my living room *and* bedroom. Which reminded me, where the hell would I even take her if she told me she'd come home with me later? Jay, the bike messenger, wouldn't be able to afford the closet in my place.

Once Bianca had my sweatshirt off, she began to unbutton a few extra buttons on her own blouse. While before, I had to imagine what was beneath the silk, now she was flaunting perfectly tanned skin and a healthy amount of cleavage. I wondered if she was wearing a push up bra or her tits were that perfectly round.

"That's stacking the deck a little, isn't it?"

She pulled her hair out of the ponytail and fluffed it up, then reached into her bag and pulled out a bright red lipstick. "It shouldn't matter *who* walks by."

When she was done, she took off her flip flops and grabbed her sexy heels from the bag, putting them on. Then she turned to me. "Ready?"

I leaned back on my elbows to enjoy the show. I didn't really give a shit what the two suits did, but I was liking watching Bianca strut her stuff a hell of a lot. "Go for it."

Just like before, she walked a bit down the grass before entering the walkway. Her hips swayed from side to side as she placed one foot in front of the other. Right before she reached the suits, she dropped the elastic band that had been in her hair to the ground. She turned, bending dramatically at the waist, and gave the two men a perfect view of her very fine ass. The one with the outstretched legs definitely noticed. Bianca stood, turned to look my way with a cheeky grin on her face, and took a few more steps. About three feet before she reached the bench, the suit pulled his legs in so she could pass.

He also followed her ass the rest of the way as she walked back to where we were sitting.

"Cute. Very cute."

"I think I need to make a few stops on the way home and pick up some things," she gloated.

"Let me guess. Bricks?"

She laughed. I loved that she just slipped off her shoes and sat in the grass without giving a shit that she might get dirty. I was pretty sure the last time Caroline's feet touched the grass, it was for a photo shoot, and she probably made one of the cameramen carry her.

My cell vibrated in my pocket. It had been doing it the entire time we rode around the city and picked up lunch, but Bianca hadn't noticed it from the back of my tandem with the sounds of the city all around us.

"Is that your phone?"

"Apparently so."

"I thought you didn't have a phone on you? That's why you couldn't give me any light to find mine when I'd dropped it?"

Shit.

"I didn't have it on my person because I'd forgotten it in the messenger bag on my bike when I went up to do my delivery."

"Oh."

My phone buzzed again.

"Don't you have to answer it?"

"It can wait."

"Are you the only messenger? Or is it a big company?"

"There are a few of us." *Pick up shovel, dig yourself deeper, Jay, you dick.*

She squinted. "You're being vague. Most men jump at the opportunity to talk about their success."

"Maybe my company is extremely successful, and I don't want to scare you away thinking I'm one of those rich men you seem to dislike so much."

"I don't dislike people because they *have* money. I dislike them because of what *having* the money does to them. It seems to cause a warp in priorities and make them think the world revolves around them."

"So you wouldn't necessarily eliminate an extremely wealthy man from your list of potential suitors just because of his wealth, then?"

"Potential suitors?" She chuckled. "Now you sound like the assholes I went to grad school with at Wharton."

"You went to Wharton?"

"Yes. Don't sound so shocked. Girls with brains use obscene four letter words and their bodies to win bets, too, you know. How about you? Did you go to college?"

I couldn't very well tell her I'd gone to Harvard, so I added another lie to the growing pile. "I went to state school. It was what my parents could afford." It wasn't a total lie. My parents *could* afford state school—to buy one...the grounds, the professors, the entire university, for that matter.

We sat on the grass for another hour eating our lunch and shooting the shit. The woman intrigued me on so many levels, and I wanted to know more about what made her tick. "So what do you do in your spare time, aside from hustling men in bets on the Great Lawn?"

"Well, I work a lot. You already know I'm a writer for *Finance Times*, but I also freelance for a few other business magazines. So sometimes I'm traveling on weekends for assignments. When I am home, I'm usually out. I'm a foodie. I like to try different ethnic places to eat with my friend, Phoebe. We've been on a Vietnamese kick lately. The last place we went to, I have no idea what I ate because we were the only two who weren't Asian in the place, and no one really spoke English. Other than that, I volunteer at Forever Grey on most Sunday mornings. It's a nonprofit that rescues retired greyhounds that their racing-obsessed owners discard when they can't run fast enough anymore. The dogs are beautiful and smart and need to be exercised, so I take two out for a run whenever I can."

"That's very nice of you."

She shrugged. "It's good therapy for the dogs and for me."

"Do you have a dog yourself?"

"I'd like to, but my building doesn't allow dogs over ten pounds. And I'm not really a small dog kind of person. Plus, with all my travel, it wouldn't be fair to have an animal cooped up in my small place. Since I left the stock market, my lifestyle has taken a hit—starting with a reduction in my square footage. My old place had a closet bigger than where I live now. What about you? What do you do for fun?"

My life for the last six months pretty much consisted of working eighty hours a week, going to mundane social engagements that my work required, and occasionally fucking Caroline when she was in town. All of which, Jay, messenger boy extraordinaire, could not reveal to Bianca. And so—I dug even deeper.

"My business keeps me pretty busy. I have some employees but the company is only a few years old, and we're still in the building stages. I try to hit the gym five days a week, and..." I needed to come up with something so it sounded like I had *some* interests. Unfortunately, when I reached into my bag full of decent lies for another, all I came up with was a handful of lint. So, I said the first thing that popped into my head. "I also whittle."

"Whittle?"

"Yes, whittle. You know, the ancient form of woodcarving. I carve various things from wood."

What the fuck? Hiking or distilling couldn't have popped into my head first? I didn't know the first thing about wood. Well, not that type of wood anyway.

Bianca looked amused. "That's not something I hear too often—whittling. What kind of things do you make?"

"Ah. I can't tell you that on the first date." I winked. "Just know I'm good with my hands, and you have some impressive wood to look forward to seeing in the future when we go out again."

"*When,* not *if,* we got out again?" She questioned with a raised brow. "You're rather sure of yourself, aren't you?"

"I like to think of myself more as persistent. I may be just a simple messenger, but that doesn't mean that I let something stand in my way when I know what I want."

The afternoon flew by, and I hated that I had to end things, but my four o'clock appointment had flown in from London last night. I couldn't very well abandon him as I had done with my entire afternoon of responsibilities. Not to mention that my secretary had been blowing up my phone with a string of urgent messages for more than an hour.

I reluctantly pedaled Bianca back to her apartment. Being a woman of her word, she didn't provide one ounce of assistance in toting her ass halfway up town. Even though I was in tip-top shape, I was sweating and winded by the time we made it to her apartment.

I wiped my brow with my sweatshirt after parking the bike. "You really didn't lend a hand at all on that ride."

She smiled. "Nope. A bet's a bet, and you lost."

I was starting to think what I'd lost was my goddamn mind. "When can I see you again?"

"Are you going to pick me up on your bicycle?"

"Does that matter?"

"No. I just wanted to know what I should wear."

"Wear something sexy." I took a step closer into her personal space, testing the waters. She didn't back up.

"Where would we go?"

"Wherever you want." I'd been dying to touch her all day, but mauling her in the park or stopping in traffic to take her mouth wasn't exactly the vibe the afternoon was giving off. But now that we were standing in front of her building and it was just the two of us, I was done resisting. Her hair was windblown from the ride, so I reached out to smooth it down and let my palm linger on her jaw so my thumb could stroke her cheek. "Name it. I'm game for anything."

"How about Ethiopian food?"

"Done." I leaned in closer. "Anything else you want?"

Her eyes drop to my lips.

Right answer.

Just as I was about to bring my mouth down to finally meet hers, something caught her attention behind me. I turned and watched an elderly woman attempting to get out from the cab.

"That's Mrs. Axinger," Bianca said. "She lives across the hall from me."

I wanted to ignore the woman getting out of the car and go back to what I was about to do, but I couldn't. She looked like she might fall, and the damn cabbie wasn't about to help. I groaned, but headed to help the woman. Bianca followed right behind me.

"Hi, Mrs. A. This is my friend, Jay."

I took the woman's arm and helped her out of the cab and up the tall curb. Once she was steady, I lifted her grocery bag from the seat and carried it behind her and Bianca as they walked to the door.

"Bianca, dear, do you think you can give me a hand getting a box from the top of my closet? I'm afraid to climb up on a chair, and I want to ship some pictures to my son out in California."

"Sure, of course. I told you to knock anytime you need anything. I'll help you put these groceries away and get whatever you need down."

After I opened the door and we were all standing in the lobby, Bianca gave me an apologetic look. "Call me?" she asked.

Begrudgingly, I dug my phone out of my pocket and handed her my cell so she could put in her number. When she was done, we swapped the phone for the small bag of groceries I was still carrying.

I couldn't very well suck her face while Mrs. A. was watching, so when the elevator door opened, I leaned in and kissed her cheek. "It was very nice meeting you, Bianca. I'll call you."

"I look forward to it."

I waited until the elevator doors closed before heading back to my bike. As I walked, I looked down at the phone number she'd typed in. She had also left me a message.

Bianca: *Whittle me something small and you'll get that kiss you were screwed out of next time.*

Great. Just fucking great. After I rode my *bicycle* back to my multi-million-dollar company, I was going to have to learn how to *whittle*.

CHAPTER 4

Bianca

I settled into bed that night in a particularly good mood thinking about Jay. But my mood was sullied when I scrolled through my email and found one from the man who'd blown me off—Mister Moneybags.

> **Dear Ms. George,**
> **Please accept my apologies for cancelling our meeting on such short notice. I'm afraid it was a personal emergency that couldn't be helped.**
> **Best,**
> **Dexter Truitt**

Really? "Best?" He wasn't even going to propose a rain check? Did he have any clue how much his "emergency" set me back? I had a deadline, and the magazine was currently without its feature story. While it surprised me that someone like him even bothered to offer an apology, this was *not* okay. I decided to write back.

Mr. Truitt,
I'm afraid your "personal emergency" has put me in
a very difficult position. We are running on a firm
deadline. If the interview isn't conducted soon, we
are going to have to cancel the entire feature. When
might you be able to reschedule?

A notification sounded within thirty seconds, signifying I'd received a new email. Dexter Truitt had written me back.

Ms. George,
How about right now?

Now? Was he nuts? He had some nerve expecting me to meet him at this time of night.

Mr. Truitt,
It's eleven o'clock at night. I'm not able to meet you
this late. When might you have availability during
working hours this week?

Bouncing my knee anxiously, I waited for his response.

Ms. George,
I'm available now. We can conduct the
interview via email. I would prefer written
documentation of my answers in any case, so
as to avoid my words being misinterpreted.

He couldn't be serious. I typed.

Mr. Truitt,
Your agreement with the magazine was for an in-
person interview. I was under the impression that
the entire purpose of this feature was so that you
could "go public." An interview conducted over
email would defeat the purpose.

Biting my nails, I stared at the screen.

Ms. George,
What agreement are you referring to? I
never signed anything with your magazine.
Therefore, there is no contractual obligation.
I simply expressed interest in being
interviewed. I've since thought better of
doing it in person. If you'd like to conduct the
interview with me now via email, I am more
than happy to offer you that opportunity.

The keys of my laptop clicked loudly as I typed even
faster this time.

Mr. Truitt,
Are you saying there was no actual personal
emergency? You lied and cancelled our interview
because you decided not to show your face after all?

Letting out a frustrated breath, I repositioned myself in
bed as I waited for his response.

Ms. George,
I did experience an emergency, but I don't

believe I am under any obligation to offer an explanation into my personal affairs. As for showing my face, well, if you want the honest truth, my unexpected change of plans afforded me the time to think twice about such a life-altering decision. I've decided that I prefer to continue keeping my identity private.

Great. There is no story now.

Mr. Truitt,
It would have been nice to know this information before we made you the feature and spent money to promote it. The entire point of the piece was to document your coming out from under the rock you've been hiding beneath. I don't believe we have a story anymore.

His response came even quicker this time.

Ms. George,
I am giving you the opportunity to ask me anything you want. Anything. I think that makes for quite a damn good story, actually. But I do have two conditions. The first is that I don't have to be photographed. I think that's pretty fair, considering I would be an open book, otherwise. Second, for every personal question you ask me, I get to ask you a comparable one. And you have to answer me. Since you seem to think baring

one's soul to the public is an easy feat, it might be nice for you to experience what it's like to be on the other side of the fence. Deal?

What was this guy smoking? Maybe I should just ask him, seeing as though I could ask him "anything." What the hell. I needed this story. And even without his face, it was better than any other exclusive we'd gotten in a long time.

Mr. Truitt,
We have a deal. Shall we begin?

Ms. George,
I'm all yours. Start with the business questions. Get them out of the way. You may work for Finance Times, but let's face it, people aren't really interested in how many shares of my company I've sold, so much as how many women I'm dating.

We'd switched to the Gmail chat feature and spent the better part of an hour going back and forth on how he came to eventually run his father's venture capital firm.

In the past five years alone, Dex Jr. had been commended for diversifying the workplace, particularly hiring more women and minorities. He was known for taking even bigger investment risks than his father had.

Dex went over what a typical day was like, chock full of meetings mostly over the phone with entrepreneurs and portfolio companies. Every client and employee signed a non-disclosure agreement whereby they could neither reveal personal information about Dex nor photograph him.

Dex said he often wouldn't sleep for days when he was close to the finish line on a deal. He ate, slept, and breathed his job.

When we'd run the gamut on the business questions, I started hitting him with the personal ones. Except, I had to think long and hard about my questions, knowing he was apparently going to hit me right back with the same ones.

Bianca: Tell me about your childhood.

Dex: I was the only child of Dexter Truitt and Suzanne Montague-Truitt. My mother's father, Stuart Montague, actually founded the company. That's where the name Montague Enterprises comes from. Stuart didn't have a son, so he left the company to my father with the understanding that I would take it over someday. My dad was pretty much an absentee father, though. My childhood was what you would expect—privileged. But my parents were never home much.

Bianca: You were raised by nannies, then?

Dex: Yes. Well, one in particular named Alice Sugarbaker. I called her Sugie.

A smile spread across my face. I thought that was kind of cute, this big, powerful man recalling the nickname for the woman who basically raised him.

Bianca: Where are your parents now?

Dex: Dad's retired, living in Palm Beach with his third wife. My mother was his second marriage. Mom lives here in the city, never remarried. I'm closer to her than my father. Anyway, you're getting a little ahead of yourself. It's my turn. Tell me about your childhood, Bianca.

Was he seriously going to follow through with this game?

Bianca: Why do you even care?

Dex: Why wouldn't I? You're no less important than I am. So, tell me. Where did you grow up?

Bianca: Staten Island. Two hard-working parents. One sister.

Dex: Nice childhood?

Bianca: I had a good childhood up until the point when my parents divorced. Then things got ugly.

Dex: I get it. Same here on the divorce front, but I'm sorry to hear that.

Bianca: Thank you. Next question. When you got into Harvard, did you decide to major in business because it was something that truly interested you or because you always knew you would have to take over the family business?

Dex: Honestly? I didn't know my ass from my elbow back then. So, yeah, I just majored in business because it seemed to make sense, given my inheritance and the expectations placed upon me. God, Bianca, these questions are fucking boring.

I laughed out loud a little. Well, fuck you, Dex!

Bianca: What do you suggest we talk about, then?

Dex: People don't care about this shit. They read your magazine because they want to know how to be successful themselves. Where I went to school doesn't matter. The truth is, this company was handed to me on a silver platter. I vowed not to waste that opportunity by making the same mistakes my father did. He wasn't honest and screwed people out of a lot of money over the years. I can say that because it's public knowledge now. I made a vow to do things differently, and that includes keeping out of the public eye.

Bianca: Why can't you be an honest man and in the public eye at the same time?

Dex: I think I've proven that you don't have to show your face to be successful. So, why bother dealing with all the social media and tabloid bullshit? They add no value. They add nothing but risk.

I couldn't even argue with that.

Dex: Ask me something interesting now. Something people would want to know.

Bianca: Since you seem to be the authority on what makes a good interview question, why don't you tell me what YOU want people to know about you.

There was a bit of a pause this time before he answered.

Dex: I want them to know that I'm more than just some entitled dude in a suit, that I wake up every day vowing to make the most of every hour and to make a difference whether big or small. I am certain there are a lot of preconceived notions about me. Almost all of them are untrue. People assume my keeping out of the public eye is a gimmick to somehow mystify myself as an elusive celebrity. The truth is...I'm just trying to grasp onto some semblance of normalcy. I'm a regular guy who wants peace in his life, Bianca. Not some big bad wolf who gets a rise out of cancelling on beautiful, brown-eyed girls from Staten Island.

That last line threw me for a loop and made my skin heat up.

Bianca: How do you know I have brown eyes?

Dex: I'm looking at your bio on the *Finance Times* website.

Feeling vulnerable that he was scrutinizing my looks, I tried to change the subject.

Bianca: What else do you think people want to know about you?

Dex: Don't change the subject off of you. You're beautiful, by the way. Let's discuss that. It's more fun than talking about me.

Bianca: Let's not.

Dex: It's my turn to ask you a question. Did you think I forgot?

Bianca: What?

Dex: What do you want people to know about you, Bianca George?

Bianca: I want to be taken seriously by millionaires I am trying to interview.

Dex: I'm taking you very seriously. And I want to know more. Now answer my question. What do you want people to know about you?

God, he was putting me on the spot. But for some odd reason, I was warming up to this man. I didn't really feel like coming up with yet another sarcastic response when, in fact, he'd been nothing but completely genuine with me this entire time. It was much less exhausting to just be honest. So, I simply answered his question truthfully.

Bianca: I'm just a girl who wants to be happy. I don't need money or a prestigious job. I left Wall Street because I couldn't hack it. It's why I do this for a living instead. I am not perfect. I do sometimes carry some preconceived notions about people of power, though. That probably comes from watching my hard-working parents get screwed over by such people over the years. But even in the little time that we have corresponded tonight, I can see that you're quite different from what I expected. I made assumptions about you that were incorrect. So, one thing I definitely want people to know about me is that I am not afraid to admit when I'm wrong.

Dex: Thank you.

Bianca: Well, you've been very open with me. So, I felt I owed you that much.

Dex: Forget the interview. What do YOU want to know about me?

Bianca: If you want the shallow truth, I'm most curious about what you look like at this point. I'm really dying to know.

Dex: LOL. Bianca George, you are definitely nothing if not honest. So...what is it...you think I don't allow myself to be photographed because I'm grossly unattractive?

Bianca: I didn't say that.

Dex: But you're thinking it.

I couldn't stop smiling.

Dex: Would you like to see me?

My heart started to pound at the prospect of getting to see what he looked like. What was wrong with me? But there was only one answer to his question.

Bianca: Yes.

A few seconds later, he attached an image. After I clicked on it, I nearly lost my breath.

Oh.

It was a photo of a man lying back on his bed. His torso was ripped...tanned...almost bronze. It almost looked fake, because it was just too damn perfect. This was probably the most amazing chest and abs I'd ever seen. The photo cut off at the bottom, only showing the top of his black boxers that had *Emporio Armani* written on the band in white. A thin trail of hair ran down the center of his defined V muscle. Holy shit.

I couldn't stop staring at it.

This was not what I was expecting. At all. In fact, I couldn't believe it. It had to be a fake.

When I was finally able to pry my eyes away from the chiseled bronze statuette of a man, I typed.

Bianca: That is NOT you.

CHAPTER 5

Dex

I wished I could have seen her face.

Fuck. I wished I could have done a lot more than that. This chat with Bianca was killing me. I was suddenly hard as a rock, knowing that she was looking at my photo.

Dex: It is me.

Bianca: I don't believe that. Admit it. You stole the picture from Pinterest. LOL.

My jaw hurt from smiling. After grabbing a pen and paper out of my night table, I wrote *HI, BIANCA GEORGE* then snapped a photo with it covering my face, making sure that my body was once again on full display. I chose to cut it off at the waist since any lower, she would have seen the rock-hard erection I was sporting as a result of this little exchange.

Dex: Believe it's me now?

Bianca: Okay, so you're attractive.

Dex: Why, thank you. But you still haven't seen my face. I'm afraid you won't tonight.

An odd sensation suddenly came over me. One I could honestly say I had never felt before. It was jealousy. But not just any jealousy. Jealousy of my own fucking self. Suddenly, Jay wanted to fuck up Dex in the worst way.

Bianca: Are we still doing the interview?

Dex: You tell me.

Bianca: I think maybe we should continue this tomorrow.

I laughed. I guess she was suddenly at a loss for words. This whole thing wasn't very professional of me, but because I had spent the entire day with this woman, I felt comfortable around her. I couldn't help it. She also made it very clear earlier that she was attracted to me, so I couldn't help capitalizing on that tonight.

Dex: Tomorrow night, then? Same time? Eleven?

Bianca: Okay. That sounds good.

Fuck yeah.

Dex: Alright. Sweet dreams.

"Sweet dreams." I sounded more like a teenage boy than a mogul. Unprofessional, but I really didn't give a shit. I'd almost called her Georgy Girl, too. That's Jay's nickname for her, you dumbass. That cocksucker, Jay. Laughing to myself, I thought about how insane this was. Dex hated Jay because he would be spending time with her in person soon. And Jay fucking detested that rich prick, Dex, for abusing his power to get to know her better.

I hadn't expected another message from her.

Bianca: Goodnight, Dex.

When had she stopped calling me Mr. Truitt? I didn't fucking care; I was just glad that she did.

Dex: Goodnight, Bianca.
Georgy Girl.

Sleep wasn't going to be happening. I was wired. Bianca's text to that douche nozzle Jay rang out in my mind: *Whittle me something small, and you'll get that kiss you were screwed out of next time.*

What better time than to stay up watching wood whittling demonstrations on YouTube.

"I need to make a stop before heading to my lunch meeting," I grumbled at Sam, my driver, as I climbed into the backseat of the dark Town Car. I'd watched damn YouTube videos for an hour last night and made a list of the supplies I'd need. I still couldn't believe the shit I was going through for a kiss from this girl. Caroline would kiss me and my cock if Sam stopped and picked up flowers before driving me to her place. Bianca had gotten under my skin.

"Where to, sir?"

"Union Square. 14th Street side."

The art supply store was enormous. Looking down at my watch, I noted I only had ten minutes before my lunch appointment, and we still had to travel across town. I must have looked as out of place wandering around looking for supplies as I felt, because a woman wearing a blue smock approached as I stood in place staring.

"Can I help you, sir?"

"I'm looking for whittling supplies. Some carving tools, balsam wood blocks, perhaps a beginner's guide."

She waved her hand over her shoulder. "Right this way."

I followed her up to the second floor and all the way to the very back corner of the store. "We have a selection of carving knives." She picked up a package containing six tools with wooden handles. "This here is a good set. It's a little pricey at just over a hundred bucks, but they're high-grade steel, and it has your chisel, a couple of gouges, and a v-parting tool."

A v-parting tool? You don't say? I have one of those myself. I took the package from the woman's hand and also grabbed two bags of wood blocks. "This will do. Thank you for your time. You're very knowledgeable."

"Anytime. We had a demonstration here a few weeks ago. The instructor gave out some good tips. If you're having difficulty, try wetting the wood."

Yes. I'll keep wetting my wood in mind.

Like clockwork, Josephine came into my office at 4:45 with a steaming cup of half decaf, half caffeinated Jamaican Blue Mountain coffee. Today though, I was too busy to look up.

"Mr. Truitt?"

"Hmmm?" Using the 7mm gouge, I notched into the wood and shaved a long line off the side I'd been working on for more than a half hour.

"Would you...like a Band-Aid?"

I'd completely forgotten that I'd Scotch taped a strip of napkin to my thumb to stop the bleeding. The blood had soaked through and turned most of the white material a lovely shade of red. It looked worse than it actually was.

"No, it's fine."

"Might I ask what you're doing?"

My shirtsleeves were rolled up to my elbows, tie was loosened, and I was leaning over my garbage pail shaving a four by six block of wood. I stopped and looked up. "What does it look like I'm doing?"

"Carving wood?"

"Very good, Josephine. I knew I kept you around for a reason."

I thought it was the end of our conversation, so I went about my carving. But Josephine just kept standing there watching me. I sighed and looked up again. "Did you need something else?"

"But why? Why are you carving?"

I responded with the God's honest truth. "I have no damn idea."

By six o'clock, I had two more makeshift napkin and Scotch tape Band-Aids and a garbage full of wasted wood. Perhaps those split leather thumb guards I saw on YouTube weren't just for pussies after all.

It was rare that I had a drink when I was alone. But I poured two fingers of Macallan twelve-year-old scotch when I got home, and found myself staring out the window at the park. The summer days were long, and the sun was just beginning to set even though it was after eight, but people were still out enjoying the weather. I watched a couple riding bicycles together and wondered when it was that I stopped appreciating things like the park. Looking down from my penthouse window, it felt a lot like I was watching from the ivory tower that Bianca had assumed I was perched in.

Bianca. The woman had taken over my thoughts for the last day and a half—consumed might have been the more appropriate term. With more than two hours until part two of our online interview, I decided to pass the excruciating wait by having Jay touch base with her. Even though I detested texting and preferred to pick up the phone or write an appropriately composed email, texting felt more like something Jay would do.

Jay: How was your stress level today? Did it require fondling your balls in the company of strange men in dark places?

I tossed back the rest of my scotch and slouched into my couch, stretching my long legs out in front of me—not entirely different than the two douche suits in the park yesterday. Only, I wasn't about to trip an old lady. Bianca took more than a half hour to answer, and I'd started to wonder if she was going to blow off Jay. But then the dots started jumping around.

Bianca: Sorry. Was in the shower. And today was peaceful, actually. I worked on a story, then went to go visit my mother. No ball fondling necessary.

For you, maybe. But now that I was thinking of Bianca in the shower, there might be some ball fondling on my end. I probably should have eased into being a perv, but I couldn't help myself.

Jay: Shower, huh?

Bianca: Get your mind out of the gutter. You're a long way from washing my back. You haven't even scored your first kiss yet.

Yet. Sometimes it was one word that exposed my competitor's hand. I smiled to myself. That kiss was a foregone conclusion in her mind—maybe I could quit slicing my fingers to shit then.

Although, I spoke too soon. She texted back before I had a chance to respond again.

Bianca: Speaking of kisses, what are you whittling me?

Jay: What would you like?

Bianca: Hmm...what is your signature piece?

I'm pretty damn good at making wood blocks into uneven sticks.

Jay: How about an animal of some type?

I'd seen some animal patterns on line with step-by-step instructions. Once I'd mastered control of the gouges, how hard could it be? There was one video where a ten-year-old boy carved a fish in less than five minutes.

Bianca: An animal sounds great.

Jay: So when is this little exchange happening? My wood for a kiss.

Bianca: LOL. I know you smirked when you wrote that last line—My wood for a kiss.

I smirked. *Again.*

Jay: Are you suggesting I'm a pervert?

Bianca: I am.

Jay: And how do you feel about perverts?

The little dots jumped and then stopped a few times. I was extremely curious at what her response would be this time.

Bianca: I actually like a little deviant in my men, I'm finding.

Although the thought of her liking a little deviant made my cock twitch with delight, something didn't sit right with me about her last two words. *I'm finding.* It made me wonder if she was referring to Dex's actions last night—sending her half-naked selfies certainly fell into the realm of deviant behavior. I wondered if she would tell me about him—about me.

Jay: Any plans for this evening.

She took a moment to respond.

Bianca: Just going to do some work later.

Hmm...technically, she was telling the truth. Dex *was* work.

Jay: How about dinner Thursday night?

Bianca: Can't. I have plans already. Friday?

Plans? Did she have a date? I had no right to grow annoyed, but that didn't stop me from feeling that way. In fact, I had a date myself on Friday night—some mundane banquet that I was scheduled to take Caroline to.

Jay: Busy Friday. Saturday?

Bianca: I'm actually going out of town Saturday afternoon for an assignment. Maybe the next weekend will work out.

There was no damn way I was waiting a full week to see her again. I didn't hesitate when I made my decision.

Jay: I'll cancel my plans for Friday. Pick you up at seven?

Bianca: OK. Sure.

Jay had a date with Bianca for two nights from now, and Dex was gearing up for his 11PM chat. What had this woman done to me?

Promptly at eleven the online chat box popped up on my laptop.

Bianca: Good evening, Mr. Truitt.

Dex: Yes, it is, Ms. George. Are you ready for round two?

Bianca: I am. I gave a lot of thought to our discussion last night, and you were right.

Dex: I usually am. You'll need to be more specific.

Bianca: I meant, that I think the article should focus more on you personally and less on the business angle of things.

I liked the sound of that. Focus more on me, Georgy Girl.

Dex: Are you telling me that your questions are going to be more intimate this evening? Because our deal still stands—question for a question, Ms. George.

Bianca: I can take whatever I dish out. You ready?

My dick twitched. *Down boy.* She was talking to Mr. Truitt.

Dex: I'm always ready, Ms. George.

Bianca: First question—Are you in a committed relationship?

Dex: I date. But, no, I'm not in a committed relationship.

It was the truth. I should probably *be* committed after the last two days, but my relationship with Caroline was open. We served a purpose for one another—attending required business functions and providing sexual gratification. Don't get me wrong—I liked Caroline, and I was pretty sure she liked me. But neither of us wanted more from what we had.

Bianca: Would you like to have children someday?

Dex: Not so fast, Ms. George. I believe you've skipped my turn. Are *you* in a committed relationship?

Bianca: No. I was, but it ended.

Dex: What happened?

Bianca: Long story. I'll give you the abbreviated version. Stockbroker. Engaged. Liar. End of Engagement.

Fuck. I needed to know more. This didn't sound like it would bode well for me.

Dex: What did he lie about?

Bianca: I've already answered two questions. I believe you're now the one who is skipping turns.

Dex: Fine.

What was the last question she asked me? Oh, yes. Children. It dawned on me that I'd been seeing Caroline for the better part of a year and she'd never inquired about whether I saw my future including a bunch of rugrats.

Dex: Yes. I do want children. But I don't want them raised by a nanny. I loved Sugie, don't

get me wrong, but I think children should be raised by their parents, if it is feasible. My turn. What did your fiancé lie about?

Bianca: Everything. Anything. You name it. He lied.

Dex: He was cheating on you, then?

Bianca: No. I don't think so. He just lied. To clients, to our boss, what his bank balance was, it didn't really matter. In hindsight, I think he got off on it in some ways.

Dex: So this factors into your dislike for rich and powerful men?

Bianca: Maybe. I've never thought about that. But I don't think my dislike of liars is related to only rich men. My father wasn't particularly rich and he lied. I just prefer the simple things in life—like the truth.

My hole I had dug for myself had just bottomed out, and I had no idea how I was going to get out of it unscathed. The smart thing would have been to stop playing this game right now, but of course I didn't. I continued for more than an hour answering and asking personal questions. The more I asked, the more addicted I became. I wanted to know everything there was to know about Bianca George. When we were wrapping things up for the evening, her last question brought me to a moment of truth.

Bianca: My deadline is at the end of the month. I'd like to finish this interview in person. We'll continue our 11PM chats in the meantime, but I'd really like to meet face to face at least once. No pictures, of course.

I hesitated before responding.

Dex: Okay. Yes. We can meet at the end.

Shit.

CHAPTER 6

Dex

Not even wetting my wood helped.

Tonight was my date with Bianca, and I hadn't been able to whittle a fucking pencil, much less an animal. Clement, my little blond nemesis as I'd come to think of him—the ten-year-old from the YouTube video—had to be a ringer. Because this shit was *not* easy. Frustrated and calling it quits, I put down the carving tool and decided Bianca wouldn't be getting a small wooden animal. I, however, was getting that kiss one way or the other.

Later in the afternoon, my phone chimed, announcing a new text had arrived. Bianca's name illuminated on the screen. I immediately swiped to open.

Bianca: Where are we going?

Jay: I made reservations at an Ethiopian place.

Bianca: Mmm. Which place? I'll look it up. I want to know how to dress.

It didn't matter how fancy the place was—it could have been a roadside trailer, and my answer would have been the same.

Jay: Wear something sexy.

Bianca: I can do that. ;-)

Jay: Good. I look forward to it. See you in a few hours.

Bianca: Okay. Don't forget my carving—I'm looking forward to our exchange.

"To Dumbo, Sam." I climbed into the backseat.

"Brooklyn? Sure thing, Mr. Truitt. Where are we heading?"

I grumbled. "Anchorage Place. The Brooklyn Flea."

My secretary had printed out a map, but it wasn't doing much good once we arrived. There had to be at least a hundred tents set up as I wandered around trying to find booth G45. When I'd asked Josephine to locate a shop that sold small wood carved crafts—such as animals, I was certain she thought she was witnessing the first signs of my nervous breakdown. I was starting to think she was onto something.

The Brooklyn flea market was apparently home to a number of handmade and unique crafters—one of which was a gentleman who also sold his wooden carvings on a website, Jelani's Kenyan Krafts. Just my luck, Jelani also sold his wares at the flea market, which happened to be open today instead of just Sunday this week, since it was the Dumbo Heritage Festival.

Eyeing a long table at the end of an aisle I'd just turned down, I was relieved to see a tall, black-skinned man wearing a colorful African hat and holding a carved wooden cane. As I came upon him, I saw that his table was filled with small, hand-carved animals. Mentally, I made a note to give Josephine a raise when I returned on Monday.

I perused the selection of carvings—admiring the beautiful craftsmanship. A week ago, I would have passed by and not taken the time to appreciate the work that had gone into these pieces—the skill and patience that they represented. But now, I was impressed by Jelani's work.

"These are beautiful."

"Thank you. Are you looking for a gift?"

"I am. For a woman."

"Ah." Jelani nodded like he understood. *That makes one of us.* He held up a small walrus. "Perhaps you can chose one based upon the special lady's spirit animal. The walrus is the keeper of secrets." He set it back down on the table and picked up another one. It was a billy goat—with two horns at the top of its head that curled back and then rounded back to the front. "The billy goat animal totem's lifestyle is about power. It's independent, strong and intelligent. They are curious, yet picky."

"I'll take the goat."

Jelani smiled. He rang me up and slipped my purchase into a small brown bag. Handing it to me he said, "Watch out for the billy goats—their horns are strong enough to impale you if you cross them."

Great. Just fucking great.

Caroline was not a happy camper that I'd cancelled our date to the banquet. I'd told her I wasn't feeling well, probably the first time I'd ever used the sick card in my life. But being here with Bianca was worth it.

She was wearing a fitted, brown dress that exposed one shoulder. The color brought out the caramel in her eyes and complemented her raven-colored hair. She was a dark beauty.

Of course, while Dex knew the answer from earlier conversations, Jay had to ask, "What nationality are you?"

"One-hundred percent Greek. You?"

"My mother is Italian and French. My father is English."

It was difficult not to stare at her from across the table. I couldn't even concentrate on the menu, which featured a bunch of stuff I didn't recognize anyway.

I'd picked Bianca up in a car I'd rented just for Jay. I figured him for a Jeep kind of guy. I had to really stop and think about what to wear, too. Dex would have probably worn a custom-tailored Armani dress shirt. Jay was more casual. I'd settled on a basic black Polo and dark jeans.

Looking around the table, I said, "I think they forgot to give us silverware."

"No. You eat Ethiopian food with your hands."

"Oh, I didn't realize."

"You've never had it before?"

"Never."

"Well, I love it, only had it a couple of times. I love trying new things."

"I love how adventurous you seem to be."

"When it comes to some things, yes." She smiled.

"I can't wait to find out more about those things, Georgy Girl." I locked my feet around hers under the table. "I'll let you order for us, since you know this food. What were you thinking of?"

"Wot."

"What are we eating?" I clarified.

"Not *what*. Wot. That's the answer for what we're getting. Wot. It's a mixture of meat, sauce and spices, like an aromatic stew. And there's this bread called injera that you use to scoop the food up with. You'll love it. You like spicy food?"

"I do."

After we ordered, I got antsy to be closer to her. So, I moved to the other side of the table.

Her tone was playful. "What are you doing?"

"I'd prefer to sit next to you. Is that okay?"

"Yes. It's more than okay."

When I placed my hand around her wrist, she looked down at my Rolex.

Her eyes widened. "That's a ten-thousand dollar watch. Does your bike messenger service do that well?"

It was twenty-thousand, actually.

Shit.

"We have good months. I reward myself sometimes."

"Nothing wrong with that. People who don't live in excess can really splurge and appreciate nice things once in a while."

Right.

She continued, "Speaking of nice things...I didn't see that you brought anything that you whittled for me."

"Don't worry. It's in the glove compartment of my car. I didn't want to press my luck in presenting it to you right off the bat."

"I'm looking forward to seeing what you made."

I rubbed my thumb along her hand. "I'm looking forward to what comes after."

Our eyes locked. God, she was beautiful, and it took everything in me not to lean in and taste those plump lips.

The waitress came and interrupted our moment, placing a large oval dish in the middle of the table. It was an array of brown and orange-looking sauces with meats and vegetables. Pieces of thin bread were rolled up around the edges of the plate.

"You're gonna have to show me how to eat this."

"Well, we basically use the bread to scoop it up. I've read that it's customary in the Ethiopian culture to feed each other, actually."

I cocked an eyebrow. "You gonna feed me?"

"If you want."

I liked the idea of this.

Feed me now.

I'll eat you later.

"I would love nothing more."

She unraveled the bread with her delicate fingers before scooping out some of the mixture. She then rolled it and gently brought it into my mouth. I made sure to touch my tongue against her hand as she did it.

She fed me repeatedly, and I eagerly awaited each and every bite. It was sensual and intimate, and there wasn't anything else in the world I would rather have been doing.

"Your turn to feed me," she said.

As I attempted to repeat Bianca's perfect feeding process, I managed to get some of the spicy sauce into the small wounds on my fingers.

"Ouch," I groaned.

"Are you okay?"

I couldn't help but laugh at myself. "Yeah. I have a couple of cuts on my hand. The spices sting. I wasn't expecting that."

"I'm sorry. How did you cut yourself?"

Well, this was one opportunity to actually tell the truth.

"Whittling."

"I didn't realize it was that dangerous."

"Yeah. It's serious business."

I tried again, scooping up some of the wot into the bread and then rolling it. When I placed it into her mouth, I let my fingers linger over her lower lip as she chewed.

"Mmm," she said. "This is so good, right?"

"So, so good," I muttered, watching the movement of her lips and yearning to lick the remnants of sauce off of them. "What other cultures don't use forks?"

"I don't know of any offhand. Why?"

"Because I'm thinking this could be like our thing."

"Yeah? We already have a thing? So soon?"

"Why not?"

The next time I fed her, I did a sloppy job. Some of the food spilled onto her chin.

"This may not be your forte, Jay Reed."

I couldn't help myself when I said, "Cleaning it up is." I leaned in and licked it slowly off her chin. When she closed her eyes and let out a little sigh, I took that as a sign that she wanted more.

Fuck the goat.

I realized that it wasn't supposed to happen this way. I was supposed to wait to get my whittling prize, but I just couldn't help it. Placing my mouth over hers, I full-on kissed her.

My hand was wrapped around the back of her neck as she moaned into my mouth while I devoured her harder, flicking my tongue around the inside of her mouth, desperate to taste nothing anymore but her.

When a waiter came by to pour water into our glasses, she pulled back. Her face was flush, and she seemed embarrassed. I, on the other hand, couldn't have given a shit who'd witnessed our PDA.

Rock hard and totally fucked, I was in no way prepared to lose this girl anytime soon. One thing was undeniable: the sexual chemistry between Jay and Bianca was off the charts. And I wasn't ready to let Dex ruin it just yet until I had a better feel for what her reaction might be if and when I told her the truth. This time spent with her was possibly all I would ever have. Jay needed to exist just a little while longer.

She cleared her throat and said, "Well, I wasn't expecting that."

"Neither was I, but you're making me a little crazy, Bianca."

It dawned on me that I hadn't been making much of an effort to get to know her better tonight, hadn't asked any personal questions throughout dinner. That was partly because I was ill-prepared to talk about myself as Jay. Dex had spent so much time getting to know her intimately that Jay apparently felt he knew everything he needed to.

It would have seemed like I was uninterested if I didn't pry into her personal life at least a little bit. So, I spent the next several minutes asking her about her childhood, her last relationship, her career—things I already knew.

I did my best to answer the questions she threw at me, but the more we talked, the more I was feeling extremely guilty for letting this charade go on.

Bianca had a hungry look in her eyes. She was most definitely attracted to me, and I was pretty sure I wouldn't be needing many wooden sculptures to get into her pants. That was messed up. Dex was pissed at Jay for even thinking about fucking her. And Jay was annoyed at Dex for judging him for thoughts that came naturally. Perhaps, Dex and Jay should have both called ahead to secure some space at the insane asylum.

From the food to the kissing, dinner was phenomenal.

Once we returned to the Jeep, she turned to me and smiled. "It's time. I want my present now."

"I guess I did things a little ass backwards tonight, huh?" Reaching into the glove compartment, I actually felt nervous about it. Handing the wooden figurine to her, I said, "This... is for you."

Bianca covered her mouth. "Oh, my God! Is this a goat?"

"Yep, a billy goat."

She marveled at it. "Look at all of the detail. I can't believe you did this."

Neither could I.

"Look at the horns!" She laughed.

"Well, I'm a horny kind of guy."

She rolled her eyes.

I winked. "You like it?"

"Yes! I would really love to see you in action at some point. Watch you whittle."

Ugh.

"Yeah. Maybe. It's something I kind of do by myself to relieve stress. I've never done it in front of an audience before. I'll have to work up to that."

"Well, clearly, based on the state of your fingers, it's not easy."

"Yes. Harder than you think."

"That makes what you carved for me even more special. Thank you."

Guilt was suddenly consuming me. "You're welcome, Bianca."

I stared out the window for a bit, trying to snap myself out of the shitty feeling. "Where would you like to go next?"

"I have to be home by ten forty-five, actually."

"Oh?"

"Yeah. I have some work I have to do."

"Work?"

"It's actually my ongoing interview with Dexter Truitt. It's via online chat."

I sucked in my jaw. "Mister Moneybags?"

"Yeah. Rather than one sit-down interview, he's scheduled me in during the evenings. Eleven each night, Monday through Friday. I guess that time works best for him."

"So, you have to bend over backwards to accommodate *his* schedule?"

Two things were wrong with that question. One: I was making Dex look bad. Two: I was getting hard thinking about her bending over backwards with her legs open for Dex. Again...fucked up.

"Actually, it's worked out well to have a set time at night. His daytime schedule is too full. It won't be forever. My deadline is coming up at the end of the month."

Funny you should say that. So is mine.

"Okay, well, we have at least an hour before I have to drop you home. What would you like to do?"

"Honestly? I would love to see where you live, if it's not too far from me in SoHo. Maybe have a cup of coffee."

"Really?"

"I hope asking to go to your apartment doesn't sound too presumptuous."

"No. Not at all."

The reality of how far I'd taken this Jay lie really hit me in the moment. Knowing that my alter-ego was going to need a place to take Bianca to, I had rented a furnished apartment through an agency on a month-to-month agreement. How had I gotten myself here? If what I'd done ever came out, it was going to sound dirty—like I'd rented a fuck pad somewhere. When the truth of the matter was, I was inexplicably crazy about this woman and kept digging myself deeper in an attempt to buy more time with her. The entire thing made no sense to me, how would I ever get her to understand that down deep I'd done all this with the best of intentions.

She smiled at me with those big brown eyes, and somehow I justified my actions...again. "What part of the city do you live in?"

I had to think. *Where did I live?* I hadn't had a chance to visit the place yet, even though Josephine had gotten me the key. This was going to be a risk, but I didn't know how to get out of it. I checked my phone, pretending to look at the time and instead discreetly checked my email for the address of my "house."

"I live in NoHo."

"That's perfect, then." She grinned.

Yeah. Perfect.

An old man who apparently lived next to me gave us the evil eye as we stood in front of my door. Then, he disappeared into his own apartment.

"You don't normally say hello to your neighbors?"

Not when they don't know who the fuck I am, no.

"That guy doesn't like me very much. He's always complaining when I play music."

Upon opening the door and getting a look at what we were stepping into, I was ready to kill someone.

This looked nothing like the furnished apartment I saw online. The décor was tacky and ostentatious with lots of white, purple, and gold accents. I was completely speechless. How the hell was I going to explain this one?

Things took an even weirder turn when I spotted a humungous portrait of Elvis hanging on the wall. And, in the other corner was a life-size statue of Liza Minnelli.

Bianca's mouth was hanging open. "This is…"

"My aunt's place," I quickly said. "She…died. And left me the apartment. I haven't had the heart to change her signature style."

"That's so sweet of you. How long ago did she pass away?"

"About a year now. Eventually, I'll redecorate, but it just seems too soon."

She rubbed my shoulder. "I can understand that."

God, I was getting so fucking sick of this. I just wanted to take her into my arms and tell her everything. Why couldn't I?

She basically answered my question when she suddenly gripped the material of my shirt and pulled me into a kiss.

That was why.

I was going to lose this.

Nope. I wasn't ready to tell her anything, because there was a very good chance I would never get to feel this again. She didn't like liars, and you, Dexter Truitt...Jay Reed... whoever you are...are a liar.

A coldness replaced the warmth of her body as she stepped away. "Can I use your bathroom?"

"Sure, it's...actually..."

Where the fuck was it?

"Let me just check and make sure it's presentable. I might have left some laundry on the floor this morning, not expecting you to come back here. Be right back."

My heart was pounding as I ventured down the hall, opening each door until I found the bathroom.

Thank fuck I checked it. There was a huge stack of porn magazines next to the toilet. Without thinking it through, I opened the bathroom window and threw them out, praying they didn't hit anyone on the head on the street below. Beads of sweat were forming on my forehead at the mere thought of having to explain that one to her.

"Everything's decent," I said, returning to the living room. "Last door straight ahead down the hall."

With every second that she was in the bathroom, I became more and more paranoid about being in this place, about what else she might find. I remembered she mentioned coffee. Considering the cupboards were likely empty, I made a decision to get us the hell out of here. We'd passed a Starbucks around the corner on the way in. I'd suggest we go there.

When she emerged, I said, "I just remembered I'm all out of coffee. How about we head out for some before I have to take you home?"

"Okay...that would be nice. By the way, why does it smell like mothballs in this place?"

That's a great question, Bianca George.

"I had to use them. Major moth problem."

I fucking hated this. I would have wanted nothing more than to spend time with her in my real apartment. The next time I ever brought her back to this place, I would make sure it was inspected from top to bottom, fumigated, and stocked full of her favorite things.

Once at the coffee shop, we nestled into a corner couch and sipped our cappuccinos. She would be mid-conversation and I'd interrupt her by eating her words with a kiss. Each time I did, she'd let out a sound. I loved the feeling of her moans vibrating down my throat.

When ten-thirty rolled around, she looked at her phone. "I really have to go."

"You can't be a little late for your meeting with Mister Moneybags?"

"No. It's unprofessional."

To be honest, it irked me a little that she chose not to cancel on Dex. I actually had to remind myself that we were rooting for Dex. And by *we*, I meant Jay and Dex. Me. Deep down, *we* were both rooting for Dex. So, why was Jay fucking pissed?

I reluctantly dropped her off at her apartment before speeding back to my actual residence.

Once home, I needed to calm down before transforming back into myself. I noticed she was online and sent her a quick message.

Dex: Running a bit late. Give me ten minutes.

Without waiting for a response, I retreated to the shower and rubbed one out to the memories of her moaning into my mouth, imagining that we were doing a lot more than just kissing.

CHAPTER 7

Dex

My release had brought me a moment of clarity.

Dex needs to win Bianca over from Jay.

As fucked-up as that sounded, if she liked real me more than the fake me, it gave *me* a better shot at her accepting that real me was worth looking past all the lies I'd told. Maybe I was fucking delusional in addition to being newly schizophrenic. But at this point, it was the only plan I had. I needed to at least start to feel her out.

Dex: Hello, Bianca. I'm here now. Sorry about the delay. How has your evening been?

Bianca: It was very good, thank you.

Dex: What did you do?

Bianca: I had a date, actually.

Dex: A date that ended before eleven? Couldn't have been very good.

Bianca: My work takes priority.
Dex: I still maintain that it could have been better if you chose not to blow me off.

Bianca: It was amazing, actually.

It *was* amazing. I could still taste her on my tongue. And there were still so many more places I wanted to taste her.

Bianca: Are you there?

Dex: Yes. Tell me about your date. What was so amazing about it?

Bianca: Well, you know how with most people, you spend a little time with them and the puzzle pieces fall into place? You sort of get the full picture after you connect a few of the odd shapes?

Dex: I suppose.

Bianca: I feel like this guy is a ten-thousand-piece puzzle, and it's going to take a long time to see the picture.

Dex: And that's a good thing?

Bianca: It is. It means he has many layers.

I wasn't sure I agreed with her. The thing she liked best about Jay was his layers—but most of them were bandages to cover lies.

Dex: Tell me what you liked best about him?

Bianca: You want the truth?

Dex: Of course.

Bianca: The way he kissed me. I could feel he was trying to hold back—but at some point, he lost the battle. I liked that his attraction to me seemed to be uncontrollable. It made me feel sexy.

I had to laugh to myself. I'd thought I was doing such a great job hiding what being around her did to me. I guess I was way more transparent than I thought.

Bianca: BTW, I think we have our roles reversed tonight. I'm the one who is supposed to be interviewing you.

Dex: I find hearing about you way more interesting than telling you about myself.

She was quiet for a minute or two after that. I knew I shouldn't be pushing, but what the fuck—I was in this deep.

Dex: Are you and this jigsaw dating exclusively?

Bianca: No. We're not there yet. I don't have any dates with other men planned, but that's not intentional.

Dex: So, if say, a handsome, young, wealthy man with a six pack were to ask you out on a date, you'd be open to the invitation, then?

Bianca: Are you referring to yourself?

Dex: Maybe...

I waited eagerly for her response. When it came, my stomach sank.

Bianca: Then, no.

My mood sucked after that answer. I was pissed and just wanted to get the rest of our chat over with. She had no interest in the real me and would rather spend time getting to know a man who lived in his dead aunt's apartment and whittled.

Dex: Why don't we get started with your interview?

For the next thirty minutes, Bianca asked me questions. Since I was feeling ornery, my answers were less candid than I'd been the last two times we'd chatted. Toward the end, she mentioned she was going to be away on a business trip and planned to use the time to go through her notes and write up a draft of her story. She'd suggested we chat next week so that she could fill in any holes in her story, and I'd agreed.

Dex: How about next Tuesday at our regular time?

Bianca: That would be great.

Dex: Have a safe trip, Bianca.

Bianca: Thank you.

Feeling utterly deflated, I was just about to shut my laptop when another message popped up from her.

Bianca: Dex? Are you still there?

Dex: I am.

Bianca: For the record, I have a firm rule that I don't date men anymore whom I have a business relationship with.

Dex: Does that rule apply after your business with a man concludes?

She took a bit longer to respond that time.

Bianca: No. I don't think that rule would apply once my business was concluded.

Fuck you, Jay. Game back on.

Dex: Good to know. Sweet dreams, Bianca.

The next afternoon, traffic was even heavier than usual. The meeting I'd slated one hour for had turned into a three-hour unproductive waste of time. I looked at my watch when the light turned red again—we hadn't made it more than four car lengths in two damn green lights. There was a heaping pile of documents waiting for review back on my desk, and my secretary would be gone by the time we made it across town. I emailed Josephine and asked her to order me some dinner to the office before she left and to pull the files I knew I'd need to get my work done tonight, if I ever arrived.

Frustrated, I rested my head back against the leather seat and stared out the window thinking about Bianca. Last night, she'd led me to believe she would be willing to go out with me—the Dex me—at the end of our chat. Which had to mean she felt some sort of connection to the real me. I just couldn't figure out how I was going to get out of the mess I'd gotten myself into. If there was one thing I had learned in business, it was that anything was possible if you wanted it bad enough. Perhaps that was the key—I needed to look at my situation with Bianca like a business problem. I'd been letting my own emotions get in the way.

What would I do if Bianca was a business I wanted to obtain, yet the owner wasn't interested in selling to me? That was easy...I'd get to know that business better—the likes and dislikes of the owner—what made him tick. Then use that to show him why I was a good fit to take over his company in a way that was meaningful to him.

I shut my eyes for a moment.

What makes you tick, Georgy Girl? What do you like and dislike and why?

I racked my brain for a few minutes and still came up with nothing I could think of that would help me gain an edge. Discouraged, I opened my eyes when we stopped at yet another red light and looked out the window again. To my surprise—the answer was right there in big bold letters. I was looking for a sign and found a literal one on the corner of West 21st and 7th Avenue. The big storefront sign was illuminated in silver letters.

Forever Grey

"Are you here for the six o'clock class, sir?"

"Umm." I looked around the room and caught a sign taped to the door advertising that tonight was a training class for new volunteers. "Yes. I guess I am here for the class." *Any chance you also have a psychotherapy session after that?* It was totally normal to make a pit stop to become a greyhound dog walker when I had a full day's work ahead of me this evening, right? Even the woman at the counter thought I'd lost my marbles. She looked me up and down.

"Umm. That's a pretty nice suit. You do realize these dogs tend to slobber a lot, right?"

"Yes. I was planning to change before we started." *My mind, perhaps?*

Suzette, as her nametag indicated, thought that was a good idea. Since we had ten minutes before class started, I filled out the registration form and went back outside to my driver. "I'm going to be a while, Sam."

He was rightfully confused. I'd basically yelled at him to stop and then marched into what appeared from the outside to be a pet facility, yet he knew I had no pets. "Is everything okay, sir?"

No.

"Yes. I forgot I'd signed up to volunteer at the greyhound rescue tonight. It's part of some charitable thing that Caroline somehow roped me into."

This lying thing was really beginning to come naturally now. It wasn't unlike criminal behavior—starting out with petty crimes—one day you're whacking a gumball machine on its side to make a plastic container filled with a broken ring pop out, and before you know it, you're robbing a bank at gunpoint.

"Why don't you take off? I'll grab a cab back up to the office when I'm done here."

After Sam drove away, I stood outside of Forever Grey and looked up and down the street to see if there was anywhere to pick up a change of clothes. Finding a Modell's Sporting Goods store, I headed over and grabbed some sweats, a t-shirt, and running shoes. Ironically, it was almost the same outfit that Jay had on when he met Bianca in that elevator. That actually seemed fitting for some reason.

Ten minutes into the class, I realized that dog walking was more complicated than I thought. Length of leash, walking in front of the canine rather than behind him to show which one of us was the pack leader, rewarding positive behavior, socializing the dog...and here I always thought you clicked on a leash, and the rest took care of itself.

My greyhound was a three-year-old named Bandit. Suzette informed me that Bandit had torn his cruciate ligament during a race and, although he was perfectly fine as a pet, he was no longer a contender when it came to dog racing. As such, his owner was going to put him down—hence how he came to be at Forever Grey.

After my hour-long training was complete, Bandit and I took a walk on our own. There was a small, local park two blocks away that allowed dogs, so we set off—me ahead of my short-leashed, canine companion. When we got there, even though the sun was already setting, it was still hot and humid. Bandit looked like he needed a break so I took a seat on a park bench. My trusty companion took a seat, too, only he faced my way and stared straight at me.

"What's the matter, buddy? I don't have any more treats for you."

The dog cocked his head and continued to stare at me.

I leaned forward and scratched his head. "You want me to pet you?"

When he inched closer to me and made a sound that sounded an awful lot like a purr, I took that to mean I was doing the right thing. Using both hands, I dug my fingers behind his ears and scratched. As he sat, one of his hind legs began to move in unison with the rhythm of my scratching. "You like that, huh." I got a kick out of watching his leg slow with the speed of my scratch, then speeding up again when I did. At one point, he suddenly jarred forward and began to lick my face.

"Guess this is as good as it gets. You're a smart dog, you know that?"

Bandit licked my face again as if to tell me he agreed with my assessment.

"Tell me, if you're so smart, what makes Bianca tick? Because I can't for the life of me figure that one out. Maybe you've even met her? Long legs, caramel eyes, comes around on Sundays. Smells damn incredible. You'd notice her, buddy. Trust me."

I was acting pretty nutty lately, although I wasn't really expecting an answer. But one came; only it wasn't Bandit that spoke.

"Got yourself in a pickle, huh?" An old lady sat down on the bench next to me. She had a head full of rollers covered by a bright, multi-colored scarf and was wearing a hot pink smock. In her hand was a bag full of birdseed, which gave me caution.

"You're not going to feed the birds right now, are you?"

"I'll wait until there aren't any more dogs left in the park." She lifted her chin toward Bandit. "From the conversation you were just having with him, it sounds like you're already in hot water. Don't need me calling the pigeons over for your dog to try to chase."

I nodded. "Thank you."

"So what did you do, anyway?"

"Pardon?"

"I don't walk as fast as I used to. Heard you telling the pooch you couldn't figure someone named Bianca out."

I sighed. "It's a long story."

"Not much I can offer these days except my time. Try me."

I didn't generally talk to strangers. Certainly, I didn't tell them problems with my love life. But, hey...why not? I was batshit crazy these days anyway. This was par for the course.

"I'll give you the short version. Met a woman—lied to her. One lie turned into two—which now seems to have snowballed out of control."

The woman shook her head, tsking. "Since you seem to care about her finding out, I take it you like this lady?"

"I do."

"Whatever it is, you need to come clean. Better to be slapped with the truth, then kissed with a lie."

My shoulders slumped. That's exactly what I'd done. Kissed her with a lie, both in the literal and figurative sense. "The funny thing is, I lied because I thought I needed to lie for her to give me a shot. But in the end, she was getting to know the real me and now that one lie is going to make her question all of the truths."

The old woman pointed to Bandit. "Is she a dog lover like yourself?"

I was too ashamed to tell her that even my dog walking stint was part of my lie. "She is."

"That's good. I have six dogs and two cats. Leave them home when I come to feed the pigeons each night. Animal lovers like us are a different breed. I always say, look at how a person treats an animal to know what's in their heart. If she's an animal lover, she already knows how to love unconditionally—it's likely she has a good spirit and has it in her to forgive an old dog like yourself for making a mistake."

"You think?"

"I was married for forty-three years. But when I first met my Walter, God rest his soul, he hit the sauce a little too hard one night and kissed a pretty bar maid."

"And you forgave him?"

"Hell no. I dumped his ass. Made him grovel for a good month, went out on a date with a guy I knew he didn't like and made sure he knew about it. But in the end—I hated the sin—but really missed the sinner."

I laughed. "Thanks for the advice. I think."

Since I'd kept Bandit out long enough, we said goodbye to the old lady and walked back to Forever Grey. Suzette was waiting in the lobby.

"I saw you coming up the street. You two seemed to have hit it off."

"We did, didn't we?" I leaned down and gave the dog one last pet.

"Will you be able to donate some time to dog walk each week? We can try to put you with Bandit if you've bonded."

I had zero available time, yet... "Sure. My calendar is full during the weekdays, but perhaps we can work something in."

"How about Sundays?"

"No," I snapped...perhaps a bit too quick. "I meant—it's hard for me to get away on Sundays but I should be able to figure a time during the week. Do you have a card? I can call you once I figure it out."

She reached behind the counter and pulled out a card, handing it to me in exchange for Bandit's leash.

"Thank you. I'll be in touch soon." *Before my sanity returns.*

CHAPTER 8

Bianca

It was starting to feel like I was being blown off. After I returned home from my business trip, I'd texted Jay to let him know I was back, and though we'd exchanged messages for a while, he didn't attempt to nail me down for our next date either. Perhaps he was just busy at work, and I was reading too much into things.

While I was a bit disappointed about it since I thought the chemistry we had on our date was off the charts, there was a part of me that also felt a bit conflicted about my conversations with Dex. Mister Moneybags had grown on me. And unless I was misreading things, he was also interested in me. My trip out of town gave me the opportunity to pull together my story about the elusive Dexter Truitt, and I'd also done some deeper research. Tonight, I had some questions about his father that I thought might be difficult, but would definitely shed more light on the mysterious man.

Promptly at eleven, the chat window on my laptop popped up. My pathetic heart started to accelerate seeing that Dex was already typing to me.

Dex: Hello, Bianca.

Was it weird that I heard him say my name in a deep, sexy voice. *Hello*, Bianca.

Bianca: Hello, Mr. Truitt.

Dex: I thought we'd moved past the formalities.

I'd nervously typed that without thinking. He was right; we weren't Mr. Truitt and Ms. George anymore.

Bianca: Sorry. Habit.

Dex: How was your week? Did you miss me?

Yes.

Bianca: I did think about you a lot.

Dex: Tell me more about that.

Bianca: Well, I was writing your story and that had me thinking about you.

I left off the fact that I'd saved the candid photo he'd sent me during our first chat and was staring at his abs while I was writing his story all weekend. That might have had something to do with why he was so difficult to get out of my head this week.

Dex: It seems that since I'm not writing a story about you, I have no excuse for thinking about you. No professional excuse, that is.

I smiled at the screen.

Bianca: Are you saying your thoughts of me are not professional?

I chewed my nail watching the screen as Dex typed back.

Dex: My thoughts were definitely more of a personal nature.

Bianca: Interesting.

Dex: They certainly were...

Great, I was going to get all hot and bothered at the beginning of the interview. Suddenly, I had no idea what to type in response. Turned out that was okay.

Dex: So how'd my story come out?

I was relieved he'd brought us back around to a work discussion.

Bianca: I think people are going to enjoy it. I just have a few more questions.

Dex: Shoot.

There wasn't really a way to soften what I needed to find out, so I went with the direct approach.

Bianca: What happened between your father and you?

He was silent for a minute.

I knew from personal experience what a horrible person Dexter's father was. I specifically chose not to divulge that to Dex. In the end, it didn't matter anymore. My need to get even with Dexter Truitt Sr. seemed less important the more I'd gotten to know his son. They were simply not cut from the same cloth.

Dex: As I've divulged before, my father was a liar and a cheat for most of his life. He cheated on my mother for the majority of their marriage and cheated business partners out of money. As a kid, I didn't really understand what type of a person my father was. I'd idolized him, in fact, even though my time with him had always been limited. By the time I was a teenager, he was all over the news for his alleged involvement in some crooked deals. Even though he was somehow always cleared of anything technically illegal, there was nothing he could do to hide the truth about himself from me anymore. So, our relationship was strained for many years because I didn't want to be associated with his bad behavior. As I've told you before, my

decision to stay out of the public eye has a lot to do with not wanting to repeat my father's mistakes. I alienated myself from him for a long time, which was wise from a business standpoint.

Bianca: And from a personal standpoint?

Dex: Well, the guy is still my father. It's not easy to be on bad terms with the person who helped give you life. We've been working on our relationship more over the past few years. He's joined a church down in Florida—thinks he's found Jesus. He also had a skin cancer scare. I think he's starting to realize that life is too short to live it like a piece of shit.

Bianca: So, you are slowly learning to forgive him.

Dex: I'm trying, yes. It's more about accepting the things I can't change and moving forward. I can't change the fact that he wasn't a very good father to me as a kid. But he wants to be more involved in my adult life now, so that's an opportunity I can choose to take or leave. I don't want to have any regrets, and I know he won't be around forever.

Bianca: I think the ability to forgive is an admirable trait.

He took a particularly long time to respond this time.

Dex: What do you consider worthy of forgiveness?

Bianca: What do you mean?

Dex: You said once that you don't like liars. Would you forgive someone who lied to you?

Bianca: It depends on the reason for the lie.

Dex: Give me an example.

Bianca: If someone lies to protect another person, then I find that forgivable. Like my mother. She lied to me to protect me. My father was having affairs and she would make up stories to make him look good. In the end, it turned out his indiscretions were what ended their marriage. So, while I don't condone lying, in the case of my mother, I'm able to forgive her because she lied to keep me from being hurt about what my father had done.

Once again, his response was delayed.

Dex: Are there any other situations in which you might forgive someone for lying?

I had to think about that. In general, there was really no excuse for lying, in my book. But I couldn't say I hadn't told some white ones in my life.

Bianca: I don't know. I guess it would just have to depend on the individual scenario.

Dex: You don't think it's black and white. Fair enough.

Bianca: How has the spotlight once again turned on me?

Dex: I think we're beyond the point where there are any rules in this process, Bianca.

Bianca: That's true. Come to think of it, I've pretty much broken every journalism ethics rule during this entire experience.

Dex: I won't tell anyone if you don't. The published product will be the same in the end. We've just had more fun along the way than most people do.

Bianca: You're right. It really hasn't seemed like work at all.

Dex: I would even venture to say I'll miss these 11PM chats when we're finished.

"Miss" wasn't the right term for how I felt about the interview process nearing an end. I'd become addicted to talking to Dex. Obsessed. It was as if my entire day revolved around just getting to eleven.

Bianca: I will, too.

We'd come to a break in the conversation. It was obvious that our interview had really run its course. I had so much information on this man that I didn't know what to do with it; it couldn't possibly all fit into a four-page article. There wasn't really a need to continue communicating. But I found him fascinating and would continue our chats for as long as I could get away with. He didn't need to know that I was virtually finished with the piece.

His next message threw me for a loop.

Dex: What happened to that guy you were dating?

That's a good question. I didn't know what had happened with Jay.

Bianca: We haven't made plans in a while.

Dex: Why not?

Bianca: I think he's been busy. We've been in touch but just haven't nailed down any dates to go out.

Dex: You don't sound too devastated.

Bianca: Honestly, between my trip and working on the feature, I haven't had much time to dwell on it.

Dex: You've been too focused on me.

Bianca: You can look at it that way, yes.

Dex: I choose to. ;-)

Bianca: What about you? What's your excuse? Why are you never cancelling on me? You must have a bevy of women waiting in the wings.

Dex: Not a bevy, but yes, I don't have to beg for dates.

Bianca: You don't say...

Dex: Want to know the truth, though?

Bianca: Always.

Dex: Lately, I haven't wanted to talk to anyone but you.

I let his words sink in. A flash of heat permeated my body. How was it possible to be so taken with someone I had never even met? I really wanted to see him—more than I'd ever wanted anything. I impulsively typed.

Bianca: How about right now? I want to see you tonight.

I closed my eyes and cringed at my assertiveness. My heart was pounding as I waited for a reply. It took him a while to respond.

Dex: Not tonight. We agreed to meet at the end, remember?

My emotional state went from hot to cold real fast. He'd implied before that he wanted to date me, yet he keeps avoiding actually *meeting* me. I needed to call him out.

Bianca: I have a feeling there will always be an excuse.

The spaces of time between his responses were getting longer and longer.

Dex: I just need to be prepared.

Prepared for what?

Bianca: Prepared?

Dex: Yes. This time with you has been different from anything I've ever experienced. You know more about me than most people. And I probably know more about you than any of the women I've dated, and yet, I can't seem to get enough. I've exposed myself to you—in

more ways than one, practically. This is new for me. Meeting you in person will be intense. And then there's the risk of disappointing you. I think that's my biggest apprehension.

Bianca: How can you possibly disappoint me if I know almost everything about you already?

Dex: You may not like what you see.

Bianca: Let me at least hear your voice then.

Dex: Not yet.

Bianca: Why not?

Dex: You'll hear me soon enough.

Bianca: Do you sound like Mickey Mouse or something?

Dex: No, I can assure you I don't. My testosterone levels are good. I suspect you'll like my voice, actually. LOL. I can't believe you just asked me that.

Bianca: I have to explore all possible reasons why you are hiding. And quite honestly, at this point, you're making me a little self-conscious, Mr. Truitt.

Dex: We're back to formalities now? Don't call me that anymore. We're beyond that. And tell me why you're feeling self-conscious when you have absolutely no reason to be.

Because I was starting to think that his apprehension was really about *me*.

Bianca: There are multiple reasons. I sometimes worry that, despite our online chemistry, you don't really have any intention of meeting me at all. I also worry that our chats have become like a game to you. And sometimes, this is the worst one, I worry that I'm being catfished, that maybe I haven't really been speaking to Dexter Truitt at all.

Dex: I swear to God, it's me. I would NEVER do that to you, Bianca. It's me.

I believed him. It was low of me to assert that. That thought had rarely crossed my mind, but deep down, I didn't actually believe it.

Bianca: Okay. I believe you. I'm sorry. I'm overreacting. I just feel like I've gotten in a little deep when I shouldn't have. This is all so unprofessional.

Dex: Fuck professional! Understand something: I do have concerns about meeting you, but NONE of them have to do with YOU.

They ALL have to do with your impression of ME.

Bianca: Do you think I'm shallow? Is it your face you're afraid of me seeing?

Dex: No. I know you're not shallow and it has a *little* to do with my face, yes.

Well, now I was just totally confused. He thinks he's ugly? Honestly, with a body like that, I'm pretty sure I could overlook it. More than that, it was *him* I wanted first and foremost, not his body nor his face.

Bianca: I'm sorry. I should have never mentioned seeing you. You already agreed to meet with me. I guess I just need to trust that and be patient.

Dex: I promise we will meet, Bianca. Don't ever be sorry about asking for what you want, either.

I needed to end the chat before I said anything else I would regret.

Bianca: I'm going to turn in for the night, if you don't mind.

Dex: I upset you.

Bianca: No. I'm fine. I think I just need to rest.

Dex: Okay.

When I didn't reply, he sent another message.

Dex: Tomorrow night. Same time?

Bianca: Yes. Goodnight, Dex.

Dex: Sweet dreams, Bianca.

I shut my laptop and closed my eyes. Feeling completely defeated, I checked my cell phone for any texts from Jay. There were none.

But twenty minutes later, there *was* a knock at the door.

CHAPTER 9

Dex

Bianca's eyes widened when she saw me standing there.

This was a mistake.

But I needed to see her.

Her eyes looked tired, like maybe she'd been crying.

Fuck.

I'd hurt her.

That's why I came; I needed to know she was okay.

"Jay? What are you doing here?"

Instead of answering her, I wrapped my palms around her cheeks and pulled her into a deep kiss, desperately letting out all of the painful frustration that had built up inside of me after our earlier conversation.

It was Jay's mouth she thought she was moaning into, but every part of me was kissing her as Dex.

I'm so sorry, Georgy Girl.

My dick was hard as a rock as I fervently tasted her. She panted into my mouth as my erection pressed into her abdomen. She tasted like toothpaste. Her braless, supple breasts were pressed against my chest. I could have easily taken her right there in the middle of her living room.

Bianca's heart was pounding so hard against mine, and I took that as my cue to kiss her harder. She grasped the back of my neck, pulling me closer. I suddenly got the urge to lift her up. So, I did. She wrapped her legs around me as I continued to kiss her harder than I'd probably ever kissed anyone.

Adrenaline was rushing through me. It was mixed with a little bit of rage because of the fact that she'd so easily let "Jay" take advantage of her. After our conversation tonight, I was more certain than ever that her heart belonged to *me*—to Dex. Yet, she still managed to let *me*—Jay—do this. Was she that weak? It made me mad.

I ached to fuck her, to express physically all of the emotions I'd been forced to bottle up tonight.

Finally pulling back and slowly lowering her to the floor, I said, "That was probably the best welcome I've ever received."

She kept her arms around my neck. "I wasn't sure if I was going to ever see you again, to be honest."

I was finding it harder and harder to look her in the eyes as Jay. Staring down at the floor, I said, "I need to apologize for not getting my shit together lately. It has nothing to do with a lack of desire to see you. Things have been crazy at work, and I haven't been able to get here until now."

Fucking liar.

"I needed this sanity check tonight," she said.

"Why?" I swallowed. "What happened?"

"Nothing. It's too much to get into. I'm pretty sure I almost lost my mind earlier. It's just...really good to see you."

No. No. No.

You didn't lose your mind.

You're right on target.

Jay needs to go—he just needed to touch you one last time.

"Everything okay now?"

"Now that you're here, yes." She smiled.

"I wasn't sure if you'd be up."

"I don't think I would have been able to sleep tonight anyway."

Me, neither.

"What happened exactly to upset you?"

"I really don't want to talk about it, if that's okay. It has to do with work."

The fuck it does. Speaking of those white lies we talked about earlier...

Rubbing my hands along the tops of her arms, I said, "Look, I really can't stay. I just..."

Needed to make sure you were okay.

Needed to see you.

Needed to touch you.

I continued, "I just wanted to say hello, to let you know I was thinking about you."

And to say goodbye.

She looked panicked. "When will I see you again?"

"I'm not sure. Work has been crazy."

And Jay needs to die.

Bianca hesitated for a while before she finally said, "I really don't want to be alone tonight. Will you lie with me?" When I didn't respond, she leaned in and gently kissed me, then said, "Please?"

There was nothing else in the world I wanted more.

Unable to come up with a legitimate reason to refuse, I nodded. "Yeah. Sure."

Bianca led me to her bedroom. It felt surreal. A yellow legal pad sat atop the nightstand. I suspected that was the side of the bed where she lay whenever she was chatting with Dex. It took everything in me not to lean over to try to see what was written down. I figured there might have been some obscenities from earlier tonight.

Bianca got into bed, and I slipped in behind her. Several minutes passed as we just lay there together. My mouth was against her back, and I let the sound of her breathing soothe me. It was as if I could feel her thoughts through each breath. I knew in my heart that despite the fact that she was enjoying the warmth of Jay's body, she was thinking about the real me, about Dex.

It all seemed innocent enough until she backed her soft ass into my dick. She intentionally rubbed against me, causing a raging hard on. After a few more times, I realized she was doing it to egg me on. Fuck, it was working. I continued to let her slowly grind against me. There was a word for this in high school: dry humping. I should have known that there was no way I could innocently sleep next to this woman.

Ready to explode in my jeans, I said, "Stop."

She turned around and whispered over my lips, "You don't want me?"

My body was in turmoil. She wanted to fuck me. And I wanted to be inside of her more than anything. But I just couldn't. I could never consider sleeping with her until she knew the truth.

I got up and ran my hand through my hair. "I need to leave."

She hopped up from the bed. "I'm sorry. I got carried away. It's been a long time. I thought you wanted it, figured that's why you came here so late. So, I wanted to let you know that it would be okay...if you wanted to. But it's fine."

My voice was louder than I intended. "I *do* want to...God, I do. But you really need to be careful, Bianca. You don't even really know me."

She let out a bitter laugh, "You're warning me against you?"

"No."

Fuck yes, I am.

I continued, "I just don't want to move too fast with you. And I just think we...should get to know each other better first."

Even though I know almost everything there is to know about you.

Letting out a deep breath, I went on. "But since I really can't resist you, I think the best thing for me to do is to go home tonight, then take you out again properly. You're not some booty call to me, Bianca."

She placed her hands over her face and spoke into them. "You're right. I was just...feeling like I needed it tonight."

I know.

Because of me.

My chest hurt. I needed to get out of here before I admitted everything. She wasn't in the right state of mind for the truth tonight.

Kissing her softly on the forehead, I said, "I'll call you soon, okay?"

She simply nodded before walking me to the door.

Try to whittle your way out of this one, douchebag.

Feeling like an absolute asshole, I drove home in my Jeep vowing that after tonight, Jay was dead.

The next morning at the office, I was distracted, to say the least. Cancelling all my meetings for the day, I did something I almost never did. I went home and did nothing.

Sitting on my couch, I watched the clock, anxious for my chat with Bianca later. Only nine more hours to go. Dread filled me.

Should I tell her tonight?

I picked up the phone and decided to dial the one person who I knew could relate to what I was going through right now.

He picked up. "Hello, son."

"How are you feeling?"

"Not bad. Just came in from a walk. About to make a tuna sandwich."

"How's the weather down there?"

"It's Florida. Hot with a chance of rain pretty much all of the time."

"Yes, that's true."

"To what do I owe this phone call?"

"I actually need your advice."

"That's not something you often seek."

"Well, this is one circumstance where I think you can actually be of some help. It involves lying. I've gotten myself into some deep shit."

"Ah. Now, this is making sense."

"I know you didn't exactly hide your affairs from Mother very well. But essentially, you always seemed to be able to get back into her good graces..."

He interrupted, "Are you having an affair on someone?"

"No, I'm not a cheater, Dad. But I lied about my identity. The woman I'm dating thinks I'm someone else."

"Are you ashamed of yourself or something?"

"It's a long story. I thought she had some preconceived notions about rich and powerful men. I made a bad judgment call. Basically, I'm going to come clean to her soon and need to own up to my mistake. I just wondered if there was a trick to admitting a lie in a way that it would result in the least amount of damage."

He chuckled. "Your mother was way too good to me, far too forgiving. She shouldn't have been. There is no trick, Dex. If you're lucky, this woman will see who you really are and forgive you. If you're not lucky, I'm afraid there is nothing you can do to convince someone you've hurt that they should give you a second chance. That's the price we pay for dishonesty. If she's got it in her mind that you're untrustworthy, there may be no turning back from that. I've learned that the hard way."

My chest constricted. "Alright."

He added, "I've lost good people in my lifetime who were right in their decision not to trust me."

"Well, I was hoping this conversation would make me feel better, but I actually feel worse now."

"Sorry, son. I'm just trying to be honest."

"Oh, the irony."

We both got a good laugh out of that. It felt weird to be laughing with Dexter Sr., bonding over our mutual indiscretions.

"Yeah." He sighed.

"I'll let you get back to your lunch, old man."

"Keep in touch."

"I will."

I was about to hang up when he said, "Dex?"

"Yeah?"

"I'm proud of you for trying to be a better man than me. I hope you get out of this mess, hope you get the girl."

"Not exactly the tongue I want to taste." Using the back of my hand, I wiped Bandit's slobber from my mouth. It was the third day in a row I'd come to take my new buddy for a walk. Jay was officially dead, and Dex was too big of a pansy ass to come clean to Bianca, so the only connection I had to Georgy Girl was a hundred-pound, shit machine whose breath smelled like ass. Sadly, he was the best friend I had at the moment.

"What are we gonna do, buddy?" I was sitting on the park bench again, and Bandit sat down facing me. Perhaps I was losing my sanity, but when he quirked one ear up, I could have sworn he was listening—wanted to help me solve my woman problems. "Have you ever lost your shit over a woman? Done something really stupid that you couldn't figure out how to make it right? I don't know...maybe take a bitch's bone and bury it when she wasn't looking?"

Bandit lifted his paw and swatted my knee. I took that as a yes. Bandit was a bone thief. "You did, huh? Did you come clean and win her heart in the end?"

Bandit opened his mouth and let out a big yawn, then rested his long face on my lap.

"I'm even boring a dog with my life." I scratched his head and sighed. "I just don't know what to do. How do I explain why I kept up the charade for so long? Admit that

I was afraid she wouldn't like me if I was who I really am? Or admit that I really *am* the asshole she thought I was and that she probably wouldn't like me much if we'd met under other circumstances?" The truth was, that was what I was really afraid of—that once she got to know the real me, she'd smarten up and find herself an honest bike messenger.

It was almost eight, and I was already an hour later than I should have been getting to the office, so I walked my new best friend back to the shelter. Suzette wasn't around when I'd arrived an hour ago but was now working the counter. "Mr. Truitt. I'm glad I caught you. I wanted to let you know that Bandit is getting relocated to our farm upstate at the end of this week."

"A farm?"

She offered an unconvincing smile. "We can only keep dogs in the shelter here in the city for so long—after three months they go upstate for retirement if they aren't adopted."

"Upstate? A farm? Are you saying what I think you're saying?" I'd had a dog that went to the so-called farm once when I was a kid. I remember the day I'd told my friend that Buster had gone to have a better life on a farm. He'd set me straight on what *the farm* really meant.

Suzette's smile was real. "God, no. It's not like that. Our farm is a nice place. A woman named Allison runs it—she's pretty amazing, actually. The only downside is the animals don't get as much interaction with people as they do here in the city where we get lots of volunteers. But it's a nice farm, and the dogs have room to run during the day."

When I looked down at Bandit, he was staring up at me. *Don't give me those sad eyes. It's a real farm. Not the proverbial farm parents used to make naïve children feel better. Didn't you hear the woman?* I kneeled down and rubbed the top of his head. "You take care of yourself. Okay, buddy?" For some reason, it felt like I was saying goodbye to the last part of Bianca I was holding on to. After a few minutes, I stood and offered Suzette the leash.

When she took it, Bandit refused to move from my side.

Suzette made kissy sounds. "Come on, Bandit. Time for Mr. Truitt to go."

The damn dog didn't budge, even when Suzette gave the collar a light tug.

"I'm sorry. They bond very quickly. Let me go grab his favorite toy."

She disappeared and came back a few minutes later squeaking a toy bone. That got his attention. "Come on, Bandit." *Squeak. Squeak.* "Say goodbye to Mr. Truitt."

I looked down at my trusty friend—my keeper of secrets—to say goodbye. But instead it wasn't what I said at all. I wasn't even sure who put the fucking words in my mouth that I vomited out. All I know is that I wasn't ready to let go of the last piece of Bianca just yet. And...I'd lost what was left of my mind.

"I'd like to adopt Bandit."

CHAPTER 10

Bianca

"What the...?"

My brain was seriously screwing with me. As I walked down 21st Street lost in thought about Dexter Truitt, the guilt I'd been feeling for thinking about him while I was kissing Jay the other night must have really started to get to me. I blinked my eyes into focus watching from a distance while a tall, dark, handsome man who looked an awful lot like Jay Reed was getting into the back of a fancy Town Car. From a block away, the man really looked like Jay, only he was wearing a three-piece suit and helping a greyhound jump into a car, rather than riding a bicycle. I laughed to myself how nutty my imagination could be sometimes and watched the dark car pull away from the curb as I made my way to Forever Grey.

Inside, Suzette greeted me. "Hey Bianca. Did I sleep through a day, or is today Monday?"

I laughed. I only ever went to the shelter on Sunday mornings. "Nope. It's Monday, alright. I came yesterday, too." I hesitated to continue what I was going to say at first, because what I was going to say might sound a little batshit crazy, but then I remembered if anyone would understand it was another dog person. "Yesterday, I walked a dog I've never walked before...and...well, I've been struggling with some things and taking him out made me feel a lot better." I decided to leave off the part that I spent the better part of an hour telling the poor dog my problems.

Suzie smiled. "The best therapists have four legs and a tail, if you ask me. Which dog is it? I'll get him for you."

"His name is Bandit."

Suzie looked surprised. "Bandit seems to be very popular lately. In fact, you just missed him. He was actually adopted by a volunteer." She pointed to the door. "Walked out less than five minutes ago."

Call it intuition, but my stomach dropped—a feeling of uneasiness crept over me, and I wasn't sure why. "Who...who adopted him?"

Suzie looked around and then leaned in. "I'm not really supposed to give out adoption or volunteer information... but...Bandit hit the jackpot. He was adopted by a guy who lives on Central Park West. Some big-wig who owns his own company."

"Was his name...Jay Reed, by any chance?"

She shook her head. "No, that's not his name."

Feeling relief, I let out a breath. "Okay. I just saw a guy on the street with a greyhound right before I came in. He reminded me of someone, and I thought maybe it was him."

"Definitely not named Jay. But if Jay looks anything like Bandit's new owner, he's welcome to come volunteer."

I laughed. "Good looking, huh?"

"Oh yeah." Suzette gathered some papers into a file and closed it on top of the reception counter. "How about if I grab Marla for you? She hasn't been out today, and you've walked her before, right?"

"Marla would be great. She's really sweet."

Suzette disappeared to the back where they kept the dogs, and I waited at the desk. After I checked my phone and found I still didn't have any new texts from Jay, I tucked it back into my pocket and looked around. The folder that Suzette had swept papers into was labeled *adoptions*. I was curious by nature, but not usually such a snoop. Glancing around the room, I found no one paying attention, so I used my pointer finger to gently lift open the manila folder—just enough to sneak a peek.

I caught the home address on the second line: 1281 Central Park West. Suzette wasn't kidding—Bandit was moving on up. Then my eyes lifted to the first line of the application. Blinking a few times, I was certain my brain was screwing with me again. There was no way it could be possible. It didn't make any sense. Not giving a shit if I was caught at that point, I opened the folder and tore the first page from inside. Staring, I couldn't believe what was written clear as day on line one.

Dexter Truitt.

My stomach was nauseous as I stood across the street in the park, waiting. I'd blown off the interview I was supposed to do this afternoon in favor of stalking like a crazy person.

Nothing made sense.

Over the last few hours, I'd connected the puzzle pieces and figured out what Dex-slash-Jay had done to me. I just didn't understand why.

Was this a game rich assholes liked to play? Screw with the working-class woman and see if you can get her to fuck you as a poor man? That was the puzzle piece that didn't fit. Because the other night Jay *could have* fucked me—I'd rubbed myself up against him, practically begged him for it. God I was so fucking pathetic. But if that was his game—why didn't he take the prize I was so willing to give? I hated that the only thing I could think of was that he didn't even want me physically. Basically, I was a mental game for him and not even my ass grinding up against his dick made him want me.

When the dark Town Car finally pulled up in front of his fancy ass building, I watched from across the street as he got out. It killed me that my heart sped up seeing him step from the car. Dexter Truitt-slash-Jay Reed was most certainly an asshole—but a gorgeous asshole at that. I almost jumped out from behind the tree I was watching from, but when Dex leaned in and helped Bandit from the car, I was too confused and mesmerized to approach.

What is he doing with the dog?

The two of them walked to a small grassy area for a minute. Dex petted the dog and said something to him after he relieved himself, then they headed to the front door of the building. Right before he stepped inside, Dex stopped abruptly, turned back, and looked around the street. Ducking back to safety behind the tree, my heart was beating out of my chest as I wondered if he could have felt me watching him.

Then, just like that, he was gone.

I stood there for almost another hour, feeling all kinds of emotions. I was angry that there was no Jay—that I'd thrown myself at a man I clearly didn't know at all. I was angry that I fell for the shit Dexter Truitt had fed me—the man was no better than his father. And I was angry that, above everything else, I was sad that the man I'd started to fall for didn't really exist.

Eventually, I decided against approaching Dex-slash-Jay and headed home to wallow in self-pity with a glass of cheap wine. I took a bath, and found myself thinking that the emotional turmoil that I was in was a lot like the stages of grief. In a screwed-up way, I had lost someone today—Jay, who never really existed.

Stage one had been shock. Even staring at the words, I couldn't believe that Jay and Dex were the same person. I'd actually made poor Suzette confirm that the man who'd just left was indeed Dexter Truitt.

Stage two was denial. I'd seen it in black and white on paper, watched the man get into a damn Town Car right in front of my eyes and verified the accuracy of it all with Suzette, yet I needed to sit out in front of his apartment for more confirmation of what he'd done.

Stage three had hit right after I polished off my second glass of wine. And it smacked me in the face with a vengeance—anger. I was pissed. Which led me to make up my own stage of healing—step 3B, I decided to call it. It was my favorite, and I couldn't wait to embrace it.

Revenge.

CHAPTER 11

Dex

Bandit had started to scratch at the door five minutes before eleven, so I was late getting to my laptop. I'd been antsy after the crap I'd pulled showing up as Jay on her doorstep following our last session. When I returned from a quick dog walk, I was relieved to find the chat window already open and a message waiting.

Bianca: Hello, Dex.

Dex: Hello, Bianca. How are you today?

Bianca: A little anxious, I suppose.

You and me both.

Dex: Anxious? About what? Is everything alright?

It took a few minutes for her to respond. But I was intrigued as hell when she finally did.

Bianca: There's something I've wanted to ask you. But wasn't sure how you'd feel about discussing the subject.

I'd already aired so much of my dirty laundry. I was curious what she could possibly feel was off limits at this point.

Dex: I've been an open book for you, Bianca. What did you want to talk about?

The answer came quick.

Bianca: Sex. I want to talk about sex.

This time it was me who needed to compose myself to respond.

Dex: Is this discussion for the article, or is what you're asking more of a personal nature?

Bianca: It's personal.

God, my cock was swelling just thinking about discussing sex with her. But I was certainly more than game if she was.

Dex: Ask away. I'm assuming our rules still stand, and I'll get to ask a question for every one you do.

Bianca. Of course.

I'd poured myself a drink earlier, and now I was glad that I did. The dots were jumping around as I gulped back half the glass in one swallow.

Bianca: How open-minded are you?

Was Bianca into kink? I'd never delved too far into that arena, but I suppose I wouldn't be opposed to it with the right partner. The thought of tying her to the bed, a little spanking and some anal play only made her that much more sexy to me.

Dex: Are you propositioning me, Ms. George?

I sucked down the other half of my drink. It did nothing to soften the steel in my pants.

Bianca: I am.

Dex: A woman who knows what she wants. I find that incredibly attractive. What did you have in mind?

It was the longest sixty seconds of my life waiting for her next response.

Bianca: A threesome with me and my friend.

I lifted my fingers to the keyboard to type a response three times, but couldn't. I was speechless...wordless. What

113

guy didn't want a threesome with a beautiful woman and her friend? Yet, for some reason, the fact that she'd suggested it made me angry on some level. I liked her—I suppose I wasn't as open-minded as I liked to think I was. To me, sharing was for fucking around, not someone you were really interested in. I wasn't sure how to respond. After long moments passed, Bianca typed again.

Bianca: Are you there?

Dex: Yes.

Bianca: Did I offend you?

She actually did. But at the risk of sounding needy, I needed to explain why.

Dex: I'm interested in you, Bianca. While the thought of being with you in any capacity is extremely appealing, I'm not certain a three-way is the right way to start things off.

Bianca: That's too bad. I think the three of us would be perfect together.

Dex: Perhaps we can try two and work our way up to three.

Given the opportunity, I was confident that I could please her so that she didn't feel the need to invite her friend.

Bianca: I'm not sure that's a good idea...

Dex: Have you done this type of thing before?

She ignored my question.

Bianca: Friday 7pm. Think about it. I'll be in the lobby of the Library Hotel if you decide to join us.

Dex: And if I don't join you?

Bianca: I've finished the article. I'll send over a copy within a week for final approval. I believe our interview sessions have come to an end. If you decide not to join, have a nice life, Mr. Truitt.

I should have been working. Or sleeping, for that matter, considering that I hadn't done much of that last night after the little chat I'd had with Bianca. But instead, I was sitting at my desk staring at a photo of her on her employer's website.

Bianca George is a Summa Cum Laude graduate of Wharton Business School who spent the first five years of her career as a derivatives trader. She joined Finance Times *in 2015 as a freelance industry expert where she pens articles from an insider's point of view.*

Nowhere in her biography did it mention she had a penchant for threesomes. I whipped my pen across the room.

Why the fuck did it bother me? What kind of a man turns down a threesome with a woman he's attracted to? Surely, a woman who was not territorial about a man whom she planned to sleep with, would be able to overlook the mere fact that I pretended to be two people. Oddly, I was less concerned with her accepting my apology now that she'd told me where her head was at. Yet, I was disappointed.

Disappointed in an offer for a threesome. *You need your head examined, Truitt.*

There was just something that I thought might be special with this girl. And not the type of special that entails her being okay with me sticking my dick in her *and* her friend all in one evening.

Shutting the page, I dove into my work. It was always the one thing I could lose myself in. Somehow, I'd managed to focus enough to study the financial forecasts of a company I was considering buying. It was late afternoon by the time I took a much-needed break. Josephine had delivered a turkey club to my desk a few hours ago, and I hadn't wanted to risk coming up for air and being distracted by thoughts of Bianca again.

If you decide not to join, have a nice life, Mr. Truitt.

Her parting words replayed over and over in my head. I dug into my sandwich and scrolled through the texts on my phone as I ate. The first one was from Caroline.

Caroline: Dinner Saturday night? I have a charity banquet to attend.

I'd been blowing her off for a few weeks now, and my head was definitely not ready to have a conversation with her yet. Not responding, I scrolled to the next. It was from my dad asking me how I was. I typed a quick, bland response and went back to the remaining messages as I polished off my club sandwich.

Buried below a dozen other texts was one from Bianca. Only she assumed she was texting Jay, not Dex. At first, when I opened it, I was confused.

Bianca: Hey. Do you have plans for Friday night?

Jay immediately typed back.

Jay: No. What did you have in mind?

Bianca: Want to meet me and a friend for some fun at The Library Hotel at 7?

What the fuck?

It didn't dawn on me until that minute. Grabbing my laptop, I opened the chat box from last night and frantically scrolled through our entire conversation. When she'd suggested a three-way with her friend, I'd *assumed* the third was a woman.

But there was no woman.

Bianca was fucking inviting Jay to a three-way with her and Dex.

When Friday night rolled around, I was no more prepared than I was the moment that she first dropped that bomb.

Shaving in front of my bathroom mirror, I lamented to my dog like a lunatic.

"Your friend is a freak, Bandit. You know that? An absolute freak!" I paused, shaking the water off my razor. Gesturing toward him with it, I said, "The thing is, the whole proposition just seems so out of character for her. But I guess it goes to show that you never really know someone. You can have dozens of intimate conversations with a woman you think is level-headed, and then they turn out to be a deviant."

"Ruff!"

"The twisted thing is—and I'm only admitting this to you, no one else—it kind of turns me on at the same time. It's like I wish I could *be* both men and fuck her simultaneously. Sick, right?"

"Ruff!"

"Yep. Ever hear the term, curiosity killed the cat? That's about to happen to me tonight. I'm so goddamn curious about what she planned on doing to me that I *can't* not show up. Because I'm a dog, Bandit. Just like you. All men are. But *unlike* you, I can't lick my own balls. So, I make crazy fucking decisions like showing up for a threesome where I'm supposed to be two-thirds of the party." I slapped some aftershave on my face.

"You know the other fucked-up part?" Laughing at myself in the mirror, I said, "I still don't know if I'm showing up as Dex or Jay."

Bandit howled and lay down.

"I know. Pathetic. Bet you wish you were frolicking upstate right about now, huh? Instead, you landed at the wrong farm—the crazy farm."

Bandit followed me into the walk-in closet off of my bedroom. I stared at the line of designer dress shirts perfectly starched and organized by color from light to dark. My eyes then landed on a smaller line of clothes in the corner—Jay's wardrobe, which consisted of jeans, casual shirts, and some hoodies. Since I still wasn't sure what I was going to say or do when I got there, I needed to dress somewhere in the middle. I chose a fitted, camel-colored sweater and wore a collared shirt underneath. Dark trousers finished off the look. I sprayed some cologne on and fastened my watch.

"Be good, Bandit. Don't be like your master, letting his dick ruin his life."

"Ruff!"

I knelt down and scratched between his ears. "Wish me luck. If I don't come back by morning, it will be because Bianca George kicked me in the nuts so hard I had to be hospitalized."

Outside, my driver was leaning against the black Town Car, waiting for me. "Where to, Mr. Truitt?"

"The Library Hotel, Sam."

From the car, I looked up toward the lights of my penthouse, wondering what things would be like for me the next time I returned home.

When Sam dropped me off at the funky, book-themed hotel Bianca had chosen in Midtown, I'd decided I would keep a low profile and try to observe her before she saw me.

We hadn't texted aside from my one response to her message, when Jay agreed to meet her at the allotted time. I was trying to minimize communication with her as Jay because, well, he was supposed to be dead.

Hiding behind a pillar, I finally spotted her. My heart nearly stopped. Bianca was sitting on a chair in the lobby with her legs crossed, wearing a black strapless dress that pushed her tits up into two mounds of creamy flesh I wanted to devour. The brightest shade of red coated her gorgeous lips. She'd stuck a matching, red silk flower barrette onto the side of her dark hair. She looked absolutely stunning, more beautiful than I'd ever seen her.

Something else caught my attention. For someone who'd brazenly requested that two different men meet her at this hotel for sex, Bianca looked awfully tense. She seemed to be breathing in and out heavily and was checking her watch every ten seconds. Something wasn't right.

I had no words, no clue what I was going to say or do. The only course of action was to wing it and then figure out how to handle the rest minute by minute. Was I Jay or was I about to come out to her as Dex? *Who the fuck knows.*

Walking slowly toward her with my hands in my pockets, I said a prayer that this didn't turn out as ugly as I fully expected it to.

When she noticed me, she stood up, brushing off her dress. "Hi."

"Hello, Bianca."

She nodded once. "Jay."

I swallowed the lump in my throat. The name had rolled off her tongue almost bitterly. Her body language was uninviting, and so, I opted not to lean in for a kiss.

Clearing my throat, I said, "I have to admit. I was really taken aback by your invitation."

"Well, it's about time you knew everything about me, Jay."

I thought I did.

Staring at her luscious lips, I suddenly felt possessive— angry. "A fucking threesome, Bianca? How did we get here? Explain why it is you feel you need more than one man to satisfy you at once? A real man should be able to do that all on his own."

"You want to know the truth?"

Ironic, but yes. "I do."

"Each of you has separate qualities that appeal to me."

"Explain."

"See...he has the most amazing brain. He's smart, ambitious, and powerful. And yet, there's a soft side that's humane, to the point where he makes *me* want to be a better person. He also expresses interest in *me,* not just physically, but in everything about me."

I swallowed. "And me?"

"You're mysterious. And I'm extremely physically attracted to you. But lately, I think about him when I'm with you. So, I thought...what better way to satisfy all of my needs than to invite you both here tonight."

My pulse raced. "I can't believe you'd want to cheapen what we have by bringing someone else into the equation. As if I could sit back and passively watch as another man's dick was moving in and out of you."

"Did you come here to interrogate me...to judge me?"

"I kind of want to know what the hell you're thinking, yeah. I thought I had you pegged, and this really threw me for a loop. How could you *ever* think I'd be willing to share you?"

She took two steps forward and spoke into my face. "If the best parts of the two of you were rolled into one man, we wouldn't have this problem."

Fuck. Me.

I couldn't hold it in a second longer. It was time.

"Bianca, there's something you need to—"

"Let me ask you something, *Jay.* How did you know the friend I was meeting here with you was a man anyway?"

"Your text."

"No. I never mentioned the *gender* of my friend. Ever." Her eyes had daggers in them.

Fuck. While I'd figured it out based on her text to Jay, she never did *say* the third party was a male. I'd been so messed up about this, I'd forgotten that she never actually specified.

It had finally happened. I'd fucked up.

"You slipped, Dex."

Dex?

Did she just say my name, or have I finally lost my mind enough to start hearing things?

"What did you call me?"

"Dex...as in Dexter Truitt."

She knows?

She knows.

This was a trap.

My heart was beating out of control. "How long have you known it was me?"

Her eyes were glistening. "Does it matter?"

"I need to know how long you've been—"

"Tricking you?" she yelled. "How does it feel, Dexter?" she shouted even louder. "How does it feel to be manipulated?"

Suddenly, I realized all eyes in the lobby were on us.

"Oh, we have an audience, Dex!" Holding out her hand, she cried, "The famous Dexter Truitt everyone! Multi-millionaire CEO of Montague Enterprises. He just showed up for a threesome with me and another man. Feel free to take photos. They'll land you some good money."

Thankfully, no one seemed to give a shit.

"Stop, Bianca."

"You want me to stop? Are you afraid everyone will know what a liar you are?"

Feeling like I had no other choice, I took her by the waist and lifted her up over my shoulder.

She wiggled her legs. "What are you doing?"

"You're not letting me get a word in edgewise. We need to go somewhere and talk in private."

"Put me down!"

"Did you really book a room?" I asked.

"No, I didn't get a room. I'm not really a whore—unlike you who agreed to a threesome with my 'friend.'"

"Make no mistake, I had no intention of sharing you, Bianca. Not with a woman. Not with a man. Not with anyone."

Still holding her over my shoulder, I arrived at the front desk. "We need a room, please."

"Oh, no, we don't!"

The receptionist awkwardly asked, "Two beds or one?"

"One, please."

"Excuse me?" Bianca asked.

"We're not using it, Bianca. We just need a place to talk."

"I'm not going to your room."

"You'll go, or the article isn't happening."

"Too late. The interview is finished."

"I'll renege my permission to publish it. I'll sue the magazine. Better yet, I'll *buy* the magazine." When the woman at the desk handed me the key card, I nodded. "Thank you."

I carried her to the elevator and put her down only after the doors closed. Pinning her against the wall, I said, "I'm not letting you go tonight until you hear me out. Do I need to carry you out of here, or are you going to walk with me?"

CHAPTER 12

Bianca

The hotel room door latched shut. With my back against it, I crossed my arms protectively over my chest. You could've heard a pin drop.

Dex sat on the edge of the bed with his head in his hands, then raked his fingers through his hair. Even as I stood there filled with anger, I wished it were me running my fingers through his mane. When he looked up at me, there wasn't an ounce of amusement in his piercing blue eyes. They displayed a seriousness that I'd never seen from him before. *Well, from Jay.*

"How did you find out?" he finally asked.

"I don't need to divulge that to you."

"Fair enough." Dex let out a deep breath. "You need to know that I always planned to tell you, Bianca. Always."

"Then why lie to me in the first place?" My voice cracked. "I've tried to figure it out but I just can't. It couldn't have been to sleep with me, because you passed that up. So, why? Just to screw with my head?"

"No!" His complexion turned an angry shade of red. "Fuck...no, Bianca."

"Then why?"

"It was as simple as just wanting to experience getting to know you without the preconceived notions you had about me. You made it very clear what you thought about 'Mister Moneybags' in that elevator. It was a split-second decision that I truly regret. A stupid lie."

"Stupid lie? You pretended to be *someone else*, Dex. There's really no bigger lie in this world than falsifying who you *are*."

"Every second of our interview, you were with the real me."

"And I preferred you, Dex. I preferred those intimate moments chatting with the real you more than anything. You ruined what could have been a good thing by bringing this alter ego into it."

"I had no way of knowing that you and I would connect so well. You seemed very closed-minded in that elevator. At the time, I didn't see how I could break through that."

"Well, I didn't know I was talking shit to your face. I might not have been so blunt."

"And that's why the whole thing was very telling. Those were your true feelings—at the time." Dex stood up and approached me. "Look...there is no real excuse to justify what I did. I don't even expect forgiveness. Blame me forever for it. But do it to my face. Be with me. Yell at me. Scream at me. Be angry with me...but *be* with me."

With his face close to mine, I could feel my legs weaken and my nipples harden. I'd always been attracted to him, but knowing that this face and body belonged to the person who'd also owned my mind for so long was almost too much to bear. I hated how badly I still wanted him.

His eyes were penetrating. I had to look away.

"How can you think I would ever be able to trust you not to lie to me again?" I asked.

"It's a chance you'd be taking. It doesn't matter how many times I promise, I know you won't believe in me right now. I have to earn your trust, and that only comes with time. You have to decide if you want to explore things with me enough to take the risk."

His phone buzzed, and he chose to ignore it.

"Who's that?"

"I don't care," he said dismissively.

"If you have nothing to hide, show me."

Without hesitation, he handed me the phone.

The jealousy monster took hold of me when I caught sight of four messages from the same person.

Caroline: Why haven't you been answering my texts?

Caroline: I'm starting to get a complex.

Caroline: I miss your beautiful cock inside of me.

Caroline: Call me or I'm coming over there tonight.

Burning up, I handed it back to him. "Caroline. This is your fuck buddy?"

"I believe I've already divulged to you in our conversations that I've had casual relationships with women."

"Why haven't you been calling her?"

Dex leaned in and spoke over my lips. "Isn't it obvious?"

As mad as I was at him, I couldn't stomach the thought of him going to be with another woman tonight. For the first time, I moved from my spot, making my way over to the window.

He followed me. "Bianca, I haven't been with anyone since the day you asked me to rub your balls in that elevator. You have completely consumed me, and I'm scared shitless that I'm gonna lose you because of one asinine decision that I made before I even really knew you."

"It was a pretty major bad decision, Dex. I just don't know. I need some time to just absorb this." Feeling suddenly emotional, I said, "Do you understand that I cared for that other person you portrayed? He was a part of my life, and he just...disappeared. I will never see Jay again. It's a strange feeling, and it's almost as if I still believe he actually exists."

"I understand. I loved the way you looked at him. Being Jay was the only way I could experience that. I'd give my right arm to get one ounce of that back right now."

My thoughts turned to the sweet greyhound I'd seen him take home. "Why did you adopt the dog? Was that a sick part of the joke, too?"

His eyes widened. "How did you know that?"

"That was how I found out about you. I saw you leaving with him. Went to the shelter and verified the name of the person who adopted him."

Dex scratched his chin and nodded in understanding. "I hadn't thought of that."

"So...are you using him, too?"

"I started volunteering there in the hopes of learning more about what you love. I knew that once I came clean to you, I was going to need all the help I could get. But soon after, I actually bonded with Bandit. It made me feel closer to you, but honestly, I fell for him pretty hard. The adoption happened because they were going to send him to some farm upstate. I worried for his safety, despite their assurances. I decided to take him home."

"So, he's living with you now..."

"Yes. He's mine. He's my dog."

"Well, that was very good of you."

"The pleasure has been mine, actually—aside from his breath. I need to do something about that."

I couldn't help but crack a smile. Closing my eyes for a moment, I said, "I found these special treats. They help. I'll message you the name."

"I'd like that." Dex smiled, and it was a reminder that I really needed to distance myself tonight before I fell deep into the trap of his charm.

"I need to go home. This has been too much for one night."

"Come home with *me*, Bianca. I promise I'll make this right."

"I can't do that."

"At least let me drive you home, then."

I hesitated then said, "Okay. But take me straight there. No detours."

Riding in Dex's luxurious car felt strange. It was a reminder of just how different this man's life was compared to that of his defunct alter ego. You could practically smell the money mixed in with the scent of leather. Dex wouldn't take his eyes off me, but he kept his distance. The weight of his stare alone made my entire body tingle. I was aching to be touched despite my anger.

I broke the ice. "So, what are your plans after this? Going to Caroline's to give her your 'beautiful cock'?"

He smiled impishly at my question. "Would that upset you?"

"I don't have any say in what you do."

"That's not what I asked. I asked if it would upset you."

"What do you think?"

"I think the fact that your face is flushed right now proves that the thought of me fucking another woman does upset you, regardless of whether you admit it or not." He reached over and placed his hand on my knee. The firm touch made the muscles between my legs pulsate. "I won't be going to see Caroline tonight, Bianca. I'll be going home to my house and curling up under my sheets with a four-legged beast who seems to think my bed is his. I will be praying to God that you find it in your heart to forgive me. And I'll wake up tomorrow morning, seizing the new day and trying like hell to get you to give me a second chance."

When we arrived at my place, Dex came around to let me out. He softly caressed my cheek as I just stood there. I closed my eyes and tried to let it all sink in.

Damn you, Dex. I just don't know if I can ever fully trust you.

Even though I wanted to say so much, the night had depleted my energy. I simply said, "Give me some time."

"Okay," he whispered.

As I headed toward my door, a thought occurred to me, prompting me to turn around.

"Do you even really whittle?"

He looked down briefly at his feet then up at me. "I tried. Those cuts were real."

I shook my head.

Two hours later, my phone signaled that I'd received a new message. This night had been so eventful, I'd almost forgotten how early it still was. The clock showed 11PM on the dot.

Dex: I know our meetings are supposed to be over, but I need to make sure you're okay.

After a few minutes of debating whether I should respond, I moved over to my laptop and typed.

Bianca: I'm fine.

Dex: You aren't. But I don't expect you to be. I'm just relieved you're even answering me.

Bianca: Did you call Caroline? Her text said if you didn't call her, she was coming over there.

Dex: I didn't call her, but she did stop by.

I angrily clicked on the keys.

Bianca: Did you give her your "beautiful cock"?

Dex: No. I told her I couldn't see her anymore.

Bianca: You shouldn't have gotten rid of your backup plan.

Dex: She was never a long-term plan. I don't have feelings for her like I do for you.

Bianca: How did she take it?

Dex: She was pissed. But I can't focus on that right now. My priority is you.

Bianca: I bet she's beautiful.

Dex: I'm more attracted to you...in every way.

Bianca: That's unfortunate.

Dex: Because I won't get to have you?

Bianca: I can't answer that.

Dex: Then, I'll spend my nights imagining it, like I have every single evening since we met. I get more excited just thinking about you than actually being with anyone else. Care to see?

A few seconds later, Dex sent a photo. It displayed the massive bulge in his gray boxers. The muscles between my legs began to contract. He looked like he was hiding a goddamn snake in there. My jaw dropped. I didn't even know what to say.

Dex: This is what you do to me, Bianca. I'm so hard that it's painful.

Bianca: Next time you send me a pseudo dick pic, you may want to make sure Bandit's paw isn't in the shot. Kind of ruins the effect.

Dex: You should go to sleep. You need to rest up for tomorrow.

Bianca: What's tomorrow?

Dex: You're meeting me at my office. I've hired a photographer to take as many photos as your heart desires for the feature. What I originally promised. I'm coming out.

CHAPTER 13

Dex

Josephine buzzed into my office. "Mr. Aster has arrived."

Looking at my watch for the tenth time in as many minutes, I blew out a frustrated breath. Hoping to get a few minutes alone with her, I'd told Bianca that the shoot was scheduled for 9:30, even though Josephine had scheduled the photographer to arrive at 10AM. Mr. Aster was fifteen minutes early, and Ms. George was fifteen minutes late. I was beginning to lose hope that Bianca was even going to show at all.

"Tell him I'll be with him in a few minutes, Josephine."

"Yes, Mr. Truitt."

I twiddled my thumbs at my desk for another ten minutes and then gave in and shot off a text to Bianca. "Since it appears you're not coming, is there any specific pose you'd like for the article?"

After another five minutes and no response, I begrudgingly went to meet Mr. Aster. He was flanked with a woman at each side.

"Mr. Truitt. Joel Aster. It's an honor to meet you. I was so excited when I received the phone call from your office yesterday."

I shook his hand. "Something's come up, and I'm going to need to get this wrapped up quickly. I hope you don't mind."

"Of course not. I know you're a busy man." He looked to the woman to his left and nodded. "Cheri can get you camera-ready with a little makeup while Breena sets up the lighting."

After showing them into my office, all three of them sprang into action. Joel and Breena started to rearrange office furniture and set up lights, while Cheri tucked a white paper bib into my collar. "I'm just going to put some moisturizer on you and then some matte foundation," she said. "You really don't need any work at all. Your bone structure is amazing, and the camera is going to love it."

As Cheri went to work, she spent a good deal of time standing in front of me with her tits right at my eye level. It was difficult not to get an eyeful with her low-cut blouse.

"Will your wife be joining us for the shoot?"

"I'm not married."

She leaned down to blot some shit on my chin and smiled. Taking in her face for the first time, I noticed she was very attractive. A mane of wild, blonde, curly hair framed her petite face. Cheri told me to look down so she could rub crap that wouldn't reflect light on my eyelids, and I was pretty sure she positioned herself for a grand view down her shirt. While it was tempting, I shut my eyes.

They were still closed after a few minutes as she went to town with powder on my face, so I tried in vain to use the moments to relax. Joel and Breena were making a lot of noise moving things around, so I hadn't heard Josephine come in until she was standing on the other side of my desk.

"Mr. Truitt. Ms. George has arrived. Shall I show her in?"

I startled poor Cheri, ripping the white paper makeup bib from my face and standing. "I need to speak to her first. Is she in reception?"

"She is."

My office was in the southeast corner of the thirty-third floor, and it was two long corridors to make my way to reception. There was a transparent glass door that led from the back office area to reception. My heart hammered inside my chest as I turned the corner and caught sight of Bianca sitting on a couch in the waiting area. She was looking down at her phone, so she didn't see me until I was almost in front of her.

"Bianca. I'm glad you decided to join us."

She stood. I knew immediately something was wrong from the look in her eyes.

"What happened?"

"My taxi had an accident. Some idiot hit us from behind, and when the crazy driver got out and started to yell at him, the guy backed up and slammed into our car a second time."

I started to pat her down, unsure of what the hell I expected to find. Holes somewhere, perhaps? "Are you okay?"

She laughed. "I'm fine. But I'm pretty late."

"Who gives a fuck? You're sure you're alright? Does anything hurt?"

"My neck is a little stiff. But it's nothing. Probably just the jerk from the impact."

"We should get you to the hospital to get checked out."

"I'm fine. I'm fine. Really."

I cupped her face and looked into her eyes. "You're sure?"

"Yes, I'm sure."

Without thinking, I pulled Bianca against me, wrapping her in my arms tight and inhaled deeply, allowing a fresh breath of calm to finally exhale out. I'd been trying to relax all morning and this...*this*...is what I needed to make it happen. I kissed the top of her head. "I'm glad you're alright."

There was no fucking way I was ready to let go of her. But she seemed uncomfortable and whispered, "Dex. Your receptionist is staring at us."

"Let her fucking stare."

"No, really. I'm fine. We should...we should get down to business."

I felt her body stiffen in my arms and reluctantly released her. Clearing my throat, I said, "The photographer and his crew are in my office setting up. Come. I'll show you around quick before taking you to my office."

My father was a natural braggart. I tended to feel uncomfortable displaying my wealth, but I was desperate when it came to Bianca. I'd do whatever it took to impress her. Before heading to my office, I walked her around the floor and showed her all of the different departments, introducing her to people as I walked. If I was being honest, my presence probably jolted more than a few. It had been at least a year since I'd stopped into some of the areas. Most days, I was buried beneath stacks of prospectuses in my office or off at some meeting.

"It's much bigger than I thought it would be," Bianca said as we left the analyst area.

I arched a brow. "I hope you're referring to Montague and not the photo I sent you last night."

Her beautiful skin blushed. "I'd like to keep this professional, Mr. Truitt."

I stopped in place a few doors down from my office. Bianca stopped a few paces after me when she realized I was no longer moving. "Mr. Truitt?" I questioned.

"I'm trying to keep it professional."

I closed the two-foot gap between us and leaned down to whisper in her ear. "Then you might want to try calling me something else. Because hearing you call me Mr. Truitt makes me hard as a rock. I've developed a rather large, visual role-play catalog over the weeks we've spent corresponding, *Ms. George*. And hearing *Mr. Truitt* from your lips is one of my favorite scenes to recall."

When I pulled my face back to look at hers, her eyes were dilated, and I watched as her throat worked to swallow. I was certain I still had an effect on Bianca George physically—that wasn't our issue. It was her trust that I needed to win back.

"Come on, I'll introduce you to Joel Aster."

I allowed Joel and his team to do whatever they wanted for the better part of an hour. Bianca stayed in the background, and at one point, I saw her chatting with Cheri, Miss Big Tits. I tried to make out what the two of them were saying as I posed for shot after shot, but it was damn near impossible. Although, I could have sworn there was tenseness in Bianca's jaw that hadn't been there before. Eventually, I called for a break.

Pulling Bianca aside, I said. "Are you feeling alright?"

"Just peachy."

That doesn't sound good. "What's the matter?"

She shrugged. "Nothing. I was thinking I'd take off now. The shoot seems to be almost done, and *Cheri* is more than happy to take care of anything you might need."

I went with my hunch. "Actually, I do need you. We're almost done here, but I thought the magazine should probably get an exclusive look at where I live."

"Where you live?"

I turned to the photographer who was adjusting his camera lens. "Joel. How would you like to take some shots in my apartment on Central Park West?"

He nearly salivated. "That would be great. I think we got enough good photos here at the office. Some shots of where you live would really give the people an insight into the real Dexter Truitt."

That's exactly what I'm banking on.

"Great. I'll call my driver. There's plenty of natural light in my apartment. I think it's safe we won't be needing the services of a makeup or lighting artist." I turned to look at Bianca. "Ms. George can let us know what she would like to see inside my apartment."

"Smart dog," I mumbled under my breath. Bandit had met us at the door, came to me for a quick pat, and went right to Bianca. She bent down and he buried his head in her chest, nearly knocking her over. *No wonder we get along so well. You're my new wingman, Bandit. Warm her up, but save me some of that, will ya, buddy?*

"Bandit. Let Bianca at least come inside."

"Your dog really seems to like her. He barely even noticed that we were here," Joel said.

"Do you blame him?"

Inside, I gave Joel a quick tour of the kitchen and living room. While he was taking in the view of Central Park, I returned to the front door where Bandit was still mauling

Bianca. Taking his collar, I gave him a slight tug. "Come on, buddy. I'll bribe you with a treat."

That bought off my wingman when he took the biscuit and trotted off to my bedroom in the back. He seemed to have commandeered that space as his place to hide his prized possessions.

Bianca was dusting off tiny, grey dog hairs from her black skirt, and I noticed her deep green blouse had a circle of wet over her left breast. "My dog seems to have left his mark on you." *My turn.*

She looked down and laughed. "He's a slobberer."

"Tell me about it. I can't get him to sleep anywhere but on my bed. Some mornings, I worry my housekeeper is going to think I've developed a bed-wetting problem."

"I think it's really sweet you're allowing him to sleep in the bed with you. But it's a hard habit to break, and dogs can become territorial when...you know...you have company."

"Perhaps he needs to get used to it right away. Are you available to stay this evening?"

Bianca rolled her eyes at me. "Are you giving me a tour, or what?"

Joel was busy taking test shots of different places in the living room to test out the natural light streaming in from the windows, so I put my hand at Bianca's back. "Of course. What do you say I show you the bedroom first?"

"What a shocker you'd suggest that?"

I gave Bianca the grand tour; she seemed curious as we walked around. Although I noticed she stayed in the doorway of my bedroom. She was trying to keep her distance, and as much as I understood that, my need to push closer was equally as strong as hers was to push me away. I got the feeling our standoff might be a test of endurance. What she didn't realize was that we'd had our first battle, and due to my own asinine self, I lost that one. But this was a war—one I planned to win.

When we got to my office, I opened the door and then quickly shut it. Coming to my apartment wasn't something I'd originally planned, and I'd forgotten the mess I'd left on my desk.

"It's a mess in there," I offered, and began to walk toward the next door. But Bianca didn't budge.

"What are you hiding in there?"

"Nothing."

She squinted. "More secrets?"

"It's not like that."

"So show me the room. What are you hiding from me now, Dex? Or should I call you Jay when you lie?" She folded her arms over her chest.

There was no way out of this one unscathed. I took a deep breath. "Fine."

CHAPTER 14

Bianca

I didn't know what to say. I just stood and stared. The oversized desk was a cluttered mess. There were piles of wood shavings, various wooden blocks that were carved and disregarded, an instruction book that was held open by a desk phone and all sorts of wooden-handled tools scattered around the long desk. But that wasn't what got to me. It was the open first aid kit, along with an assortment of crumpled up, bloodied paper towels and at least half a dozen Band-Aid wrappers.

Dex was standing behind me. Neither of us had said a word since he'd flicked on the light. I turned to face him.

"Why?" I asked.

"Why what?"

"Why did you tell me you whittled?"

"You want the truth?"

"Of course, I do."

He raked a hand through his dark hair. "I have no fucking idea. I wanted to sound like a regular guy, I guess."

My lip twitched. "You have no idea what regular guys do for hobbies, do you?"

"I was raised privileged, Bianca. If I'd told you that I fenced competitively in high school and spent my weekends at sailing regattas, what would you have thought?"

He had a point. One lie can easily snowball into so many. "For the record, I've dated mostly *regular guys* and none of them whittled, Dex."

"So noted."

"Pretty sure most of them didn't say things like '*so noted,*' either."

He smiled half-heartedly. I could see he felt bad for what he'd done. In fact, I was certain he had been beating himself up over it on a regular basis even while he was lying to me daily. I stopped at the doorway when Dex flicked off the light. "I'll give you this much. You committed to the character."

He grumbled. "Or I should *be* committed."

After my tour was over, Joel was all ready to take photos. He did a series of Dex standing at his window with the view of Central Park, followed by some of him standing in front of the massive fireplace that was the center of the living room. But it was the ones that he took of Dex sitting on the couch that I liked best.

Joel had just taken a break from shooting when Dex's cell phone rang. He excused himself and went to sit on the couch to talk to what I assumed from the side of the conversation that I'd heard, was his secretary. As Dex was talking, Bandit slunk up on the couch and lay next to him, resting his long face on his master's lap. He mindlessly stroked the dog's head while he went about the conversation with Josephine. From the other side of the room, Joel lifted his camera and started taking photos of what we both saw. I could only imagine how intimate the photos were going to come out.

By the time Dex hung up, Joel was starting to pack up his camera equipment.

"You're all done?" Dex asked.

"I think I have more than enough. You'll be very happy with the results."

Dex nodded, then looked at me. "Do me a favor, Joel? Take one more. I'd like a photo with Ms. George."

"Of course."

Dex extended his hand toward me, and I felt foolish making a stink over a silly picture, so I went to stand next to him. He wrapped his arm around my waist and pulled me close. Joel snapped some shots and then Bandit decided to get in on the action. He jumped up between us, one paw landing on each of my and Dexter's chests. We laughed while Joel took a few more.

There was an awkwardness when Joel was finished gathering his things and packing his camera up. Well, at least, I felt it. Joel extended his hand. "It was a pleasure to meet you, Mr. Truitt. I'll have these photos to your office within two weeks."

Dex nodded. "Thank you."

"Are you heading uptown?" Joel turned to me. "Perhaps we can split a cab?"

Before I could answer, Dex cut in. "Actually. I need to go over some last minute things about the article, Bianca. Do you think you can stay for a few minutes?"

It wasn't smart for me to be alone with him. "I'd love to, but I have an appointment I need to get to."

Dex was not going to make it easy. "Two minutes. I'll have my driver take you wherever you need to go after we're done so you don't have to waste time grabbing a cab."

He walked Joel to the door before I could answer. When he came back to the living room, I was sitting on the couch rubbing my neck. It was really starting to hurt.

"Your neck is still bothering you?"

I nodded. "It's muscular. Nothing a warm bath or a heating pad won't take care of."

"Scoot up."

"What?"

Dex motioned for me to sit on the edge of the couch cushion. "These fingers can't whittle for shit, but they can rub a mean massage. Let me at least help you with that."

Again, he didn't wait for my answer. Instead, he slipped off his shoes, stood up on the couch, and swung one leg over to the other side of me. Then, he settled in behind me, enveloping me between his parted thighs.

I was about to object, when his fingers pressed into my neck. *God, that feels good. Two minutes won't hurt.*

Dex wasn't lying; he could definitely give a mean massage. His thumbs rubbed up and down either side of my spine, and he applied firm pressure, kneading a circular motion to relieve the tension in my muscles. Loosening up, my head dropped until my chin was practically resting on my chest. I lost track of time as he quietly rubbed and pressed in all the right places. At one point, he guided my head to the left side and focused on an area on the right at the top of my shoulder blade. A little mewl escaped my lips before I could catch it. After that, even though my neck was relaxed, I started to feel *other things* tensing up. Dex was getting aroused, and since I was sitting between his legs, I could literally feel his erection swelling up against my ass. *God it feels so good.*

A large part of me wanted to enjoy it, to relish the feel of his fingers pressing into my achy neck muscles and his firm cock nudging at my ass cheeks as it grew. But then I remembered the *other time* I felt Dex up against my ass. Only it wasn't Dex...*it was Jay.* The night he'd showed up at my place unannounced, and I practically dry humped him. He'd spent an hour online with me as Dex and then must have raced over to my apartment to spend the next half hour as Jay. He didn't even require a break between his lies. Realizing that was like having a bucket of cold water thrown over me.

I abruptly stood. "I should go."

Dex stood with me. "I'm sorry. Don't go. I tried everything. Even thinking about the time I walked in on my grandmother having sex with my grandfather, but not even *that* calamity could stop my body from reacting to having you near me. I didn't ask you to stay to get physical with you. I wasn't going to try to seduce you."

Oddly, I believed him. "Why did you ask me to stay then, Dex?"

"I wanted to make sure you were feeling alright from the accident this morning. But I also wanted to see if I could convince you to go on a date with me. Can we start over? I know I fucked up royally—just give me the chance to show you I'm a man you can trust."

That was half of the problem. Trust was an issue to begin with for me. I knew I had some daddy issues that were at the root of many of my doubts. But I also knew that it was nearly impossible to be around Dex without something physical happening between us. And being physical with him before I was able to forgive him and truly trust him again, would be a big mistake.

"I need some time, Dex."

"How much time?"

"I don't know."

He looked panicked. "Can we at least continue to chat in the evenings?"

"That's not a good idea."

"Bianca...what can I do?"

I actually felt bad for him. Reaching out, I touched his cheek. "Give me time. At least a few weeks."

He searched my eyes. Finding I was serious, his shoulders slumped. "Fine."

I pushed up on my tippy toes and kissed him on the cheek. "Take care of yourself, Dex."

CHAPTER 15

Dex

"Damn you, Clement."

Sometimes when I got frustrated about the Bianca situation, I spent my time watching YouTube videos of my whittling nemesis. The kid could whittle anything with precision without getting a single cut on his hands. It pissed me off, yet invigorated me at the same time.

Do better, Dex.

I needed to step up my game.

"Nice haircut, by the way," I spoke to the computer screen, referring to his straight blond hair that was exactly the same length all the way around like a bowl.

I shouldn't have been torturing myself like this, but lately, it seemed harder and harder to sanely occupy my time outside of work. Bianca didn't want to resume our evening chats or see me at all for a few weeks. That basically meant several days of Dexter going slowly insane and nearly blind from jerking himself off.

I vowed to use these days wisely. Just because she didn't want to see me, didn't mean I couldn't let her know I was thinking about her. I liked to refer to this period of time as *Operation Get Bianca Back.*

Step one: learn to actually whittle so you can make her romantic wooden things. All the wooden things! I bet if I put my mind to it, I could whittle a goat that might be half as good as the one I bought at the Brooklyn flea market.

I turned to Bandit who was sitting beside me watching Clement whittle away. "That's genius, right? Show her I'm putting in the effort. It's heartfelt and original at the same time."

"Ruff!"

I typed in: *how to whittle a goat.*

Unfortunately, there weren't any videos fitting my exact specifications. I randomly clicked on the first clip that came up in my search.

It was some guy with an Australian accent holding a chubby baby girl. There was an actual goat sitting next to them.

"Come on, Bree, say Dada."

Every time the man would say the word, "Dada," the goat would let out a long *"Baa."*

The baby would just let out a belly laugh each time the goat made a sound.

"Say Dada."

The goat responded, *"Baa."*

Giggle.

"Say Dada...Dada," the man repeated.

"Baa."

Giggle. Giggle.

What in the ever-living fuck was I watching?

The man turned to the goat. *"Mate, can you stop for a bit? She won't say it if you keep making her laugh."*

"Baa!"

Giggle. Giggle. Giggle.

The video ended. I immediately hit replay. It was addictive, and dare I say, my mouth hurt from smiling.

Turning to Bandit, I said, "Imagine that? Talking to a pet like a human being and expecting it to understand?"

"Ruff!"

The title of the video was *"Pixy and Bree Say Dada."*

"This is so ridiculous," I said, discreetly bookmarking the video. This guy, Chance Bateman, had an entire YouTube channel featuring various videos of his two children and the goat. These would come in handy someday when I wanted reassurance that I wasn't the only person in this world off my fucking rocker. *Fuck it.* I subscribed to the channel.

Even though I'd vowed not to call Bianca, that didn't mean I couldn't pull some tricks that would make it impossible for her to resist contacting me. When the phone rang, I suspected it might be her.

I picked up. "Bianca...I—"

"You are out of your mind." She sniffled. She was either laughing or crying. *She was laughing.*

"You're laughing, though."

"Dex Truitt...I may have to edit the article to include a disclaimer at the end noting that you have totally lost your marbles."

"Yes, but you're laughing."

"How did you even get it into my apartment?"

"Let's just say your maintenance guy is going to have a really nice Christmas this year."

"It scared the living daylights out of me. I thought it was a real person, that someone had broken into my apartment and was readying to kill me."

"You're laughing, though!" I repeated again.

"I am," she conceded. "You are totally nuts."

I'd purchased the Liza Minnelli statue from the owner of Jay's fake apartment and decided to have it transported to Bianca's. I'd asked him to set it up in a way that she'd see it the second she walked in the door. Making light of crazy Jay's antics was definitely a risk, but I did it in the hopes that she could eventually learn to look back at that time with humor.

"Well, now you have to figure out a way to rid my apartment of the mothball smell from that damn place."

I'd been laughing before, but now I was laughing even harder.

"I'll send for it tomorrow."

"Goodbye, Dexter."

"Goodbye, Bianca."

After I hung up, I looked at Bandit and smiled victoriously. "She loved it."

On Sunday, I found myself at The Brooklyn Flea. Some people had drug dealers; I had a wood dealer. Coming upon the tent with the sign that read Jelani's Kenyan Krafts, I walked over to the familiar vendor.

"Hi, I bought a wooden billy goat off of you some time ago. I'm not sure if you remember."

Still wearing the brightly colored hat from last time, the old man looked me up and down. "Yes. I do remember you," he said in a strong African accent. "Are you interested in something else?"

"Actually, I need to ask you a strange favor."

"Okay."

"I've tried everything online and nothing seems to be working. I need to learn how to whittle and was wondering if I could pay you to teach me."

He bent his head back in laughter. "It took me years to learn how to do this, been perfecting my craft since I was a little boy growing up in Kenya."

"I can imagine that doing it as well as you do would take years, but I'm just really looking to be able to carve something not even half as good without slicing my fingers off. Even if it looks pathetic, as long as it's recognizable, that will do."

"Boy, why on Earth would you want to even bother?" He squinted at me. "Is this about that woman?"

"You're a smart man, Jelani."

"Ah. That makes more sense."

"Look, I know it sounds crazy. When I bought that goat from you, I told her I had made it myself. But she eventually figured out the truth. I regret ever lying to her and was hoping to prove how sorry I am by actually showing a real effort to make her something similar. Basically, I'm desperate, very close to losing the only woman I've ever had true feelings for. I'd do or pay just about anything for your expertise."

He let out a deep sigh before jotting down an address. "Meet me at 2PM this afternoon here."

I didn't have enough time to go over the bridge to Manhattan and come back before then, so I hung out in Brooklyn, grabbed a coffee, and walked around aimlessly until it was time to head to the address in Williamsburg.

At 2PM on the dot, I knocked on the door and waited.

The old man opened and said nothing as he stepped out of the way so I could enter. His head was completely bald, which I only now realized since he normally wore that African-themed hat. He led me down to a wood workshop located in a dingy basement.

"I don't know why, but I pictured you with a full head of hair under that hat," I said just trying to make conversation. He didn't seem amused. It was a bit of an awkward start as I looked around. "So this is where the magic happens, huh? How did you get started in wood carving?"

"My grandfather taught me. We used to sell them to tourists back in Nairobi."

He'd set out some tools on a table and gestured for me to sit next to him.

"The three main things to remember are to always go slow, have a very sharp knife, and keep your hands protected." He handed me some cut-resistant gloves. "I'm not going to tell you what to do. I'm going to show you. Watch and do as I do."

Jelani had already drawn with pencil the pattern of the animal onto two pieces of wood. In silence, I followed every movement he made. We practically said nothing the entire time. It took nearly two hours because that was how slow we were cutting the wood.

Toward the end, Jelani turned to me. "I have no hair because of chemo. I'm in the middle of treatment. Colon cancer."

Oh, no.

"I'm sorry. I didn't know."

"It's alright."

"How are you feeling?"

"There are good days and some very bad days. Today is a good day."

"I'm glad to hear that."

I pondered the fact that you never quite know what crosses people are carrying. My problems with Bianca seemed trite, in comparison.

By the end, I ended up with a half-decent goat, although it was pathetic compared to Jelani's. But still, it was mine, and I could proudly take full credit for it.

"I can't thank you enough for taking the time to do this." Reaching into my pocket, I took out a wad of cash.

Holding his hand out, he said, "No."

"Please..."

Jelani pushed my hand away.

"I have to give you something," I insisted.

"Then, come back once a week."

Did he just say what I thought he did?

"You want me to come back and do this again?"

"Yes. I appreciate the company. It helps take my mind off things. When you live alone, you think too much. This was like therapy for me."

His request blew me away, but there was only one answer.

"I can do that."

CHAPTER 16

Bianca

Stepping out of my apartment on the way to work, I noticed a black Town Car parked out front. My heart jumped. Dex had broken his promise not to see me, and I couldn't say I was disappointed.

The driver got out and came around.

He nodded. "Ms. George."

I waited for the window to roll down or for Dex to emerge but neither happened.

"Where is Dex?"

"Mr. Truitt instructed me to be at your disposal this week."

"He's not here?"

"No. He would like me to safely see you to your destination."

"Oh. Um...okay. Thank you."

He opened the back door and let me in. After giving him the address to my building, I immediately picked up the phone.

Dex answered, "Bianca."

The sound of his deep, soothing voice gave me shivers.

"What are you doing?"

"It's more comfortable than the back of my tandem bike, isn't it?"

"*Jay's* bike, yes." I shook my head. "I can only imagine how fast you had to work to make the bicycle thing happen that day, by the way."

"Let's just say I was highly motivated."

"What's with the chauffeur service?"

"I thought you'd like a break from dangerous taxis. And I was looking for a change of pace. I've been cabbing it to work. Sam is at your beck and call all week."

"It's really not necessary."

"I know that. But if I can't be with you, at least I know you're safe and sound in good hands."

"I can't use it tonight," I said.

How exactly was I supposed to tell him that I'd accepted a date with a co-worker?

One of the editors at work, Eamon Carpenter, had asked me out. The word "no" had been at the tip of my tongue until I realized that it might benefit me to go out with someone other than Dex. I'd be breaking my own self-imposed rule not to get involved with men I worked with, but it would be a test as to just how deep into Dex my heart really was. We weren't exclusive, so I was able to justify it. I absolutely knew that I wasn't going to let things get to a physical level with Eamon, in any case. So, I figured there was really no harm.

I felt compelled to be honest with him.

"I'm going on a date tonight. I don't feel right taking your car."

There was nothing but dead silence on the other end of the line. I swore he'd hung up.

"Are you there?"

"Yes." He began to trip over his words. "I'm just a little stunned, to be honest. I haven't been...I mean, I..."

"You haven't been what?"

"I haven't been seeing anyone. I just assumed..."

He was having trouble saying it.

"You assumed that I wouldn't date anyone during this break?"

"I guess I was just hopeful." More silence before he asked, "Where is he taking you?"

"Bistro Nine." I sighed. "It's nothing serious, Dex. I don't plan to let him...do anything."

His breathing became heavier.

"Are you okay?"

"I have to go," he abruptly said.

"Alright, I—" He'd hung up before I had a chance to say anything further.

Later, when I arrived at the office, there was a package sitting on my desk. Upon opening it, I realized it contained the photos from Joel's shoot at Dex's house. Dex was supposed to have chosen his favorites to be used for the article. From the ones that he vetted, I would choose three or four images.

The first couple of shots were of Dex in front of his window overlooking the park. I marveled at his beauty: his lustrous black hair, his tall stature, his impeccable clothes, his big, masculine hands. In one of the pictures, he reminded me of a more handsome version of James Bond as played by Pierce Brosnan, but with more facial hair.

There were two more shots featuring him in front of his fireplace. The next couple of photos were from the ones he'd shot of him and Bandit on the couch.

My heart clenched. The last one was framed and had a note on it. *Mr. Truitt wanted you to have this. It's not for the article.*

It was the photo of Dex, me, and Bandit, the one where the dog had a paw on each of us. It was making me emotional. He'd clearly sent this over before our conversation this morning. Guilt set in.

Damn you, Dex.

The reality was that I didn't want to go on this date with Eamon. I was forcing myself to do it to prove that I still had the capability to connect with someone else in the event that my heart was to be destroyed by Mister Moneybags. It was a self-protective mechanism. Deep down, I knew that...but Dex didn't.

I was sure Eamon could tell I was preoccupied. I kept checking my phone to see if Dex had texted. He hadn't said a word since my date revelation this morning, and it made me wonder if I'd royally screwed things up.

I mentally scolded myself for obsessing over Dex while on a date with another man.

Trying to make conversation to move my mind into a different place, I said, "What's new on your end at the magazine? What's the next project?"

"I'm setting up an interview with Harry Angelini of Markel Corporation next week. But honestly, your exclusive with Truitt is all anyone seems to be talking about."

Great. So much for getting my mind off him.

"Yes. It went really well."

"I haven't had a chance to read the first draft, but people keep saying how thorough it is, as if you'd spent months with him."

"It was...an ongoing format." I cleared my throat. "I found that to be better than rushing it."

"I think you might have something there."

The waiter came by with a small plate. "Some dessert for you."

"We didn't order dessert."

"Yes. Well, actually, it was courtesy of someone who called in and wanted you to have it."

When I looked down at the plate, I nearly gasped. Sitting atop a drizzle of caramel were two gigantic chocolate balls.

"What is this?"

"It's tartufo. Ice cream balls."

Balls.

My face felt flush. *Dexter.* It had to be.

"Okay. Thank you."

"What was that all about?" Eamon asked.

"I'm not sure," I lied. "Will you excuse me? I have to use the bathroom. Please start on the dessert without me."

Once in the stall, I texted him.

Bianca: Are the ice cream balls from you?

Three dots immediately appeared on the screen.

Dex: Yes. Enjoy them.

Bianca: You really shouldn't have.

Dex: Well, I know you like balls. And I wanted to apologize for my strange behavior this morning. You have every right to see whomever you want.

Bianca: Thank you, but no need to apologize. Your reaction was understandable.

Dex: I've instructed Sam to wait outside of the restaurant in the event that you need a ride. If he's not parked, he'll be circling around the block. I'm not using him tonight anyway. If you decide not to take advantage of the ride, that's fine. But he's there if you need him.

Bianca: That's very nice of you. Thank you. What are you doing tonight that you don't need a car?

Dex: I've decided to stay in.

Bianca: Okay. Well, have a good evening.

Dex: You too.

His sudden change of attitude seemed weird. I almost wondered if he was practicing reverse psychology, although I would never really know for sure.

When I returned to the table, Eamon had devoured his ball and paid the bill.

"Was it good?" I asked.

He licked his lips. "It was great."

A few minutes later, I looked down at the time and said, "This has been really fun. But I have to be up early in the morning, so I think I'm going to head home if that's okay."

"Can we share a cab?"

"Actually, I have to stop somewhere on the way back, so I'm going to just head out alone."

"Okay, sure."

He seemed very disappointed, but truly, it was better not to lead him on. I really shouldn't have gone on the date in the first place if my heart wasn't in it.

I told Eamon I needed to stop back in the bathroom on the way out, so that he would exit the restaurant first.

Once outside, sure enough, I noticed the Town Car parked across the street.

I waved. "Hello, Sam."

"Good evening, Ms. George," he said as he opened the door for me.

I nearly had a heart attack when I saw who was in the backseat.

At first, I thought it was Dex. But no. It was the Liza Minnelli statue. Sinking back into the leather seat, I began to laugh hysterically.

"Sorry about that, Miss. He made me do it," I heard Sam say. "Where to?"

Where was I going?

There was only one place I wanted to go tonight.

"Mr. Truitt's place, please."

CHAPTER 17

Dex

Bandit was barking like crazy. I twisted the shower handle to turn off the water so that I could hear what was making him go nuts. He wasn't generally a barker. In between his *ruffs*, the faint sound of the doorbell buzzing echoed under the bathroom door.

Shit.

Stepping out, I grabbed a towel, wrapped it around my waist, and headed to the front door. When I looked through the peephole, no one was on the other side. But Bandit was still going crazy, so I opened the door and poked my head out into the hallway. My heart started pounding when I found Bianca standing in front of the elevator doors looking down.

"Bianca?"

She looked up. "Dex. You didn't answer. I thought you were out."

"I was in the shower." The doors to the elevator she was standing in front of slid open, and she turned to face them, then glanced back at me, and then back at the waiting car. She was clearly pondering her departure. After a few heartbeats, she made her decision. "I should go. It was a mistake coming over here. I'm sorry."

"Bianca! Wait!"

She froze with one foot inside the elevator car. I didn't give a fuck that I was still dripping wet and only wearing a towel, I ran down the hall after her. "Don't leave. Please." I caught her elbow and waited as she again deliberated. When she finally nodded, I let out a deep breath. There was no way I was giving her any time to change her mind again, so I quickly steered her away from any available escape and into my apartment.

Although I'd managed to get her into my place and close the door behind her, she stayed just barely inside and looked down at her feet. "Well, this is a nice surprise," I said.

"I shouldn't be here."

"I think you're wrong. *This* is exactly where you should be. Where you shouldn't have been tonight, was on that date."

Bandit had been standing near my side and chose that moment to walk to Bianca. He sat down directly on her feet and pushed his head into her crotch. She smiled and scratched the top of his head. *Good boy. Remind me to buy you a bone. From an elephant.*

"Our dog seems to agree with me."

Her head whipped up. "*Our* dog?"

"Yes. I feel like he belongs to both of us since he helped bring us together."

"If I'm not mistaken, he actually helped break us apart. I saw you at the shelter. That's how I uncovered who you really were, remember?"

I took a step closer. "I don't see it that way."

She scoffed. "Then you need glasses, Truitt."

Another step. "I don't need glasses to know you look beautiful right now." Her hair was down and had a wavy, windblown look to it. She looked absolutely breathtaking wearing a simple, black strapless dress. Her lips were painted a blood red and when her tongue darted out to wet them, I was unable to stop staring.

"Dex..." Her voice was low but there was a warning tone to it. She must have known how much looking at her was affecting me.

"Bianca..." I mimicked her and took a hesitant step closer. When she didn't run, not that she had anywhere *to* actually run with her back against the front door, I took that as a sign to keep moving in. She looked down, and I got the sense that she was trying to maintain her control. Too bad I wanted nothing more than to make her lose it. "Your date ended early. Did Eamon not do it for you, the way I do?"

She squinted. "How did you know his name was Eamon?"

Shit. "It doesn't matter. You ended it early. What matters is that you're here now and not with that ass-wipe."

"He's not an ass-wipe, and it *does* matter. How did you know his name?"

"My driver paid the maître de to get the name on your reservation."

"Why?"

"Because I needed to know who my competition was on the chance that you'd like him enough to go out with him for reasons other than an attempt to forget me."

Her eyes widened. "You're so full of yourself. You think my date had something to do with you? *Newsflash, Dexter Truitt*, the world does not revolve around you."

"Really? That's a shame. Especially since mine seems to revolve around you as of late."

We stared at each other. There were clearly a million thoughts going through her head as her eyes jumped back and forth. Unfortunately, she settled on the one I had hoped she'd rid herself of already. "I should go," she whispered.

I felt desperate. I closed the little gap that remained between us. The heat from our bodies was radiating, and the smell of her perfume engulfed my senses. When I glanced down, I realized her chest was rising and falling as rapidly as mine. I couldn't let her leave. I just couldn't. "Don't go."

"I need to."

Recognizing I was out of time and she was about to bolt, I used the only thing I knew was her weakness—her attraction to me. Taking her face in my hands, I cupped both cheeks, and planted my lips over hers. "Stay. Don't leave." Then I devoured her mouth. She opened without hesitation, and my tongue dove right in finding hers. Feeling her physically surrender to me so easily was a complete turn-on. I pressed my body into hers, pinning her between the door and my naked chest. Her tits pushed up, beckoning to be set free from her strapless little dress, and the feel of her bare skin against mine was fucking incredible. I wanted to lift her up and cradle her in my arms as I carried her back to my bedroom.

I was just about to, too, when Bianca nudged at my chest. Her voice was breathless, and she didn't sound like she actually meant one word. "Dex. We need to slow down."

I leaned my forehead against hers. "I've been trying to slow down since the day I met you. I seem to only have one speed when it comes to you, Georgy Girl."

Her lip twitched. "Georgy Girl? Isn't that what Jay used to call me?"

"Yes. But it's what I've called you in my head since the first day I met you."

She pondered that for a moment. "I do like it. It's sweet."

"There's a first. Not sure a woman's ever called me sweet before."

"That's the thing with you, Dex. On the outside, you appear to be something very different than what I keep catching glimpses of on the inside."

Her sexy red lipstick was smeared. I rubbed it from her face with my thumb. "Oh yeah? Is that a good thing or a bad thing?"

"It's a good thing. It means deep down inside you're not the jerk that you show people on the outside. The one who lies to women in elevators."

A flash of what I saw when the elevator lights flickered on that day popped into my head. "I thought you were stunning the first time I saw you."

"I didn't think you were so bad yourself."

"I'm so unbelievably attracted to you. For weeks I haven't been able to think about you without getting a hard on."

Bianca blushed. "I think I feel that attraction digging into my hip right now."

I grinned, but didn't make an attempt to move. "Sorry."

"No, you're not." She shoved at my chest. "Go put some clothes on. We need to sit down and talk. And you can't be in a towel."

"I could take it off."

She waved her hand in the direction of my very visible erection then shook her head and pointed down the hall to my bedroom. "That thing is distracting. Go. And don't come back until it's less...bulgy."

I needed a full ten minutes to get my head screwed on straight. Not to mention get my raging hard on under control. Bianca was here instead of on her date. It was a start. If I could manage to keep my dick out of my head, maybe I stood a chance after all.

I dressed in a pair of jeans and a plain, dark t-shirt before spraying on some cologne and slicking back my wet hair. Then I double checked that my bulge was adequately deflated and headed back to the living room. Bianca was looking out the window.

"Can I get you something to drink?" I asked.

"Are you having something?"

"I was going to open a bottle of wine. Do you like red?"

"I do."

It took me twice as long to open the damn bottle since my kitchen counter faced the living room where Bianca was staring off. I couldn't stop looking at her. She was gorgeous—a man would have to be blind to not see that. But it was more than that. I felt a pull to her that was there the first time I'd met her, even before the lights turned on in that dark elevator. We were connected in some way; I was sure of it. I just needed to show her it was more than physical.

"Here you go." I handed her a glass.

"Thank you." She turned back to the window.

"You look pretty deep in thought there."

She sipped her wine. "I suppose I am."

"Well, I'm de-bulged and all ears."

Bianca glanced down and sighed. "Such a shame to have wasted it."

Trying my hardest to be on my best behavior, I bit my tongue. "Why don't we go sit, so we can talk?"

After we sat, I waited for her to speak first. The key to getting Bianca to forgive me was going to be patience, so I figured I'd start practicing with the easy things. She traced the rim of her glass a few times with her finger and then said, "My date was a nice guy."

I closed my eyes briefly and then opened them. "I suppose if you're dating someone other than me, I'd like them to at least be a nice guy, for your sake."

"Thank you."

I couldn't help myself. "To clarify, just because he might be a nice guy doesn't mean I wouldn't like to beat the crap out of him right now."

She shook her head, but smiled. "You don't have to worry. I'm not going to go out with him again."

I sipped my wine, watching her over the brim of my glass. "I might have just lost some of my urge to beat him senseless."

We were sitting on the couch next to each other, and Bianca twisted her body so that she was facing me straight on. "I wanted to like him. I wanted to have the tingles as he spoke during dinner, and I wanted *to want* to go home with him after we ate, to have mind blowing sex."

I know I probably deserved for her to feel that way after the shit I'd pulled, but hearing her say that really hurt. "Well that makes one of us."

"I don't want to want to be with you."

"Yes, I'm getting that loud and clear."

She set her glass down on the coffee table and then looked me in the eyes. "But as much as I don't want to feel a certain way, I do. I've tried to force myself to stop thinking about you, and I've tried to distract myself with another man. Yet here I am at the end of my date tonight."

I set my drink down next to hers. "Listen to me, Bianca. I fucked up. I know I did. I've apologized, and I'll keep apologizing over and over again. But you can't deny that there is something going on here that is worth taking another chance on." I caressed her cheek. "Take a chance on me, Georgy Girl. Take a chance."

CHAPTER 18

Bianca

I finally admitted to myself that I was more afraid *not* to take a chance than I was of getting hurt again. Sometimes the reward is worth the risk.

I looked into Dex's eyes. "You'll always be honest with me?"

"I swear on it."

I bit my bottom lip. The truth was, I couldn't imagine never seeing this man again. He was right. Something was there between us. Something I'd never experienced before. Our connection was so strong; it was impossible to move on. "Okay."

Dex's face lit up, like I'd just flicked the lights on Christmas morning and he'd found a room full of presents. It was really adorable. "Okay? As in you're giving me another chance?"

I needed to be serious, but couldn't help but smile at how happy he seemed. "Yes. But...we need to slow down. I want to start over."

"I can do that."

"Starting over means dating. Getting to know each other. I want to know the real Dexter Truitt."

He inched closer to me on the couch. "I'm an open book."

"Good. We should probably start with a date."

"I'd like that." He inched closer again so that our knees were now touching. I was wearing a skirt and when his hand went to my bare knee, I felt it all over. His thumb gently rubbed at my skin.

Goosebumps were prickling from his touch, yet I managed to say, "I don't have sex on the first date."

He leaned in. "What *do* you do on the first date?"

My mind may have wanted to slow things down, but my body had other ideas when he began to wind my long hair around his hand. "Not much."

He spoke over my lips. "How about kiss. Do you kiss on the first date?"

There was nothing more than I wanted than to kiss him again. Well, maybe there were *other* things I wanted even more, but that was definitely going to have to wait, too. I abruptly stood.

"I need to go."

Dex stood. "Because you don't trust yourself to stay here in my apartment with me?"

"I don't and you know it. You know I'm attracted to you physically, and I can see that you're going to make it very difficult for me if I stay. So I'm going to remove myself from this situation. Because we're going to take it slow."

He didn't hide his disappointment. "When will I see you again?"

"Friday night. You can take me out on a proper date as Dexter Truitt. I think a public place is safest for now."

Dex's grin was wolfish. "If you think being in public with me will keep me from mauling you, then I suppose you need this date to get to know me better."

I rolled my eyes, even though I secretly loved him admitting he couldn't control himself around me, either. "Goodnight, Dex."

"Goodnight, Georgy Girl."

I had the worst first-date jitters I'd ever had—which may have had something to do with the fact that it wasn't really our first date. I'd just discarded the third dress I'd tried on and was now sitting on my bed in only a bra and panties taking a minute to relax. Eyes shut, I took a few cleansing breaths and started to focus on the sound of my meditation balls humming as I massaged them in the palm of my hand. I rolled my neck a few times, loosening up my posture, and just when I began to find my calm, the doorbell buzzed.

Shit. I grabbed for my phone and was shocked to realize that it was already ten minutes to seven. I must have wasted almost an hour trying on clothes and attempting to meditate, when I'd thought it was more like fifteen minutes.

Shit. Shit. Shit.

Covering myself with a bathrobe, I went to the door and pressed the button for the intercom.

"Dex?"

"The one and only."

I buzzed him up. There wasn't time for me to get dressed, but I quickly ran to the bathroom mirror to fix myself. Even though I'd done my hair earlier, changing in and out of dresses had made a mess of it.

When I was done, I unlocked the door and waited. Dex stepped off the elevator, and I watched as he walked down the long hall to my apartment door. God, he was really handsome. He wore a dark sportsjacket with dark slacks and a gray dress shirt, sans tie. But it was the way he strutted toward my door full of swagger and confidence that made my pulse race. There was actually a little flutter in my stomach as he neared my door.

Dex took my face into one hand and gave me a chaste kiss. After, he spoke over my lips, "I thought you wanted to go slow?"

"I do."

"Answering the door in that robe and looking at me like that isn't exactly the way to go about doing slow."

I shook my head, hoping to wake up my brain. "Sorry. I lost track of time. Come in. I just need a few minutes." I opened the door and went inside my apartment, but turning back, I found that Dex hadn't followed me in. He was standing inside my open doorway.

"I think I should wait out here."

"What? Don't be ridiculous. Come inside."

His eyes dropped down to point to my breasts. I was fully covered, but my silky robe wasn't doing a damn thing to hide my pert nipples. They were poking through the lace of my bra and thin cover up, looking as anxious and excited as I felt. I folded my arms across my chest. "That's your fault."

"My fault?"

"Yes. If you weren't all…" I waved my hand up and down. "…all dark and sexy looking, they wouldn't be saluting you. And you kissed me. What do you expect?"

He grinned. "Dark and sexy looking?"

I rolled my eyes. "Just come in and sit down."

"Okay. But I can't guarantee I won't be all sexy looking."

I disappeared into my bedroom and left Dex sitting in the kitchen. After another rummage through my closet, I finally settled on a red dress that I loved. It was one of those colors that turned heads, and the only time I'd ever worn it was when I went out to a bar with my friends from work. I'd attracted more attention than I'd ever had that night. So much so, that I never wore it again. But tonight I was feeling greedy and wanted Dex to be unable to keep his eyes off of me the same way I seemed to be unable to keep mine off of him.

The look on Dex's face told me I'd made the right decision when I walked into the kitchen. He was looking at some pictures of my nieces that I had hanging on the refrigerator and turned when he saw me.

"You look..." he trailed off. Then made a face. "Maybe you should change?"

I frowned. "You don't like my dress?"

"I fucking love the dress."

"I don't understand."

Dex walked to me. "You look beautiful. Red is definitely your color. But that dress...I'm going to get myself into trouble tonight, and I know it."

Dex had taken me to one of the most exclusive spots on the Upper West Side. The Chapel restaurant was an old church converted into a high-end eatery. Featuring original stained glass windows, it was popular not only for the ambience but for its eclectic fusion cuisine. It took weeks, if not months, to get into this place.

Unfolding my cloth napkin, I said, "I'd ask how you managed a reservation, but I assume you can pretty much get whatever you want in this city."

"Well, if that isn't the most ironic statement of the year. I most certainly *cannot* get whatever I want. If that were true, I'd be underneath this table right now with my head between your legs."

I clenched my muscles. "You're such a horny bastard."

He played with his watch. "I've never tried to hide that fact from you. And your face is turning redder than that gorgeous dress. You know you love the thought of my head buried beneath your skirt, my mouth getting you off. Admit it."

I did.

"It's a pleasurable thought, yes."

"You've learned through the course of our talks that I'm damn good at what I do for a living, but what you haven't yet realized is how damn good I am with my tongue. That's not something I could have described in an interview, of course. It's just something I'll have to show you when the time is right."

Dex had an unbelievable ability to appear so composed when he was talking dirty in public places. I would bet anyone watching him from afar could have easily assumed we were just talking business. I, on the other hand, was squirming in my seat.

He wiggled his brows. "By the way, I brought you something."

"Oh?" I grinned.

He took it out of his inside pocket. It appeared to be another little wooden animal. Unlike the last one that he'd given me—that Jay had given me—this one was far from perfectly carved.

"I made this for you," he said proudly.

"What is it?"

"It's a goat. You can't tell?"

"Oh, I see," I lied. I couldn't tell what it was. "This is all your handiwork?"

"Yes. I've been taking lessons from a master whittler. By the time he's through with me, I plan to whittle you the world, baby."

"That's really not necessary. Why do you feel the need to continue that part of your façade?"

"It's not about that...at all. I think I accidentally developed respect for an art I'd originally made a mockery of. And now, I truly enjoy trying my hand at it. I'm also in a very disturbing, one-sided competition with a ten-year-old YouTuber." He cracked a smile. "Is that weird?"

"Yes." I laughed. "But you're a little eccentric and weird yourself... in a good way. So, it fits." I looked down at the barely recognizable goat. "This is precious, though. I'll cherish it even more than the first one, because it's really yours."

"Good." He winked.

After we finished our meal, my attention turned to a couple who'd just arrived. They were sitting diagonally across from us. The woman was tall and gorgeous and much younger than the man. Her blonde hair was parted to the side and pulled back into a low bun. A thin strand of pearls lay atop her champagne-colored, satin, sleeveless top. A bright red Birkin bag that I knew must have cost in the tens of thousands sat on the ground next to her seat.

When the woman's date got up from the table, her eyes locked with mine before she started to type something.

Dex's phone suddenly vibrated, prompting him to look down and check it. He then turned around and looked straight at the blonde. She was now smiling directly at us.

What the hell?

"Fuck," he whispered under his breath.

"That woman just texted you?"

He gritted his teeth. "That's Caroline."

Caroline.

My stomach sank. Suddenly, the woman who had seemed attractive seconds ago became ten times more gorgeous in my mind—more threatening. I realized the mouth that was curved up in a smile was the same one that had been habitually wrapped around his "beautiful cock."

Riddled with jealousy, I asked, "What did she just text you?"

Dex knew he wouldn't be able to get away with hiding it, so he simply handed me the phone.

Caroline: So, this is the reason you won't fuck me anymore...

I gave it back to him.

Caroline noticed that he'd shown me the text and began typing again.

When his phone buzzed, I asked, "What does it say?"

He reluctantly turned the screen toward me.

Caroline: Make sure you tell her that you like anal play.

A rush of adrenaline hit me. "Oh, really?" I huffed. "Good to know."

Dex looked like he was getting angry. "She's fucking with you, Bianca, because she sees you checking my phone."

When Caroline's date returned to the table, the texting stopped, and her attention turned back toward the older man who was wining and dining her.

"I'm sorry," Dex said.

"It's fine. We can't change anything that happened before we met."

He could clearly see that I wasn't really okay when he said, "Let's get out of here."

"No. Then she'll know she upset me. I don't want to give her that satisfaction."

"Yeah, well, the alternative...staying....is making you miserable. I'm not going to accept that." Dex placed a wad of cash on the table to cover our bill and signaled for me to follow him.

I forced my eyes away from Caroline as we passed her table and exited the restaurant.

We made our way into the Town Car, and Dex instructed Sam to just drive around for a while until we knew where we wanted to go next.

Dex took my hand in his. "I'm really sorry about that."

"You don't need to apologize again."

"I'm glad we at least got to eat before she showed up."

I stared out the window for a bit before I said, "I've never been a jealous person. I wish it didn't upset me so much." It was hard to admit how I felt, but seeing her—especially how beautiful she was—really did catch me off guard. In a weird way, it made me want him more because I suddenly felt insecure and possessive.

"I think it's adorable that you're jealous. And it's also a bit of a relief, because it shows me that you care about me at a time when I really need that reassurance."

"I'm the one feeling self-conscious right now. She was absolutely stunning."

"She's physically beautiful. But so are a lot of women. It takes more than a pretty face to get me to the point of obsession. That's where I am with you, Bianca. Not only are you the only woman I care to be with physically right now, but I fell for your mind long before my dick became impossible to control." He squeezed my hand. "And you want to talk about jealousy? Do you have any idea what a wreck I was every single second you were out on that date? But it's good to be open about this kind of stuff. We should be honest about our feelings, especially when it helps us determine where we stand with each other."

Speaking of honesty, something had been really gnawing away at me for some time now. It was the one secret I'd kept hidden from the get-go. I'd given him grief about his deception when I was hiding something of my own. It felt like the right time to confess what brought me to him in the first place.

My palms felt sweaty. "I have to tell you something."

Seeming concerned by my tone, he loosened his grip on my hand. "Alright..."

Here goes.

"I've knocked you for your dishonesty. But I haven't been completely truthful with you about something. There's a piece of information I've been keeping from you since the day we met."

"Tell me this doesn't have to do with another man."

"No."

"Thank fuck."

"Well...not in the way you might think."

"What are you talking about?"

"There was a reason I volunteered to interview you. It wasn't just for curiosity's sake."

"Okay...what was it, then?"

"Your father was the reason."

"My father..."

"Yes."

"What about my father?"

"My mother used to work for him."

"Your mother...worked for my father? What did she do at Montague?"

"She was his secretary for a time."

"You're kidding."

"No."

"God, he went through so many secretaries. How long did she work for him?"

"I'm not sure. Several years."

"Well, that's certainly longer than most."

"I know. Your dad fired her, though, and that led to some serious money problems for my family because we were dependent on that paycheck. Dexter Sr. apparently paid very well. We'd become accustomed to having that security."

"What happened after that?"

"Well, I was too young to remember but from what my mother told me, my dad's company downsized around the same time, and he lost a good portion of his income. That was sort of the point where my parents' marital problems really started. My father had an affair around that time. So my mother losing her job was really the beginning of the end."

"And you associate all of this bad stuff happening with what my father did. That was sort of the catalyst."

"Yes. I realize it wasn't directly his fault, but it made me want to somehow get back at him by conducting the interview with you. I had originally planned to make it difficult for you. But that never happened, of course, because I soon realized that you were nothing like your father."

"I can't believe you kept this from me."

"Well, I think you can understand the need to hide an uncomfortable truth."

He nodded. "I certainly can, and I don't blame you for not wanting to admit your original intentions. I just wish you had opened up to me about it sooner. I wouldn't have held it against you. You didn't know me then, and honestly, my father was a shitty human being, so you had every reason to want retribution."

"I would never want to do anything to hurt you now, Dex. Please believe that. I feel so foolish thinking back to that time."

"You know what I think?"

"What?"

"We've both made mistakes—especially me. I think we've done enough lying to each other and enough apologizing. Why don't we stop dwelling on the past. Let's stop letting other people get in the way of our happiness, too, whether that's fictional Jay, Caroline, or my father. Let's just move on." He kissed my forehead. "Unless you have anything else to confess?"

"I don't." I smiled. "Thank you for understanding. And you're right. No more focusing on the past."

"You could've told me something far worse, and, honestly, at this point, Bianca, I'd have let it slide because I want you too damn much. I can't go back. You could've told me you murdered someone, and the next thing I'd know, I'd be harboring a fugitive."

"You're crazy, Dex."

"I know you have trust issues, and I know I've contributed to them. But I really do want to help undo some of the damage."

"It goes far beyond what happened with us. My father's affair, his leaving us when I was so very young, really made me an untrustworthy person, in general. There's no man a girl is supposed to trust more than her father. His betraying my mother when times got rough conditioned me to always wait for the other shoe to drop. I won't let you take all the blame for my hesitation with you. It goes far beyond you or... Jay."

"Okay, then we've established that we both have the same fear."

"The same?"

"Yes. You fear that I'll turn out like our fathers, and that's exactly my own fear. I worry that even though I know right from wrong, that I'm somehow genetically predisposed to being a bad person. Honestly, the Jay facade made me wonder more than ever. The fact that I was capable of pulling that off—of deceiving you—served as evidence in my own mind that my fear is warranted. How much control do I really have over my actions if I was able to make a split-second decision like that? So, I worry, too. But at some point we just have to let go and see what happens."

He was right.

I happened to look down at that moment and noticed that he looked like he was packing a snake in his trousers. "Oh, my God. Are you hard?"

"Yes."

"How can you have gotten an erection when we were in the middle of a serious conversation?"

"Do you really have to ask that? When am I *not* hard around you?" He pointed to his skull. "I've been talking to you with this head. My other one downstairs has a mind of its own."

"Too bad you're not really Jay," I joked.

"What do you mean?"

"Well, if that relationship were real, we would've been dating for a while by now. We'd probably be home participating in all the things you are imagining at the moment," I teased.

"That's just cruel. I already hate that guy enough as it is." He placed his hand around the back of my head and brought my face into his, speaking over my mouth. "Let me ask you this. What can I get away with tonight?"

"Well, I don't trust myself to be alone with your 'beautiful cock,' so we're not going back to your place or mine."

"Okay...so then where can I have my limited way with you?"

"Honestly, the only place I'd probably trust myself to let you touch me is a crowded theater. At least there, I would know it could only go so far with other people around."

Without hesitation, he called the driver. "Sam, head to the Lincoln Square Loews Cinema."

CHAPTER 19

Dex

Perfect. The entire back row was empty. We'd gotten here so late that all of the good movies were sold out, but it didn't matter. I wasn't here for the show.

When the lights dimmed, I placed my hand on Bianca's knee. We at least attempted to watch the very beginning of the movie—some bank heist comedy.

A few minutes into it, she turned her head toward me. Bianca was looking at me when she should have been watching the movie, and I knew that was my signal; she was giving me silent permission to start what she knew I'd come here for.

I felt like a teenager, so excited about the prospect of feeling her up for the first time. Turning my body toward her in my seat, I held the back of her head as I brought her lips to mine and growled into her mouth as I began to kiss her hungrily. There was something wildly erotic about testing the limits in a crowded theater. Having the back row to ourselves was the best of both worlds; no one was looking, but you still got the thrill of doing something naughty in a public place.

With each lick of my tongue against hers, I wanted more. My hand slid up her thigh and under her dress until it landed on the elastic of her underwear. Her hips wriggled beneath my hand as I slipped my finger underneath. Her panties were drenched; she was so aroused, and it made me wonder if she'd been like that all night.

I closed my eyes in euphoria as I pushed my index and middle fingers in and out of her wet pussy. It was all too easy to imagine what it would feel like wrapped around my painfully hard cock. I knew without a doubt I couldn't go much longer without knowing what that felt like.

I yearned to suck on her breasts but her dress wouldn't allow me access without unzipping it from the back. Instead, I lowered my mouth to devour them through the fabric before kissing my way back to her mouth again.

I whispered in her ear, "I can't wait to fuck you."

"I'd let you if we weren't here. That's why we *are* here."

"I know."

She ran her fingers through my hair as she kissed me harder. I continued to finger fuck her while massaging her clit with my thumb. When she tightened repeatedly against my hand, I knew she was coming. It hadn't taken much.

There was nothing sexier than watching her scream out in silence as she climaxed. I couldn't wait to hear what she sounded like when she came with me inside her in the privacy of my bedroom.

When she stopped moving, I slipped my finger out and took it into my mouth, savoring every bit of her taste.

She placed her hand on my erection and whispered in my ear, "If we had something to cover us, I'd return the favor."

That was the moment I knew a garment of clothing was about to be sacrificed.

I took off my jacket and covered myself. Her hand slipped underneath and worked to unzip my pants. My engorged cock sprung free and Bianca began to jerk it slowly. Relaxing my head back, I wondered how the hell I was going to manage this quietly when it felt better than anything I could remember aside from what I'd just done to her moments ago.

I just about lost it when she licked her palm before repositioning it around my dick. She pumped harder and within seconds, I came in her hand until my limp body collapsed back into the seat. Her wet hand totally undid me.

Bianca smiled impishly as I used my designer jacket to discreetly clean up my load. I hadn't pulled this shit since the early years of high school.

"I won't be taking this to the cleaners."

"I hope that wasn't your favorite suit jacket."

"It only cost two thousand dollars. But that hand job was worth more."

"I didn't realize it was that expensive. I should have just used my mouth."

"You are evil, Georgy Girl," I said before smashing my lips against hers.

"When will I see you again?" We were in the back of my Town Car and almost to her building. I didn't care that I sounded desperate, and I'd asked her the same exact question just the other day. The ball was in her court—why pretend it wasn't?

"Well, tomorrow night I have a work thing. I won't be home until pretty late."

"That work thing isn't Eamon, is it?"

She smiled. "No. But if it was, it would be work, not a date. I wouldn't disguise a date as a work thing."

Our fingers were entwined as we sat side by side. "I hope you mean that you wouldn't disguise a date because you aren't planning on having any. Outside of me, that is."

She bumped her shoulder to mine. "Is that your way of asking me to be exclusive with you?"

"I expect if I'm not fucking you, no one else will be inside you either."

"You're so crass."

I shrugged. "Maybe. But can you really tell me the thought of my cock in another woman sits right with you?"

"No. It definitely doesn't."

"Then it's settled. My cock will continue his relationship with only my hand until such time as your pussy decides to put it out of its misery."

She laughed. "You're so romantic."

We pulled up at the curb outside of her building, and I made no attempt to open the door. "I'm not letting you out of this car until you tell me when I'll see you again."

"How about the day after tomorrow? Thursday."

"I have a dinner meeting up in Boston."

"Well, Friday I have dinner plans with my mom at her house. She's watching my two nieces overnight so my sister and her husband can have a date night out and the house to themselves after. But you're more than welcome to come, if you want."

"It's a date," I said immediately.

She chuckled at my eagerness. "Perhaps before you agree to come with me, I should warn you that my sister's kids are little holy terrors."

It didn't escape me that Caroline had once asked me to go to a family function. An excuse rolled from my tongue before the invitation was even fully out of her mouth. Yet with Bianca, I had no hesitation at all. Even more fucked up was that, as she painted a picture of something I'd normally run the other way from, I found myself thinking that perhaps seeing her with her sister's kids in action might be a glimpse into my own future.

I brought our entwined hands to my mouth and kissed the top of hers. "I don't scare that easily."

"Say that after you meet the twins from hell and sit in rush hour traffic to Staten Island."

Turning to face her, I cupped her cheeks in my hands. "Did you say rush hour traffic? I can think of a few ways we can pass the time back here on the way to Staten Island Friday night. I'll bring a cheap jacket this time."

CHAPTER 20

Bianca

We'd had a change of plans for Friday night. My afternoon interview wound up being in New Jersey, so I'd told Dex to meet me at my mom's house, rather than my going back through Staten Island to Manhattan at rush hour only to turn around and come back. Plus, after I thought about the prospect of Mom meeting Dexter *Truitt*, I decided it might be best to tell her alone who Dex's father was. It had been so many years since Mom lost her job and my parents divorced, but if I was initially harboring a grudge against Dex for his father's actions, there was a possibility Mom could feel the same. Or worse.

"Hey, Thing One." I let myself into my mother's house and one of my sister's daughters, Faith, ran up to greet me at the door. She barreled into my legs and I lifted the featherlight four-year-old into the air. Her face was covered in chocolate and she had on a headband with tiny red horns, the kind that came with a devil costume. "The horns finally came out, huh? I knew they were in there somewhere, and it was only a matter of time." I shifted her to my hip and went to find the other little monster. It was quiet; I hoped they didn't have my mother tied up somewhere already.

"Mom?"

"In here, sweetheart!" Mom's voice yelled from the kitchen.

I walked in to find Hope, Faith's twin, standing on a chair stirring something at the table while wearing white angel wings. Mom was taking the large, silver mixing bowl from the nearby KitchenAid Mixer. She smiled warmly. "I have two assistants today."

Kissing Faith on the forehead, I said, "I see that. And one of them is in costume."

"I'm an angel, Aunt Bee!"

"Far from it. But your wings are pretty. Did Grandma take you shopping in the costume store today?"

Faith nodded her head rapidly. "She said you'd do our makeup later, too."

"Oh she did, did she?"

My mother kissed my cheek. "I actually didn't tell them that. We never even discussed makeup today." She turned to my niece. "Faith, what did Mommy tell you about lying?"

Faith covered her nose with both hands. "I'm not lying."

Mom and I chuckled. Then Faith spilled whatever it was that she was stirring all over the table and floor, followed by Hope getting half a head of her hair stuck in the mixing spoon Mom had given her to occupy her mouth while we mopped up the mess her sister had made. After we finally finished cleaning up the kitchen and the two terrors, I popped in a *Full House* DVD and poured Mom and I a glass of wine.

We sat at the kitchen island where we could still keep our eye on the girls watching TV in the living room. "So. Tell me about this man you're seeing who is coming over."

I took a healthy gulp from my glass before answering. "Well...he's handsome, smart, and successful."

"Sounds perfect so far."

"He's definitely not perfect. We actually got off to a pretty rocky start, but we managed to weather it through. I think that's what I like the best about him. He doesn't pretend to be perfect. When he made a mistake, he didn't try to make any excuses. He owned up to it."

Mom's smile was sad as she looked down. "Owning up to your mistakes is important in a relationship."

I knew she was talking about Dad. Even after all these years, what he'd done still saddened her. I covered her hand with mine. "Can I ask you something, Mom?"

"Of course."

"If Dad had come clean about what he'd done, had owned up to it, do you think you could've stayed together? Could you have truly trusted him again once he'd broken your trust?"

"Sweetheart, it wasn't Dad's fault we didn't stay together."

Never once in the fifteen years since the split did my mom come clean over what Dad had done to her. She was the type of mom who wanted to protect us at all costs. But my sister and I had overheard enough fighting about his affair to know the truth.

The doorbell rang, and I looked at the clock on the microwave. I must've lost track of the time. "I guess that's Dex. I didn't realize it was so late."

"Dex?"

"Yes. His name is Dexter, but he goes by Dex." I'd have to fill her in on his last name another time. Maybe it was better that way. She would get to know him independent of any negative feelings that she might still harbor toward his father. "I'll get the door."

"I'll get the brownies out of the oven."

I took a deep breath before opening the front door. It had only been a few days since I'd seen Dex, but I'd thought about him non-stop since our night in the back of the theatre. In fact, I was finding it difficult to focus on anything *but* Dexter Truitt the last few days. My heart rate was out of control when I opened the door and took in his handsome face.

Dex smiled, and I swear my knees got weak like a teenage girl. He held a big bouquet of colorful flowers in one hand and a bottle of wine in the other. Leaning in, he kissed me gently on the lips then looked over my shoulder inside the house. The twins were glued to the television. "They good for a minute there?" he whispered.

"*Full House* is better than duct tape and rope."

Dex abruptly hooked an arm around my waist and pulled me outside onto the front stoop, shutting the door behind me. Before I could even realize what was going on, my back was pressed up against it. He took my mouth in a serious kiss. "I missed you," he groaned when it broke.

"I missed you, too."

He leaned his forehead against mine and then his eyes trailed down to my cleavage. I'd picked out a dress with a lower neckline than I'd normally wear. "My mouth needs to taste those so fucking badly. We skipped second base and went to third."

"Not here."

"No. Not here. But tonight."

I cleared my throat. "Okay."

"Okay?"

I nodded. "Second base later, but don't try to slide home."

He closed his eyes. "I'm about to meet your mother. Could you please not use words like *sliding home*? I'm already at

191

enough of a disadvantage being a Truitt, I don't need her to think I can't even control my own erections."

I looked down. "Yeah...about that..."

Dex was acting weird. I wasn't sure if he was pissed I decided not to tell my mom who he was before he arrived or if just being at my mother's made him feel uncomfortable, in general. But his body language was stiff, and I could see the tension in his face. He was also being unusually quiet. When my sister called to check in on the girls, Mom went to the living room to put them on the phone, and I took the opportunity to feel out Dex while I put the flowers he brought my mom in a vase with water.

"Is everything okay?"

"Fine."

I furrowed my brows. "Why do I feel like you're upset with me? Are you angry because I didn't tell my mother who your father is yet? Because I was planning to...I still am. I guess I was just stalling and ran out of time and then thought I really want her to get to know you for you and not be tainted by something that has nothing to do with the person you are."

Dex closed his eyes. "It's not that."

"Then what's bothering you?"

"What's your mom's first name again?"

"Eleni."

"I recognize her. I didn't go to my father's office often, but I must have met her at one point because as soon as I saw her I knew I'd seen her before."

"Well, she didn't seem to recognize you. Does that make you uncomfortable that you know who she is, but she doesn't really know who you are? Because I'll tell her right now if you want."

"Do you see the irony in that question?"

I hadn't until he pointed it out. "Yes, but this time it's my fault that you're not being forthright. I put you in this position. It's not the same as when you weren't honest with me."

"Feels just as shitty to do it."

"So, I'll tell her. I don't want to make you uncomfortable."

"No, don't. Not while I'm here tonight anyway. I feel like shit enough putting a face to one of the many people who my father treated poorly. I'm sorry that he affected your family, Bianca. I truly am."

My heart broke a little. I knew what it was like to grow up with a father whose actions I wasn't proud of. And as far as I knew, my father only ever hurt my mother. I couldn't imagine having to live in the shadows of a man who openly embarrassed his wife with affairs and fired loyal workers without so much as a thought. "You're not your father. We said we were going to put our past behind us. Please don't feel badly for something you had nothing to do with. In the end, even my own resentment toward your father was somewhat misplaced. Sure, my family struggled a little when my mom lost her job. But plenty of families go through difficult financial times. It was my father's actions that made my family fall apart. I think I just wanted to blame someone else. It's time to grow up and put the fault where it really lies."

I finished arranging the flowers, and Dex reached out and pulled me close to him. He caressed my cheek and then leaned in to kiss me, but the moment was disrupted by a certain little devil. Fearless, she ran right up to Dex. "Who are you?"

She'd been so hypnotized watching the TV, she hadn't even noticed him walk through the living room and into the kitchen with me. Dex stood from his chair and crouched down to speak to Faith at eye level. "I'm Dex. Your Aunt Bianca's friend."

"Do you sleep in the same bed?"

My eyes widened. "Faith! What kind of a question is that?"

She ignored me and continued to speak to Dex. "When I go to Aunt Bee's house, she lets me sleep in her bed. When Daddy goes away for work, Mommy lets me sleep in her bed. If you're going to sleep in Aunt Bee's bed, then I'm going to have to sleep on the floor."

Dex's lip twitched, but he answered her with sincerity. "You won't have to sleep on the floor."

"Are you going to marry Aunt Bee?"

Dex responded before I could. "If I'm lucky, maybe someday."

"Could I be the flower girl? Cause there's only one, and my sister picks her nose. So you don't want her."

I started to laugh, until I realized that Hope had walked in and overheard her sister. "I do not pick my nose anymore!"

Faith leaned in with a devilish smile and whispered to Dex, "She stopped yesterday." These girls were going to be hellions when they were teenagers.

Dinner was a myriad of spills and arguments between the angel and devil. In between, Mom and Dex talked a lot. He was definitely a charmer, and it was interesting to see him in action. She'd put on an old Duke Ellington CD for background music during dinner, and he'd quickly picked up on her affinity for jazz music. Then he won her over by spouting off his favorite songs by jazz artists like Lester Young and Bill Evans, both of whom I'd never heard of. By the time dinner was over, Dex's last name could have been Manson, and I wouldn't have been worried. He'd insisted that Mom and I sit down while he and the girls cleaned up. The entire scene was comical to watch. We sipped wine while he took turns lifting the girls to put dishes up in the cabinets. If I didn't know better, I'd have even thought he had the ability to tame wild beast four-year-olds.

"I like him. He seems genuine," Mom said.

Dex was bending over to load something into the dishwasher, and my eyes were glued to the way his jeans hugged his firm ass. "I like him, too."

I was mid-sip, still ogling the view when Mom sighed. "Does he have a nice father for your dear old mom?"

I choked, coughing some of my wine through my nose. It burned like hell.

Mom laughed when I finally stopped sputtering and caught my breath. "What? I'm old. Not dead."

On the ride back to my apartment, I let Dex get to second base. We laughed as he discreetly felt me up in the back of the Town Car. He even managed to drop his head and take the taste he wanted while somehow shielding me from the driver and passing vehicles. Who knew how many uses a sports jacket could have?

When we pulled up to my apartment, I noticed there was a considerable bulge in his pants. "Do you want to...come inside?"

"That depends on what you're inviting me to come inside of. Are you asking me up and I'm not allowed to touch you, or are you asking me to *come inside*."

My body wanted the latter more than I could explain. I squeezed my thighs together to quell the desire burning between my own legs. Yet...I just wasn't ready to go there with Dex. It wasn't that I was holding back because I didn't trust him anymore—my heart seemed to have moved past the distrust that he'd initially made me feel. Instead...I was realizing that having sex with Dex was going to mean something...possibly something monumental in my life. And maybe I was just a little scared. I turned to him. "I want you more than I've ever wanted anyone."

Dex looked into my eyes. "That's good. Because the feeling is mutual. Although I'm sensing that wasn't the end of your statement. That there's a *but* coming..."

I smiled. "I wish there wasn't. It's just..." I had no idea how to put what I was feeling inside into words. I was confused by my own emotions, so it made explaining things pretty difficult.

I'd looked down, trying to gather my thoughts into coherent sentences, and Dex put two fingers under my chin and lifted until our eyes met. "I'll wait as long as it takes. It doesn't matter why you aren't ready. I'll be here when you are."

"Thank you."

We made out for a while after Dex walked me to the door, but he made no attempt to come in. When we finally said goodbye, I leaned my head against the closed door and listened to his footsteps as they walked away until I couldn't hear them anymore. I hadn't thought about it in years, but a flash of my dad the night he moved out came back to me in that moment. I was sitting in my room crying while he was making trips back and forth carrying boxes to his car. I didn't want to see him, but I also couldn't bring myself to stop listening for him either. I remembered listening to his feet clank against the tile of the hall floor with every trip he made. The last time he went out to his car, I didn't realize it would be his last trip. I'd listened to his footsteps as he walked to the door, the sound becoming more and more distant. Then I waited for the sound to come back again. It never did. He never walked into our house again. He was gone.

CHAPTER 21

Dex

Bianca was out of town the next three days on a trip to the West Coast for an interview. Though I'd felt like our relationship had truly started to push past the crap I'd pulled, something was still not sitting right with me. I'd racked my brain trying to figure out why Bianca's mother looked so familiar, but I couldn't seem to place where we'd met. And she certainly didn't seem to recognize me either, albeit years had passed and I wasn't a teenage boy anymore.

Throughout the day, I was swamped at the office. Even though I was able to immerse myself in my work, an unsettled feeling lurked in the background. By the end of the day it had grown and caused me to lose my concentration. Unable to focus, I picked up the phone and decided to call my father. On the second ring, my secretary walked in and placed a stack of papers she'd just finished photocopying on my desk. I hung up the phone, thinking better of calling him to fish around for details and instead spoke to Josephine. "Before you leave for the day, can you make some last minute travel arrangements? I need to fly first thing in the morning. I'll also be needing a rental car once I land."

"Of course. Where do you need to be?"

"West Palm Beach. I'm heading down to see my father."

Palm Beach International Airport was the total opposite of JFK, that was for sure. Everything seemed to move at a slower pace. It was a weird thing to feel almost relaxed at an airport. The vibe was definitely different down here.

Since I wasn't staying more than one night, I had no checked luggage. I dialed my father as soon as I exited the sliding glass doors. The heat and humidity outside nearly melted my face instantly.

"Dad, where are you right now? I flew down, just landed at PBI."

"Am I dying and don't know about it?" he joked.

"What do you mean?"

"Why else would you be visiting me? It's been how long since I've gotten you down here?"

"Well, I have to talk to you about something important, and I figured I'd kill two birds with one stone, come see you personally. It's been a while."

"It certainly has."

"Are you home?"

"No, actually. I'm at The Breakers."

"I'll meet you there. I'm just getting my rental car, and I'll head straight over."

"Okay, son. See you soon."

After I picked up the Mercedes, I drove over the bridge that connected West Palm Beach to the exclusive island of Palm Beach. Driving past the famous Mar-a-Lago Club with its high hedges, I remembered my parents dragging me to a party there as a child and seeing Donald Trump. We'd spent many winters and holidays down in this posh, private community.

Driving down the road, to my right was a view of the aquamarine-colored ocean. To my left were the mansions—some Spanish-style, some with more modern glass-encased architecture. Tourists and residents leisurely strolled the sidewalks in beach attire, looking like they didn't have a care in the world; I envied them.

I finally arrived at the The Breakers, a Renaissance-style resort where my father often met other retired CEOs for lunch. I knew he also spent a lot of time at a millionaire's club down the road on Peruvian Avenue.

The breeze from the palm trees was a welcome contrast to city life. I couldn't help but wish that Bianca were here to soak in some of this fresh air with me. That reminded me to book a vacation for us as soon as she was ready. I imagined how amazing it would have been to frolic on the beach with her here. I just knew her luscious ass would look amazing in a bikini.

Walking into the hotel reminded me why my father loved it down here. The whole island catered to the glitterati. He was totally in his element. It was a palatial explosion of pastels and money.

I'd texted him at the valet station, and he met me in the lobby.

My father offered a quick hug, patting me on the back. "Dex...so good to see you, son."

"You, too."

I wasn't sure if it was the lighting or what, but my father looked a lot older than the last time I'd seen him. Despite that, he was in pretty good shape for his age because he made a point to stay active every day.

"We were just having lunch out on the balcony. Smoked salmon and capers prepared by Chef Jon. Why don't you join us?"

"Who's we?"

"Myra and some friends."

Myra was my father's most recent wife. She looked like many of the women down here: heavily blonde, Chanel-clad and tweaked by lots of plastic surgery. Let's not forget the small fluffy dog by her side at all times. I was pretty sure Caroline would turn into a Myra someday.

"I was actually hoping that you and I could talk privately."

"Is something wrong?"

"No. I just have some questions for you."

"Alright. Let me just tell them I'll rejoin them. We can take a walk along the beach."

"That sounds good."

I'd dressed for the occasion today, wearing khaki pants and a pink Polo shirt. *When in Rome.*

After he returned, we ventured down to the water. Rolling up my pants and holding my shoes in one hand, I walked alongside my father amidst the crashing waves as the tide came in. Shells crunched under my feet, and a few seagulls nearly grazed my head as they flew by.

"So whatever happened to the situation you called me about? The girl you lied to about your identity?" he asked.

"Well, miraculously, she's decided to forgive me. We're working on things. I haven't earned her trust one hundred percent yet. She's actually the reason I came to see you. Well, more specifically, her mother is the reason."

"What about her mother?"

"She used to work for you. You fired her years ago."

My father laughed. "That narrows it down to a few hundred people, then."

"I met her the other night and immediately recognized her, which was odd. She must have worked for you longer than most, because I don't remember many people from those days."

"What's her name?"

"Eleni George."

He suddenly stopped dead in his tracks and turned to look me in the eyes. "Eleni Georgakopolous."

"No, Eleni George."

"Georgakopolous. It's Georgakopolous." He walked over to a rock. "Come sit. I need a bit of a rest."

"You sure her name was Georgakopolous?"

"Yes."

"Hang on." I quickly typed out a text to Bianca.

Dex: Random thought. I never asked you... George doesn't sound like a Greek name. Is that short for something else?

She responded right away.

Bianca: Yes. I shortened it a while ago for work purposes. No one could seem to spell my last name. My legal name is actually Georgakopolous.

Dex: Good to know.

"What did she say?" my father asked.

"She said her last name is really Georgakopolous."

He nodded. "Let me guess...your girl...she has big, golden brown eyes, gorgeous dark hair, and killer curves?"

"Yes."

"The apple doesn't fall far..."

"If you were so fond of her mother, why did you fire her?"

"Fire her?" My father laughed incredulously. "Is that what she told you?"

"Yes. Bianca said you gave Eleni the ax and that it devastated their family financially. It set off a chain of events that they never recovered from."

"Let me tell you something about Eleni Georgakopolous. And I can tell you this because we're both grown men, and also because I'm not with your mother anymore."

"What?"

"That woman was like...sexual napalm. I've never in my life experienced anything like her."

"Sexual what? Excuse me?"

"Eleni was my secretary, yes. And I was her boss. But we were also lovers, Dex. She was cheating on her husband with me."

"What?"

"It went on for several years. She wasn't the only woman during that time, of course—you know your dear old dad— but she was the only memorable one."

It sickened me to think about my father and Bianca's mother.

"Wait...you need to back up."

"Alright. I'll explain anything you need."

"She was cheating on her husband...with you? And then you *fired* her on top of that?"

He shook his head. "No. I never fired her. Her husband found out about the affair and forced her to quit. They may have told their children a different story. I would have never fired her, because I couldn't quit her. I would've never let her go. She was too addictive."

"God, that's fucked up. This went on for years?"

"On and off, yes."

"I can't believe it."

"What's so hard to believe? If her daughter is as beautiful as she was, surely you can understand?"

"No. I can't understand cheating on your wife—my mother—to begin with. But knowingly wrecking someone else's marriage? That I definitely cannot understand."

"Her husband never gave her what she needed."

"She told you that?"

"Yes. There was so much more to her than he ever saw. He wanted her to just be this complacent wife. But she was a pistol with fire inside. The husband was apparently a good, hard-working man, but he didn't get her, and he wasn't... affectionate."

"And you were...affectionate? That doesn't sound like you at all."

"Maybe adventurous is a better term. I gave her what she needed. You really want me to spell out what that means?"

"No. Spare me. Please."

"What we had was very passionate—sometimes volatile. In the end, she decided she wanted to save her marriage for the sake of her children. That was when things ended between us. But apparently, from what you're telling me, that didn't work out for her after all. I assume any trust that was broken couldn't be repaired. I'm sorry for any part I played in disrupting her family structure, but I don't regret our affair.

It was one of the most memorable times of my life. I still think of her from time to time, and that's rare for me."

"I don't even know what to say. I want to be mad at you, but I suppose you couldn't have known I would meet and fall for her daughter someday."

"I certainly didn't."

"This is so bad. Bianca and I promised each other that there would be no more secrets. How am I supposed to tell her that her mother is not exactly the saint she thought she was? How do you tell someone that their entire view of their childhood is wrong?"

My father seemed to ponder my question then said, "Okay, listen. Now you may not agree with what I'm about to say, but I'm going to say it anyway."

"What?"

"I think sometimes in life there are exceptions to the 'honesty is the best policy' rule. In a case like this, no one stands to gain anything from your telling her what you know. Think about it, Dex. What happens if you tell her and Eleni denies it? What then?"

I challenged him. "Or to the contrary, when Eleni finds out who I am...what if she confesses everything to her daughter anyway?"

"Then you play dumb. No one needs to know we had this conversation. I'm certainly not going to tell anyone."

"I don't know. I really don't think I can keep this from her."

"It's one thing to tell the truth when it's for someone's own good. But nothing good can come from this. All I'm saying is to think about it. Don't rush into anything. There is no logical reason to drop this kind of a bomb now. It's been so many years. Leave it alone. That's my very strong suggestion. If Eleni wants to come clean, let her. But it's not your responsibility to explain."

Staring up at a plane flying overhead, I said, "I am going to have to really think about this."

"Try not to stress yourself out. Life is too short. I'm learning that more and more every day as I see friends dropping dead from heart attacks left and right." He stood up from the rock and kicked the sand off his feet. "Come on. How about a game of golf?"

Carving the giraffe's neck wasn't easy. I followed as closely along as I could while Jelani demonstrated the correct movements of the knife as we sat under the lamplight in his basement. My mind just wasn't in it today.

After only one night in Florida, I'd flown back just in time for my weekly whittling session at his Brooklyn apartment. While Jelani's lessons were always a quiet, meditative experience, spending time here also made me feel like I was contributing to society by looking after him.

Jelani never complained, but I knew his cancer treatments were wearing on him. He mostly stayed home aside from setting up shop at the Brooklyn Flea on weekends. He also had very few family members who checked in on him. A nephew took him to his appointments but sometimes had to cancel. I insisted he call me the next time that happened. While he wouldn't take any money from me, I was prepared to pay for whatever he needed if he'd let me.

"How are you feeling?" I asked.

"I have to push through. If I let myself dwell on it, I'll feel sicker. It's part of why I ask you to come here. Watching you attempt to carve is like pulling teeth, but it gets my mind off things. The mind has incredible power over the body. Speaking of which, tell me what's on *your* mind."

"You can tell something is on my mind?"

"You've whittled the giraffe's neck so thin, it looks like a pencil. You're not concentrating today."

I chuckled. "You got me."

"So, tell me. What is it? Does it have to do with the Greek goddess?"

"How did you know?"

"Wild guess. Tell me the problem."

I spent the next several minutes summing up my Florida trip, explaining the discovery about my father and Eleni.

"So, now my father has me second-guessing whether telling Bianca the truth in this case is a good idea or not. He did have a point. Why put her through that pain if no one stands to gain anything?"

Jelani shook his head. "Your father is wrong. Here's why." He took the giraffe from me then proceeded to walk over to a tool bench and grabbed a small saw. "This is you right now," he said, displaying the pathetic animal. He then sliced the neck off slowly until the giraffe's head and neck fell to the ground.

What the?

"Why did you do that?"

"I'm putting him out of his misery. You couldn't even concentrate today because this secret you are keeping has already begun to fester. It's eating away at you faster than his neck was disappearing. Secrets and lies will always slowly do that until they eventually come out."

"Like the head falling off," I said.

He nodded. "Yes. There is never a reason to hide the truth about anything. The truth shall set you free. Ever hear that?"

"Yeah."

"You can't risk Bianca finding out you knew about this. Even if you don't tell her, you have very honest eyes, Dex. She'll be able to read you. And then that will be the end of you. You've already lied once. There is no second chance here. It's not worth the risk. Never mind what your father said. From what you say, he's a serial liar. It's in his nature. Just tell her the goddamn truth, and don't come back here to whittle unless your mind is with you." He handed me a fresh piece of wood to start on a new giraffe. "Now, focus."

I took it. "Yes, sir."

Sometimes, the truth was hard to hear, but I appreciated the harsh reality check more than he knew.

Later that afternoon, I still wasn't completely sure about what to do.

Bandit was ecstatic to see me. I'd picked him up from the high-end doggy day care, and we were both heading over to Bianca's.

Needing to talk it out in order to make a decision fast, I rubbed his head as I spoke to him in the backseat of the Town Car.

"Okay, so my father says I'd be creating a mess by bringing up the past now, but Jelani thinks I'd be a fool to hide anything from Bianca at this point. You know, if you could talk, that would be really helpful. A third trusted opinion would be most appreciated right about now."

"*Ruff!*"

I knew what I wanted to do, what my gut told me to do.

"If you bark one more time, Bandit, I swear...I'm just going to have to tell her the truth."

"*Ruff!*"

"Alright. If this blows up in my face, I'm gonna blame you."

I'd made up my mind; I was going to tell her tonight.

CHAPTER 22

Bianca

A small, wooden giraffe was staring me in the face as I opened the door.

"You're getting better," I said, taking the figurine.

"You think?"

"I'm going to have to clear some shelf space for all of them." Bandit had bolted past me into my apartment. "He didn't even give me a chance to greet him." I said, watching the dog run into my bedroom.

"Is he okay to go in there?"

"It's fine." I smiled, looking the gorgeous man in front of me up and down.

Dex was dressed casually in a pair of khakis and a white Polo. The shirt fit him like a glove. It was really hard not to slip my hands underneath the fabric and rub them along his muscles. His chunky watch completed the look—millionaire casual. Taking in a deep breath of his cologne, it really hit me how much I'd missed him. I could only imagine those women down in Florida ogling him.

"You definitely look like someone who just came back from Palm Beach."

"I didn't have time to change. I landed, headed to Jelani's, picked up Bandit, then came straight here."

It was really great to see him, but Dex seemed off; I wasn't sure why. He definitely appeared preoccupied with something. I couldn't help feeling a little self-conscious, because he hadn't even hugged or kissed me yet. My body ached to touch him, but my pride kept me from making a move.

"Is everything alright?" I asked.

Scratching the scruff on his chin, he said, "There's something I need to talk to you about."

My heart sank.

Right after he'd said it, the doorbell rang.

"Shit," I said.

"Are you expecting someone?"

"Yes."

"Who?"

"It's my father."

Dex looked panicked. "Your father?"

"Yes. I wasn't sure if you were stopping by. He's having dinner here."

"You haven't told him about me, have you?"

"No."

"What about your mother? Did you tell her yet?"

"No. I haven't gotten around to it yet." I walked toward the door. "I'd better let him in."

As I was about to open up for my dad, Dex whispered behind me, "Bianca, do *not* tell him my identity, okay?"

"So you own your own business? Is it something I'd be familiar with?" Dad was trying to strike up a conversation with Dex, who was being uncharacteristically quiet. Whatever he came to tell me was clearly weighing on his mind.

"Probably not. It's a financial firm. Nothing too flashy."

I hadn't had a chance to tell Dex yet, but the article I'd written was green lit and had been moved up on the magazine's schedule. It was originally slated for publication in the fall, but the editor-in-chief loved it so much, she moved it to next month. Dex had said he didn't want my parents to know who he was when he walked in, but the article would take care of that for us sooner rather than later. I also didn't want him to downright lie to my father. Looking between Dex and my dad, I thought to myself, lies were how so many things ruined my early relationship with both men.

"Dex is being modest, Dad. He runs a very successful company. In fact, that's how we met. I interviewed him for an article in *Finance Times*." I looked over at Dex, who was staring off into space until I caught his eyes. "You'll actually get to learn *everything* about him in two weeks. The magazine is running with my article as the cover story next month."

Dex's eyes grew. "Next month? I thought it was coming out in the fall."

"They moved it up. Apparently, my editor thinks the world has waited long enough to get to know you. By this time in a few weeks, all your secrets will be told to the world." I winked. Of course, I was kidding, but it looked like the thought made Dex pale.

"Can you excuse me for a moment? I need to use the bathroom."

Dex was gone for a few minutes, so after I got my dad a beer, I went to check on him. I knocked lightly on the bathroom door. "Dex? Are you okay in there?"

He opened the door. "I'm actually not feeling too well."

I felt his forehead. His naturally tanned skin was sallow and his skin was a little clammy. "Do you think you're coming down with something? Maybe you should go to my room. Lie down for a bit."

"I should probably go. I don't want to get you and your father sick."

I was definitely disappointed, but I really wanted to believe maybe Dex's strange behavior was the result of him not feeling well. Although inside, my gut was twisting that his behavior was from something else entirely—something that didn't bode well for us long term. I just had that bad feeling. "Okay. If you think you'd feel better in your own bed."

Dex's eyes searched mine. I went to turn away and walk back to the living room when Dex grabbed my elbow and pulled me back. He cupped my cheeks with both hands. "Being in my own bed would never feel better than being in yours. Mine is lonely without you even though you haven't been in it yet."

His words were so sweet, such a contradiction to his sad face. "Well, I hope you feel better."

He nodded. When we walked back to the living room together, we found Dad bonding with Bandit. The dog's two hind legs were on the floor, but the rest of his body was sprawled across my dad's lap on the couch.

"Seems like you've made a friend."

Dad scratched behind Bandit's ears. "I always wanted a dog. Is he a rescue dog, Dex?"

"Yes. He is, actually."

213

"I didn't know you always wanted a dog, Dad? How come we never had one growing up?"

Dad's voice was low, the same way he spoke whenever we were forced to discuss my mother. She was definitely a subject we both avoided, although sometimes it was inevitable. "Your mom never wanted one."

Bandit climbed off Dad's lap and went to sit at Dex's side. My father stood. "How about a beer, Dex?"

I answered. "Dex was actually going to leave. He's not feeling well."

"That's a shame. My daughter so rarely allows me to meet anyone that she's spending time with. Thought I might finally get a chance to put some of those embarrassing childhood stories to good use."

Dex raised an eyebrow. "Embarrassing stories?"

My father walked to the kitchen as he spoke and grabbed a beer out of the refrigerator. "In kindergarten, my little princess had a crush on our neighbor's oldest son—Tommy Moretti."

I turned to Dex. "You should probably get going since you don't feel well."

Smiling, Dad twisted the beer cap off and extended it to Dex. Both men completely ignored me while Dex took the bottle from my Dad's hand. He continued, "Anyway, Tommy was about eighteen or nineteen. Bianca was maybe seven. She befriended Tommy's little sister so she spent a lot of time over at the Moretti house."

Dex turned to me and whispered, "Older men even back then, huh?"

I rolled my eyes. My father continued, "Of course, Tommy was more interested in girls his own age than seven-year-olds, but that didn't stop my little princess from crushing on him. A few times we found some of Tommy's things at our house, and Bianca would just play it off as she must have brought it home by accident. There was a pair of his gloves, some aftershave once, a baseball hat. It wasn't until Bianca's mother cleaned her room one day that we caught on that she was starry-eyed for the boy."

"What did she find?" Dex asked.

I closed my eyes, knowing what was coming next. Lord knows my older sister tortured me about it for years.

"Bianca was apparently going into the bathroom after Tommy shaved and collecting all the little hair shavings from the sink. She had a baggy under her mattress with a year's worth of stubble." My father chuckled and took a swig from his beer. After that, Dex said he would stay for a bit. One beer turned into four, and by the time we were finished eating dinner, Dex had enough embarrassing stories about me to last a lifetime. I might have wanted to kill my father if I hadn't found it oddly sweet how many crazy little things he remembered.

As I packed away the leftovers in the kitchen, I watched my father and Dex bonding in the living room together. The two were really enjoying each other's company. Over the last two hours, they found out they had quite a few things in common, other than their mutual enjoyment of embarrassing Bianca stories. Both men liked to fish, something I couldn't picture Dex doing so easily. And they were both into old Chevy cars. Looking at them sitting together and laughing in the living room, it warmed my heart.

"I should get going." My father looked at his watch. "I have to stop at the pharmacy and pick up medicine before it closes," Dad said.

"Medicine? Are you sick?"

Dad walked to me. "No, princess. Blood pressure is just a little high so they put me on some medicine. Pretty common at my age."

"Okay."

Bandit was scratching at the front door. "Why don't I walk out with you. Looks like Bandit needs a walk," Dex said.

"Let me grab a sweater, and I'll go with you."

I walked to my bedroom and went into the closet. Before I could pull a sweater from the pile on the top shelf, Dex was shutting the bedroom door behind him.

"Your dad's a really nice guy."

I wished I didn't feel the need to constantly put him down. Why did a compliment to him always feel like it was an insult to my mother? "He can be at times, yes."

Dex came up behind me as I was putting on the sweater and squeezed my shoulders. "I'd like to walk your father out alone, if you don't mind."

I turned around. "Oh. Okay. I guess?"

He kissed the top of my head. "Thank you. Perhaps you can just mention you just remembered a work call you needed to make or something?"

"Okay. But you're coming back after you walk Bandit, right?"

Dex pulled his head back, the relaxed face he'd been wearing the last two hours was suddenly gone again. "Yes. We need to talk."

Just like Dex had requested, I feigned an important work call and excused myself from taking the dog for a walk. After saying goodbye to my dad, the two men left together. The last thing Dex said was. "I'll be back in ten minutes."

I waited the ten minutes. But ten turned into twenty, and twenty turned into forty. Before I knew it, Dex had been gone more than an hour. Finally, feeling anxious, I sent him a text.

Bianca: Are you coming back?

CHAPTER 23

Dex

"What's on your mind, son?"

I'd been lost in my head the last ten minutes, not knowing how to start the conversation I wanted to have. I had asked Bianca's dad to join me for Bandit's walk, then was nearly silent the entire five-block walk to the park. "Sorry. There is something that's bothering me."

"Would you like to talk about it?"

"I don't know where to begin."

"How about at the beginning? I'm in no rush. The pharmacy can hold until the morning, if need be."

I took a deep breath. "Okay." There was a park bench to the left of the walkway we were on. I motioned to it. "Would you like to sit?"

"I'm fine. We can keep walking if you'd like."

Not knowing any other way to break the news, I blurted out, "You know my father. My name is Dexter Truitt."

Bianca's father, Taso, stopped short in place. He looked me in the eyes. Finding I was dead serious, he said, "Maybe we should have a seat after all."

"She was going to live with her mother. I might be old school, but a girl belongs with her mother if it's at all possible. There was never any fight for custody. I didn't want her to hold a grudge against the woman she needed to look up to." Taso shook his head and sighed. "Eleni didn't want to lie to her. It was all my idea. I didn't fight her for custody of the girls, agreed to the support she wanted, and promised I'd never miss a visit with my daughters. In exchange, I asked her for two things in return. One of them was to say it was me who had had the affair. Eleni wouldn't come right out and say it, wouldn't lie to the girls, if asked. But she promised to never tell them outright. The night I left for good, I apologized to the girls for what I'd done to break up our marriage. All the years that followed, they never asked anything else about my supposed affair, and Eleni never told them anything different."

"Bianca harbors a pretty heavy grudge against you still."

Taso's shoulder's slumped. He took off his glasses and rubbed his eyes. "I know. When I came up with the plan so many years ago, I figured they were kids and would get over it. Bianca, though, she could never really forgive me."

I realized in that moment how much trust Bianca was placing in me by giving me a second chance. She'd never even afforded her father that same opportunity. I turned to Taso and looked him straight in the eyes. "I have to tell her."

He stared at me for a long moment. "I understand. She's not a little girl who needs protecting anymore. She's a grown woman who deserves the truth from a man she clearly cares about. The lies were what ended things between Eleni and me. I loved her. Part of me still does, if I'm being honest. But when I figured out what was going on, I gave her a second chance. Thought maybe we could move past it, if we worked hard enough. A few months after, things had just started to settle down again, when I caught her in another lie. Went to her office and found...well...I'm sorry...you don't really need to know the details."

After that, we sat and talked for a while longer. When my phone buzzed in my pocket, I realized I'd been gone for more than an hour. Taso saw me check my phone.

"My daughter?"

I nodded.

"You should go. Get this off your chest. She's a big girl, loves her mother. She'll eventually understand that sometimes when one person makes a mistake, it's not always only that person's fault. She'll get over it. Just make sure you're there for her when she needs to work through it."

We both stood. I extended my hand to Taso. "Thank you for understanding."

"Take care of my little girl."

Knowing it was the right thing, didn't make it any easier. I stood outside of Bianca's door for a few minutes before finally growing a pair and knocking. She answered almost immediately and stepped aside for me to enter. Bandit charged ahead and disappeared inside.

"I was starting to think you weren't coming back."

"Sorry about that. I was talking to your dad, and we must have lost track of time."

"You two seem to have hit it off. I hadn't really thought of it until I watched you together, but you sort of remind me of my dad." She scrunched up her nose. "Is that weird?"

"Only if that makes it weird for you."

She smiled. "Would you like a glass of wine?"

"I'll take something stronger, if you have it."

Bianca went into the kitchen and brought us each back a glass. Mine was filled with an amber liquid. When she sat down and looked at me expectantly, I gulped back half of it without even a sniff test.

She got right to the point. "Something has been troubling you since you knocked on my door earlier. What's going on?"

I took a deep breath. "There's something I need to talk to you about."

"Okay..."

"It's something you're not going to be happy about."

It was her turn to drink some liquid courage. She tossed back half her wine glass and then looked me straight in the eyes. "I prefer the truth, even when it's something I might not want to hear, Dex."

"Alright." There was no easy way to say it, so I just let it rip. "My father had an affair with your mother."

The floor was going to be worn from her pacing. Bianca had her silver stress balls singing a mile a minute in her hand as she walked back and forth. I'd explained what I knew from my talk with my father, and now she was trying to make sense of the lies. She'd passed through the disbelief stage and moved on to angry in the last fifteen minutes.

"Why would he lie and make me hold it against him for the better part of twenty years?"

"He was trying to protect you."

She froze. "By lying to me? Lying doesn't protect anyone but the liar."

"I think there are two kinds of lies. A lie to protect something and a lie to escape something. He wasn't trying to escape anything."

"So you think it's okay that he let me spend all this time thinking he was a cheater?"

I rubbed the back of my neck. I needed to be careful here. Bianca was only beginning to trust me again, and it probably wasn't a good idea to have her suspect I was okay with any lying at all. So instead of giving her an opinion on whether her dad did the right thing by lying, I decided to refrain from having that conversation. I'd been giving her distance, but I felt like she needed physical comforting almost as much as I needed to give it to her.

Stepping into her pacing trail, I covered her hands with mine. The low hum of her stress balls quieted. "Come here." She hesitated at first, but then let me wrap her tight in my arms.

"God, Dex. I feel like my entire life was a lie. I thought my dad was the bad guy, and my mother was the good guy, but in truth it was the opposite."

"I don't think there was a good guy or a bad guy. I think one person just made a mistake and the other tried to make it so that mistake wouldn't keep you from seeing all the goodness in that person."

She was quiet for a long moment. When she finally spoke, her voice was shaky. "My mom's a cheater."

"Don't let it define her. People make mistakes, Bianca."

She pulled her head back. "Do you see your father as a cheater?"

"Yes, but that's different. My father didn't make one mistake. His entire life was a series of affairs, lies, and cheating. It wasn't one mistake, it was a thousand lies."

"How do I know my mother isn't the same way? For all I know, she had a thousand affairs, too."

"You'll talk to her. You're not a kid anymore. She'll tell you the truth."

Bianca had another glass of wine, and we talked for a while longer. Then she asked me to stay the night. She wanted me to hold her, and I wanted nothing more than to give her whatever comfort she needed. I'd stripped out of my clothes but left my boxer briefs on before slipping into bed. Tonight wasn't about sex, even though I'd be lying if I said her ass didn't feel spectacular as I molded my body around hers from behind. I kissed her shoulder once as we spooned in the darkness. "Get some sleep. We can talk more in the morning, if you want. Okay?"

She sighed. "Okay."

After a few minutes, her breathing had slowed and I thought she had fallen asleep. Her voice was a whisper when she spoke. "Dex?"

"What do you need?"

"Thank you for telling me the truth tonight. I know it couldn't have been easy to do."

"It wasn't. I hate the thought of causing you any pain, and I knew this would be very difficult for you to hear."

"It was. But having you here really helped me get through it."

"I'm glad."

"I mean it. That was a horrible truth to face, and you made it bearable."

I kissed her shoulder again. "I get it now. We can get through anything together as long as we're honest with each other."

I had no idea at the time, but getting through *anything* wasn't always possible.

CHAPTER 24

Bianca

When the flame from the single flickering candle fell into my line of sight, I turned to him. "Again? Are you serious?"

Dex snorted then offered a deep, mischievous laugh that I felt through my core. This was becoming a thing. Every day this week was an apparent celebration.

About ten restaurant employees converged upon our table and began to sing the happy birthday song to me. This might have seemed normal except for two things. Number one, it wasn't my birthday. Number two, it was the third time this week that Dex had told the staff at different restaurants to bring out a piece of cake in celebration of my turning another year older.

Dex Truitt had quite the odd sense of humor, which I already knew. But I really appreciated his attempts to try to take my mind off of the situation with my mother. He knew I was putting off confronting her about the affair and the lying.

Dex and I decided to just enjoy the week without worrying about anything other than just being with each other. After all, what was done in the past was done. Even though I had to address it with my mother, there was no rush because the damage had already been inflicted.

I nodded toward the staff after they finished singing. "Thank you." I turned to Dex. "Why do you do keep doing this again?"

"The birthday cake?"

"Yes."

"Because I get to hear that same beautiful, embarrassed laugh over and over again. That alone makes it all worth it." Dex would always say the same thing once we were fully left alone: "Make a wish and blow." The way he said blow always sounded suggestive.

Despite his dirty mind, he continued to hold back on pressuring me to have sex. He was being ultra careful, almost *too* careful to not make any mistakes with me. We hadn't slept in the same bed since the night Dex told me about our parents. Even then, he'd been cautious, intentionally holding back. Most evenings, he'd insist on sleeping at his own place after dropping me off.

Dex's voice snapped me out of my thoughts. "You know this isn't just your problem, Bianca. It's *our* problem. It involves my father just as much as it involves your mother. The blame doesn't lie with any one person. Take some of the weight off of your shoulders and give it to me. I would take all of the burden, if I could."

It was the first moment in my life that I felt like I had a partner in crime. I was starting to realize that, perhaps, Dex might have been here to stay.

"You're not going anywhere, are you?"

"I couldn't go if I tried, Bianca. Why did you even ask that? Have you been waiting for me go somewhere?"

"I don't know. Maybe on some level I have. I think it just hit me that I have you, that you're not going to leave me."

"You're finally realizing this?"

"I think I am." I smiled.

Dex reached across the table and took my hands in his. "I've never felt connected to anyone like I do to you. It feels almost chemical. We haven't known each other for that long, but in some ways, it seems like a hundred years, doesn't it?"

I fully agreed.

"It does."

"And I know this is going to sound strange, but I feel like this was all meant to happen, even the stuff with our parents. As sordid as it all may have been at the time, they had a connection, just like we do. And maybe there's something to that. Maybe the predisposition toward each other is genetic or something. I don't know. All I know is that..." He took a deep breath in and seemed to stop himself.

"What?"

Dex shook his head. "Nothing."

"You were about to say something then stopped."

"I was. I was about to say something...but it's so important that I don't feel like now is the right time. I don't want it to be tainted by your anxious state."

Hmm.

"Well, my anxiety isn't going to pass until I decide to confront my mother."

"I think I should be there when you do."

"My mother's birthday is this Sunday. Alexandra wants to have us over to celebrate. My sister really wants to meet you."

I'd told Alexandra all about Dex's identity but hadn't had a chance to break the news about our mother's affair yet.

"Well, then I'll go with you to the party," he said.

"The problem is, I don't want to make a scene on my mother's birthday, but I'm not sure I can hold it in, since it will be the first time I will have seen her since finding out."

"Why don't we just take it one moment at a time and see how things go?"

"Alright."

Making a wish, I finally blew out my candle.

"I just can't believe this," Alexandra said. I could hear that she was crying.

"I know. I'm really sorry to have sprung this on you tonight, but I didn't want you to be caught off guard on Sunday in case I lose it with Mom."

I'd decided to call my sister and tell her the full story about our mother and Dexter Sr. She was just as shocked as I'd been to learn the truth about how the demise of our parents' marriage really went down.

"Honestly, it just makes so much sense," she said.

"How so?"

"Why Dad always seemed so sad when he was supposedly the one who'd had the affair."

"You know, you're right. That never did make much sense."

Alex sniffled. "I hope it was worth it."

"The affair?"

"Yes. It cost her marriage, cost us everything."

"In a weird way, though, it brought me Dex. If it weren't for my thinking that his father wronged Mom, I might not have ever volunteered so hard for that assignment. It's like the universe gave me something in return."

"You really care about him, don't you?"

"We've been through a lot, but yes, I'm pretty sure I'm falling in love with him." It was the first time I'd admitted it aloud, but there was no doubt in my mind how I felt about the man. "In fact, I'm certain of it."

"Wow. I guess it's definitely time for me to meet him, then."

"Yes...long overdue. You'll love him. He's extremely charismatic and down-to-earth. Mom took to him right away. Of course, she had no clue who his father is."

"Well, that's about to change. The sooner you tell her, the better."

"Okay, Sunday it is, then."

Dex stood just outside of my bedroom with his arms crossed. With a seductive gaze, he watched me intently as I tied my hair up.

Wearing a black, button-down dress, you would have thought I was going to a wake instead of my mother's birthday party. I was definitely not in the mood to celebrate anything, and my nerves were acting up because I knew that once the celebration wound down, I would be talking to her about the affair.

"You're extremely tense," he said, slowly approaching my spot at the mirror.

"I am."

Dex came up behind me and placed his hand on my ass. "Don't be. I've got your back."

I pushed my tush into his hand. "That's not my back."

He squeezed. "You have the most amazing ass, but I *was* being serious."

I turned to him and wrapped my arms around his neck before giving him a peck on the lips. "I know."

Dex looked into my eyes for a while before he said, "I want to help you relax before we leave."

"How are you going to manage that?"

"It's time your pussy became acquainted with my mouth."

CHAPTER 25

Dex

I'd started out just teasing her. As she lay back on the bed with her black dress hiked up to her waist, I kissed up and down her thighs and over her stomach. Her breathing was heavy, and it was hard to tell if that was from anticipation or nerves.

There was only one way to find out and that was to press my tongue against her clit. The moan that escaped her was all the confirmation I needed that she was more than okay with this.

With each movement of my tongue, I wanted her to know how badly I'd wanted this, how good it felt to finally taste her. My cock was beyond ready to explode as I dove my mouth into her while she moved her hips beneath me. I pulled her thighs toward me to bring her body up closer against my face, and inhaled her.

It felt so good to give her pleasure that I'd almost forgotten it wasn't supposed to be about me. This was about getting her to come so hard against my face that she had no choice but to be relaxed tonight. Yet, I was the one with the rock-hard erection and an insatiable need to keep devouring her, to prolong this.

I'd always loved going down on women, but I could honestly say that never before had I felt like I could come from the act alone. With Bianca, it was different. Giving her intense pleasure, watching her bodily sensations override the thoughts in her mind was truly as arousing as it was fascinating.

Aside from a thin landing strip, she was mostly shaved. I knew she'd feel the effects of my stubble rubbing against her tomorrow.

I came up for air long enough only to lick my fingers before sliding them inside her while I continued to eat her out. I loved the feel of her hands gripping my hair for dear life. If that didn't mean she was enjoying it, I didn't know what did. When I sensed she was close, I slowed down my pace, only to have her push my head deeper into her. Apparently, I was a fool for thinking I was the one in control. Applying more pressure, I felt her beautiful pulsating pussy climax against my tongue. I kept at it unwaveringly until her hips stopped moving.

Bianca's body was limp as she lay back on the bed.

"Wow," she breathed out. "That was...wow."

"We're going to be late," I said with a smug grin. "After the party, I'm taking you back to my place tonight. And anything and everything you let me do...I'm gonna do to you. Get dressed while I go to the bathroom."

With her taste still on my tongue, I ventured into the bathroom and jerked myself off, replaying the last several minutes in my head, feeling like there was no going back after tonight; I needed to be inside her later.

Bianca's mother greeted us at the door to her sister's house. "It's so good to see you again, Dex."

"Happy birthday, Eleni."

Bianca looked around. "Where's Alexandra?"

"She just went out to grab some candles for the cake. I told her not to bother, but you know your sister. She wants everything to be perfect. I told her it was better not to burn the house down with the number of candles on my cake this year."

Bianca looked at me sheepishly. "What do you know...a birthday cake this week that's *not* for me."

Looking confused, Eleni asked, "What's that?"

"Dex has been telling the staff at every restaurant we've gone to this week that it's my birthday. I've had four cakes and four serenades."

"Gotta love a man with a sense of humor. Do you have an older brother by any chance, Dex?" Eleni teased.

Oh the irony.

A tall, blond guy saved me from the awkwardness of that comment.

"Dex?" He extended his hand. "Brian...Alexandra's husband. Nice to meet you."

Offering him a firm handshake, I said, "Good to put a face to the name, Brian. Bianca's told me a lot about you."

"Where are the girls?" Bianca asked.

"They tagged along with Alex to the store." He pointed to a plethora of appetizers that were laid out on the granite island. "Help yourself to some food. I've got a mini bar set up in the corner there."

"Thanks, Bri." Bianca smiled but when her brother-in-law walked away, I could tell she was starting to freak out a little. She was staring off into space, her gaze fixed on an electric fireplace built into the wall.

Rubbing her back, I asked, "You okay?"

She blew out a shaky breath. "Yeah. I'm not going to talk to her until after the party. I don't want to ruin it."

I spoke low. "Okay. Whatever you're comfortable with. Let me make you a drink. What do you feel like?"

"A rum and Coke would be great."

After preparing her drink, I noticed an influx of commotion at the front door. Bianca's sister had apparently returned with her daughters. I stayed back in the kitchen, letting Bianca have some time with her nieces.

The sound of a woman's heels nearing the kitchen caused me to straighten my posture. I flashed a smile as her sister approached me. My smile quickly faded as an uncomfortable familiarity set in.

I knew her.

I just couldn't figure out why I seemed to know her.

I couldn't even remember what I'd said to her during our introduction. It was all a blur because I was too focused on her face, trying to decipher the mystery.

My mind was racing, our conversation moving in and out of my brain like Formula One cars speeding around a racetrack.

Smile.

Nod.

Speak.

Repeat.

Why was she so familiar? Goddamn it, Dex. Think.

At some point during dinner, as I continued to sneak looks at Alexandra, the realization hit me like a ton of bricks. My throat felt like it was closing up.

Without excusing myself, I got up in search of an escape so that Bianca couldn't sense my sudden panic. Inside the confines of the bathroom, I looked at myself in the mirror. Beads of sweat were forming on my forehead. My heart was pounding so fast that it felt capable of breaking.

Alexandra's face was familiar because it resembled one I'd looked at every day for half of my life.

She looked just like my father.

It took me ten minutes to gather up enough energy to head back to the dining room.

Bianca took one look at me and seemed confused. "Are you okay, Dex?"

"No...I think I caught some kind of bug."

"Oh, no!"

"Yeah. Um...I need to leave. I'm so sorry. I know you were counting on me being here, but I really don't want to get anyone sick."

And there I was, right back to lying. But telling the truth in this case—at this very moment—was simply not an option. Telling Bianca that I suspected her sister could be my father's daughter based on the resemblance alone was *not* an option. But more than that, the unthinkable—that Bianca's paternity could be in question—wasn't an option. I couldn't even go there until I did the math and confronted my father. Couldn't even fathom it.

"Are you sure?" The look of fear in her eyes seemed to match my own, albeit she was worried for a totally different reason.

"I'm positive. I'm really sorry."

"It's okay. Don't be."

As I was walking out the door, all I could think was that I wished I'd told her I loved her earlier this week at the restaurant. I'd stopped myself, thinking it was too soon. Now, I wished I'd told her how I felt before everything changed in an instant.

Flustered, I hadn't even dialed my driver before leaving, so I was standing outside in the cold with no ride. It was starting to rain as I began to walk, weaving through people and traffic. Picking up my cell phone, I dialed my father.

His wife answered, "Hello?"

"Myra, is my father home?"

"Yes. Is everything okay?"

"Please put him on the phone."

My father's voice came on a few seconds later. "Dex?"

"Dad...I need you to think, okay?" The words were coming out faster than my mind could conjure them up. "When you and Eleni Georgakopolous had the affair...exactly how many years ago was that?"

"I told you it was ongoing..."

"Twenty-seven...twenty-eight years ago? What? Think!"

"Hang on." He paused. "It started about twenty-nine years ago and went on for about six years."

My stomach was turning.

"When you had sex with her...did you use protection?"

Please say yes.

After a pause, he said, "I can't remember every single time, son."

236

"How can you *not* remember?"

"I think she said she was on the pill, but honestly…it was so long ago."

I raised my voice. "You never used a condom?"

"No. Never."

"How could you do that?"

"I guess I trusted her. It wasn't responsible. Anyway, why are you asking me all of this?"

"I saw Bianca's sister tonight for the first time."

"And?"

"Dad…" I swallowed. "She looks like you."

Silence.

"You think she's my daughter?"

The rain started to pelt down on me.

"I think there's a chance."

"How can you be sure that you're not just looking for similarities because of what I told you about the affair? You might just be paranoid and looking for trouble."

"No. I wish that were the case. The thought never even entered my mind until I saw her face. She resembles you too much. But, God, I could have never imagined that you would have been so irresponsible as to allow this possibility. How could you do this?"

"Nothing is confirmed. And even if what you're saying is true…what are you so worried about?"

"You can't possibly be asking that? You're telling me that you could technically be the father of my girlfriend's sister, that you were sleeping with their mother during the time period when both women were conceived. There are only a couple of years between them. Now I can't even be sure whether I'm in love with my own sister! How the fuck can you not know what I'm worried about?"

People on the street were staring as I yelled into the phone.

"Calm down, Dex."

"Don't tell me to fucking calm down. The only thing that will get me to calm down is to wake up from this nightmare!"

I couldn't even remember hanging up the phone. The next thing I knew, I was in a liquor store, leaving with a large bottle of Fireball in a brown paper bag.

When Sam pulled up outside, there was only one place I could bear going.

"Where to, Mr. Truitt?"

I took a sip and relished the burn of the alcohol sliding down my throat. "Brooklyn."

CHAPTER 26

Dex

This shit is disgusting.

Not that I cared. By the time I arrived in Brooklyn, I'd already made a dent in the repulsive tasting bottle of alcohol. I'd told my driver not to wait, so when Jelani didn't answer his buzzer, I took up residence on the stoop of his house and proceeded to swig from the brown paper bag like a homeless person. Oddly, as I sat there for more than an hour in the dark, I started to wonder if this was what a homeless person felt like on the inside. Granted, they didn't have a multimillion dollar penthouse overlooking the park to go home to, but I felt homeless at the moment—like I had no anchor, no one to turn to. In the months I'd known Bianca, she'd somehow become home in my heart and having an actual place to go had become meaningless. I took another big swig from the bag and relished the warmth that traveled through my body. I could see how people used drinking to replace warmth in their cold lives.

I must have nodded off for a while, because one minute I was contemplating the meaning of life while drinking my new cinnamon tasting best friend, and the next my feet were getting kicked.

"Trying to see how the other half lives, my friend?" Jelani was standing over me and smiling as he roused me back to consciousness. I stumbled as I climbed to my feet, feeling the full effect of the alcohol on my balance now.

"I didn't know where else to go."

Jelani nodded as if he understood and invited me in. He spoke as he unpacked some groceries from a canvas satchel that was slung across his chest. "Woman or family problems?"

Isn't that ironic? "Both."

"How about some coffee?" He motioned to the bottle I was still clutching. "I think that might be a better idea than whatever you have in that brown paper bag."

Jelani ground some beans and put up a pot of coffee in an old silver percolator on the top of his gas stove. While he was busy, I took a seat and checked out the new carvings he had lined up on the kitchen table. The first one was a small walrus, the same spirit animal Jelani had suggested I buy the first time we met. "I bought the billy goat, but you were right in suggesting the damn walrus."

"Ah. The keeper of secrets." He set two cups of black coffee on the table and slid one in front of me. "Your lady friend has some skeletons in her closet that have brought you to question if she is the right woman for you?"

"You could say that."

Jelani sipped his coffee, contemplating me over the rim of the mug. "We have an old saying where I come from. *Smooth seas do not make a skilled sailor.* As men, we become stronger by learning to ride the waves while keeping the ship on course."

"Yeah...well..." I scoffed. "This one is more like a tsunami. You got a lot of sailors who survive a tsunami?"

"There is no problem too big that God cannot solve."

I sipped the bitter, black coffee and decided it needed a little something if God was going to get involved in this conversation. I was pretty pissed off at the big guy in the sky at this point. Pouring a shot of Fireball into my coffee, I stirred it in with my finger while Jelani looked on. After a medicinal gulp from the mug, I set it on the table and looked at my unlikely friend. "I fell in love with a woman."

Jelani smiled.

"And tonight I found out she and I...we very likely might have the same father."

Jelani's smile fell. Then he slid his mug to my side and motioned for me to pour him some Fireball.

"You wanna know something screwed up?" I'd just explained the whole sordid mess with my father to Jelani.

His brows arched. "There's something more screwed up than that? How much of that nasty stuff you have left in that brown paper bag?"

We both laughed. "I'm not sure I care if she is my sister. Even drunk and thinking we might share DNA doesn't make me want her any less."

"Many royal families keep their blood lines intact by marrying within family. The Monomotapa monarchy in Zimbabwe practiced incest on a regular basis. The king frequently married his daughters and his sisters to produce pure-blood offspring." He paused. "Cleopatra married both of her brothers."

"Got anything more recent? Say in the twenty-first century?"

Jelani forced a smile. It was then that I realized how much the bones in his cheeks had become pronounced. I'd been so caught up in wallowing in my latest drama, I hadn't even noticed he'd lost more weight. "You're not eating. Is your treatment making you feel worse?"

As usual, he acted casual. "It has its bad days and good days."

"When was the last time you ate a real meal?"

"Not too long ago. Soup is my friend these days."

I stared at him. "Tomorrow night. I'm taking you to dinner at my favorite restaurant."

"I suspect you might be the one feeling too nauseous to eat tomorrow after drinking that stuff."

We were both quiet for a minute. Eventually it was Jelani who spoke. "You need to tell her."

"I know."

"Everything will work out how it was meant to be."

I sure as shit hoped he was right. Because today, more than ever, I realized what was meant to be was me and Bianca.

The coffee had woken me up, but not completely sobered me—which as far as I was concerned was a damn good thing. The Uber dropped me off in front of Bianca's building, and I stood there motionless for a solid twenty minutes staring up at her window. I could see from the street that her bedroom light was on, but I wasn't sure if she had left it on when we were leaving earlier in the evening. I needed to grow some fucking balls—actually go into the damn building and check if she was home—and then suddenly the light flicked off, and I got my answer. *She's home.* I took a deep breath and went for it before I changed my mind.

"Dex?" Bianca opened the door just as I raised my hand to knock a second time. She took one look at me and was immediately concerned. "Are you okay? Is the sickness worse or something?"

"Can I come in?"

"Of course. Of course." She stepped aside.

Bianca locked the door behind me. "You look terrible. You should be in bed." She reached out to feel my head. *God, I'm so fucking in love with you.* "You're not warm. No fever, at least."

I couldn't stop myself. I wrapped her in my arms and pulled her against me, giving her the biggest, tightest hug I've ever given anyone. I might have been crushing her a little, but I couldn't let go. After a long time like that, she finally attempted to pull back a little.

Our noses were barely inches apart when she looked up at me. "You're not sick. Are you?"

I shook my head.

"What's going on? Does it have something to do with my mother? Was it freaking you out that you were going to see her and knew what she had done? I had a feeling it was going to upset you more than you realized."

I nodded. Suddenly I was a fucking mute even though I had so much that needed to be said.

Her beautiful eyes turned sad. "Go sit. I'll pour us some wine, and we can talk."

She extricated herself from my arms and headed toward the kitchen. Just before she was out of reach, I suddenly grabbed for her and caught her hand, pulling her back against me. She smiled, thinking I was being playful, but I was dead serious. If this was going to be our last moment as who we'd become to each other, if everything in our fucked-up lives was about to change, I wanted one last kiss.

Taking her beautiful face in two hands, I kissed her until there was no doubt that she meant everything to me. After, she blinked a few times as if she had to work to get herself back into reality. "You're scaring me, Dex," she whispered. "That kiss felt an awfully lot like goodbye."

If this was the beginning of the end, it was *not* how I wanted her to remember our last kiss. I caressed her face. "I love you, Bianca. I fucking love you so much."

She looked surprised at my declaration. Hell, it surprised the crap out of me, too, that the words slipped from my mouth. But even after I'd put it out there, I was glad I told her. She needed to know the truth. The whole truth. Bianca pushed up on her tippy toes and kissed my lips softly, then pulled back to look into my eyes. "I love you, too, Dex."

I wished I could freeze time and stay in this moment forever. But too soon, Bianca was readying for our talk. "Go. Go sit down, and I'll pour us that wine so we can talk."

She smiled at me from the kitchen. Was I a total asshole for dumping on her that I was in love with her a few minutes before I said what I came to say? She was beaming as she poured two glasses of wine. It seemed that my affirmation had quelled the worry she'd had over what I'd come to talk to her about, and here I was about to rip her apart. God, I hoped

I didn't make things harder because I was a selfish bastard and wanted one last kiss if things didn't turn out for the best.

Bianca set two glasses of red wine on the coffee table and settled onto the couch across from the chair where I sat. I hadn't noticed what she was wearing until that moment. Rather, what she wasn't wearing. Namely—very much clothes. She had on skimpy, black boy short underwear and a light pink, spaghetti strap tank top that hugged her beautiful, naturally tanned skin. When she raised her glass to sip her wine, I saw she wasn't wearing a bra under the tank and her nipples were fully erect and pointing at me.

Fuck.

Fuck.

Fuck.

My mouth watered staring at them. It was agony to force my eyes shut and remind myself: *She could be your sister. She could be your fucking sister.* When I reopened my eyes, I could have sworn her luscious nipples had doubled in size. I scrubbed my hands over my face. "Do you think you could put a robe on or something?"

Bianca looked down and noticed what I was seeing. "You don't like my nipples?"

"I like them very much. Too fucking much. I can't concentrate while they're taunting me."

She laughed as though she thought I was amusing but then went to grab her bathrobe. I chugged my full glass of wine in the two minutes that she was gone. When she came back out wearing a sexy, red silk robe that was hanging open, I grabbed her glass and finished it off, too.

Seeing the two empty glasses, Bianca fastened her robe and sat. "Talk to me."

I didn't know where to begin. I took a deep breath, followed by a mental snapshot of her as if it was the last time I might ever see her, and then opened my mouth. "Your sister is the spitting image of my father."

CHAPTER 27

Bianca

"How is this even possible?"

Dex raked his fingers through his hair. "I called my father after I left. He confirmed that the timeline could work. And that he never used protection."

"You must be imagining it. Alexandra is so much like my father. They have the same mannerisms, the same sense of humor, they even hold the fork in the same exact odd way!"

"Those things are learned. Not genetic."

"They both have bushy eyebrows."

"That's a fairly common trait. I'd venture to guess that afflicts half the population of Greece."

"You're wrong. You have to be wrong."

Dex took his phone out of his pocket and hit a few buttons, then scrolled until he found whatever he was looking for. Turning it to face me, he extended it palm up. I could see he'd called up Facebook. "It's my father's page. Scroll through some of his pictures."

I hesitated, but eventually curiosity won out. The first picture I landed on, almost stopped my heart. It was as if I was looking at a computer-generated picture of my sister turned into a man. It had to be a coincidence. I swiped again.

My sister's eyes.

Swiped again.

Alexandra's chin.

Swiped again.

Her smile. *Alexandra's beautiful smile*. Tears welled in my eyes.

Dex reached out his hand and attempted to cover the phone to stop me from looking further. I knocked it away, needing to see more. I swiped and swiped...looking for some semblance of hope that all of the previous pictures were just a bad angle or something. But by the time I frantically reached the end of the pictures, tears were falling.

Dex dropped to his knees and knelt in front of me. "I'm sorry. I'm so sorry."

He tried to hold me, offer me comfort, but I couldn't let myself let go yet. I needed to know more. "Did your father know?"

"He claims to have had no idea."

"Does my mother know the truth?"

"I don't know."

"She only started working there a year before Alexandra was born. What the hell did she do? Jump in bed with the boss the first chance she had?" I wasn't really asking Dex a question, even though I had so many.

"I don't know what really happened. My father was vague on all the details. Sadly, I got the impression it wasn't because he was intentionally being ambiguous, but rather it was because having an ongoing affair was a regular occurrence for him during his marriage, and he can't keep them all straight in his mind anymore."

"I just don't understand, Dex. How do you have a child that clearly looks like another man and move on? They just ended the affair after she got pregnant, and neither of them ever bothered to question paternity? Everyone just moved on with their lives?"

Dex squeezed my hands. "The affair didn't end, Bianca. My father said it went on for close to six years."

I'm not sure if it was my brain's protective mechanism, or if I was just really that naïve. But I still hadn't had my moment of epiphany. "Six years? Alexandra and I are only four years apart."

Dex stared at me, looking deep into my eyes waiting for the click.

5

4

3

2

1

"Oh my God!" I stood before running to the bathroom. "I think I'm going to be sick."

I felt like someone had died. There was a hollow in my chest, a sort of achy emptiness, yet that emptiness weighed so heavy. After two hours of talking, crying, and polishing off two bottles of wine, Dex had asked me if I wanted him to leave. I wanted just the opposite—him to stay forever and tell me tomorrow morning that tonight was just a bad dream. Yet now that we were lying in my bed in the dark, the craziness that he could possibly be my brother was really seeping in.

Neither of us said a word for a long time. My back was to him, and his hand was resting gently on my hip until his squeezed and broke our silence. "Ever hear of the Monomotapa monarchy from Zimbabwe?"

I laughed. What the hell was he talking about? "No."

"Know anything about Cleopatra?"

Ahhh. So that's where his mind was at? I turned over to face him. It was dark, but my eyes had adjusted enough to see his. "I do, actually. You know she wasn't really Egyptian. Her family roots trace back to Macedonian Greece." I knew that wasn't what he was talking about, but I figured I'd screw with him a little.

It worked. I heard the smile in his voice. "Oh yeah? Figures you'd know that, Georgakopolous. Anything else you learned in history class?"

"She had a thing for bad, heavy eye makeup."

"Wiseass. You know exactly what I'm referring to."

I sighed. "Are you saying you don't care if I'm your half-sister or not?"

The levity was gone from his voice. "I don't know what I'm saying. The only thing I'm sure of is that I'm in love with you. And there's no way I'm ready to let you go. No matter what."

"You say that now. But men look at their sisters very differently than women look at their brothers. There is no way in hell that you'll be able to think of me sexually, if there really is a chance that we're related, Dex."

I saw the whites of his eyes going back and forth as they looked into mine. Finally, he reached for my hand. "Don't judge." Then he pulled it down his body until my hand was covering his dick. His rock-hard, fully erect, dick.

I gasped as he wrapped my fingers around it demonstrating that he was *definitely* able to think of me that way still.

"That answer your question?"

"I guess so."

Dex chuckled as he brought my hand back up to his lips and kissed the top. Then he leaned forward and kissed my forehead. "Get some sleep. We'll figure out where to go from here tomorrow."

"Okay." I turned over, and Dex pulled me flush against him, my back to his front, wrapping me in a tight hold. Even though I could clearly feel his erection, the hold didn't feel sexual. It felt...protective.

With his warmth wrapped around me like a blanket, it didn't take long to succumb to sleep. "Good night, Dex," I whispered.

"Good night, my Georgy Girl."

The following day, Dex called from his office in the middle of the afternoon to check on me. Actually, it was one of several times he'd contacted me to make sure I was okay. I hated the sick thought that flashed through my head suddenly.

He's just doing the protective brother thing.

Shut up!

I hated my brain sometimes.

Dex sounded tired. "How are you feeling?"

"Do you really want to know?"

"Of course."

"I think I was in shock most of yesterday, but now it's starting to sink in. And the reality is scaring me."

"You're not alone, Bianca. I'm scared, too. In fact, I can't recall anything that has ever scared me more in my entire life."

Sadness crept in. I longed for the time before this came to light. "I miss you."

"I'm still here," he whispered. "I haven't gone anywhere." After some silence, he continued, "We need to know. It's killing me. Are you ready to find out? I won't push you unless you're ready."

I never ended up having the conversation with my mother the night Dex left my sister's. Now, that conversation was going to be a totally different ball game because I'd not only be telling her about Dex's identity but also confronting her about whether Dexter Sr. could have fathered Alexandra and me. What a clusterfuck.

"Where do I start? I feel so helpless," I said.

"I need to work on convincing my father to agree to a DNA test. I think you need to have the conversation with your mother and sister as soon as possible. We can't put it off any longer—especially now."

"Okay," I agreed. "I'll call an emergency meeting tonight at my sister's. We need to get Alexandra to agree to a test as well."

"Do you want me there when you tell them?"

"Actually, I'm thinking it might be better if I handle it alone. It's going to be a lot for my sister to take in. I think she would be more comfortable if it was just me."

"Okay, fair enough. Whatever you think is best. I just wanted to be there to support you if you felt you needed me. Didn't want you to have to handle the tough stuff alone."

I hated what I was thinking in that moment.

He apparently could sense something in my silence. "Tell me what's on your mind right now."

"You said you didn't want me to handle it alone, and that made me realize that I might have to get used to a life apart from you. Maybe the sooner I figure out how to do that, the better."

Dex sounded almost angry. "Don't say that, Bianca. Don't even think it."

My tone changed from quiet to insistent. "It's true, Dex. I think we need to seriously prepare ourselves for the worst. We're in denial."

"Do you think I'm going to just disappear from your life if things don't turn out in our favor?"

"Well, we certainly can't remain...close. That would be too painful, don't you think?"

"Actually, I think the opposite would be far more painful. I can't imagine my life without you. If it turns out..." He hesitated. "God, I can't even say it. I can't even fucking say it."

I spoke for him. "If the worst happens..."

He gathered his composure and said, "*If* the worst happens, I will always want to be in your life. As crazy as that sounds, I care about you way too much to let you go."

I was confused as to what he meant. "So...we'd be... what...like friends?"

"I don't think we could really put a label on it but—"

"You're gonna want to see me with other men?"

Dead silence.

"Fuck. No...I can't even fathom that. But I'd have to suck it up somehow because I'm going to want to protect you even if it kills me. I don't want you to ever just disappear from my life."

I could feel my eyes getting moist. "You say that now... but it will be too difficult, Dex. I don't think I can handle seeing you with other women, seeing you get married, have children someday. God...those kids...they'd be my—"

"Please, Bianca! Don't go there. I'm begging you not to think about it like that right now, okay? Just let us have these days of denial. It's the only good thing about this time of waiting. Alright? I'm not saying to pretend it's not happening, but try not to *go there*. Okay? Can you do that for me, baby?"

I shut my eyes tightly to fend off the tears. "You shouldn't call me 'baby'....until we know."

"Fuck that." I could sense that he was gritting his teeth when he said, "You're my baby and my Georgy Girl. And I'm gonna call you whatever the fuck I want. I'm not going to hide my feelings until the day...the *second*...I absolutely have to."

I sniffled away my tears. "I hope that second never comes."

Sitting side by side on my sister's couch, they were both completely speechless. Alexandra looked like she was going to pass out. I hated everything about this, but it had to be done. And I was glad it was finally out, because holding it in had been killing me.

I'd spent the past half-hour coming clean to them about what I knew and what I suspected. Dex had given me some pictures of his father as a younger man so that I could show my sister the resemblance. She didn't dispute it; she couldn't.

My mother was, of course, shocked to learn about Dex's identity in the first place but once that was revealed, she didn't seem all that surprised about my suspicions regarding Alexandra's paternity.

She finally spoke, "I really didn't think..."

"What?" I cried. "That we would figure this out? Have you never noticed how much she resembles him?"

"I *have* noticed. But it wasn't apparent until she got a bit older. By that time, it was too late. Your dad *is* your father in all the ways it matters. He loves both of you more than life. The technicality of it truly wasn't going to make a difference."

"But you do admit that it *is* possible...that not only could Dexter Truitt have fathered Alex but that he could be *my* father, as well?"

"I can't rule it out. I made a huge mistake in putting us in this predicament. But I was young and reckless. I'd felt trapped at the time, and Dexter was my way out of it. I wasn't thinking about long-term repercussions, and I certainly could've never predicted that one of my daughters would end up in love with his son years later. I'd give anything to take my decisions back, but I just can't do that."

My mother was crying, and my sister, who'd been quiet, abruptly got up and ventured to the other room.

I followed her.

"I'm so sorry, Alex."

The room was dark. She sat on the bed and covered her face. "It's not your fault. I just need some time to process this."

"Take all of the time you need."

She suddenly turned to me. "Why doesn't she seem more upset? Does she have any clue how much this is going to impact all of our lives? Not only mine...but especially yours?"

"I think she's in shock. It seems like she's just been in denial all these years. She never thought we'd figure it out."

"Does Dad even suspect anything?"

"He has to have suspected," I said. "Unless he's never actually seen Dexter Truitt? Honestly, even knowing what I knew, I wouldn't have thought this was possible until I actually saw the resemblance."

"You look like Mom," she said. "I look like neither one of our parents. But I still never suspected anything."

"I know. Me neither."

Alex stood up in a panic. "We need to get this test soon. I have to know."

"Dex is working on getting his father to agree. He's going to handle all of the logistics once we can get his father's consent."

"What if he doesn't agree?"

"Then, I suppose we can test ourselves against Dad," I said.

"This whole thing is such a mess. Please tell me you didn't sleep with Dex."

"We've come close...but never took that step."

Alex let out a relieved breath. "Thank God, Bianca. Could you imagine?"

That was the thing. I *could* imagine it. And that fantasy didn't feel any different than it had before this nightmare. I couldn't exactly admit that to her at this point. My romantic feelings for Dex hadn't wavered, and that was going to have to stay between him and me.

I didn't think anyone else could possibly understand.

CHAPTER 28

Dex

As I buttoned my shirt, I looked down at Bandit who was standing at attention and listening to me ramble.

"You might have technically humped your sister, you know. Aren't dogs inbred all of the time?"

"Ruff!"

"You're fine, though, right? It wasn't the end of the world. Nobody judges dogs. Why should they judge me?"

He just stared at me, panting with his tongue hanging out.

"It still seems a little fucked up. Shouldn't I feel differently about her, Bandit? Knowing what I know? But I don't. I want her. In some ways, I don't even *want* to know the truth. And I certainly can't stand back and bear witness to her moving on with her life. I want her with *me*." Spraying on some cologne, I looked over at him. "What do you think about a move to Europe? I heard incest is not as frowned upon there. We can all be happy there: you and your inbred ass, me, Bianca, and our two-headed baby. What do you say?"

"Ruff!"

When I realized I was running significantly late for my dinner with Jelani, I quickly fastened my watch.

"Be a good boy," I said before heading to the door.

Since he hadn't been feeling too well, I opted to take Jelani out to a restaurant in Brooklyn, so he could be close to his house if he felt he suddenly needed to go home.

After I'd ordered four different family-sized platters at the Italian restaurant, my gaunt-looking friend said, "I didn't realize we were expecting an army."

The waitress had set down large portions of chicken and eggplant Parmesan, lobster ravioli, and vegetable lasagna.

"You need something that sticks to your bones. And you're taking the leftovers home with you, too."

I let Jelani do most of the talking. My mind was elsewhere as he told some stories from Kenya and spoke about whether or not to renew his spot at the flea market for the upcoming year.

At one point, he raised his voice and interrupted my thoughts. "Dex, I've been talking to you for a half hour, and you've been staring off into space half of the time."

Shaking my head quickly, I said, "I'm sorry. I'm just feeling very anxious tonight."

"About the test..."

"Yes. My father finally agreed to do it, but only after he returns from his vacation in Turks."

"Well, at least he agreed to cooperate. That was half the battle, wasn't it?"

I sighed. "Yep. So, it's going to happen in about a week."

Twiddling my thumbs and bouncing my knees up and down, I looked around the restaurant.

Jelani sat in front of me with his arms crossed, and I stopped my fidgeting long enough to realize he'd been quietly observing me.

"Dex..."

"Yeah?"

"Go to her."

"What?"

"Your mind is not here. Stop wasting time here in this restaurant trying to get skinny old me to eat. Go to her and spend the rest of the night with her. If there's one thing I've learned since getting sick, it's that each day is precious. If things don't end up in your favor, at least you'll have these days. Don't waste them. Live in ignorant bliss for a little while longer."

There truly wasn't anything I wanted more in that moment than to go to Bianca.

"You sure you don't mind?"

"Of course not. Life is good. We've been here long enough, and I have food for the entire week."

"You'd better eat it."

Jelani chuckled. "Thanks for looking out for me, Dex. You're a good man."

It was a full moon out tonight. After I dropped him back home, I had Sam head straight to Bianca's. I hadn't thought to call or text first, so I was disappointed to find that she wasn't home. Still, I thought better of chasing her down. She might have been with her sister, still dealing with the after effects of dropping that bomb.

Rather than text to ask her whereabouts, I opted to go back to my place and change out of my clothes.

Back home, I'd just gotten my pants off when there was a knock at the door. Bandit started to bark like crazy. The only person who was allowed to bypass the doorman was Bianca. My heartbeat accelerated.

When I opened the door, my breath caught. She looked so incredibly beautiful, dressed casually in jeans and a fitted, leather jacket. Bianca's hair was damp from the drizzle outside. Her eyeballs moved back and forth as she looked at me, seeming like she'd been searching for something and had finally found it.

Then she practically fell into my arms. I embraced her tightly for the longest time, cherishing the feel of her heart pounding against mine. It was confirmation that her feelings for me remained unchanged.

Whispering into her hair, I said, "I went by your place. You weren't there."

"I was with Alex. Brian watched the girls so that we could have dinner out and talk."

I pulled back to look at her face. "And you came straight here after?"

"Yeah. My sister could tell my mind was on you the entire night. She told me to just go see you."

"That's funny. Jelani did the same thing to me, told me to go to you. I guess we're both pretty transparent, huh?"

Bianca's eyes trailed down the length of my body. It was then I realized I was still shirtless, dressed only in my underwear. Desire pooled in her eyes as she continued to stare at my half-naked physique. Knowing full well what she was thinking, my abs clenched and my cock stiffened.

My words came out in a hoarse whisper, "It's okay to want me." Brushing my hand against her cheek, I added, "Lord knows, I want you so fucking badly."

"I'm learning that you really can't fight what comes naturally. And that bothers me, because what if the news isn't in our favor, and I still can't shake it? What, then?"

"Then, we move to Europe," I said without hesitation.

"What?"

I placed my hand on her cheek. "I'm kidding." *Sort of.* "Look," I said. "People can tell us how to think, but they can't tell us how to feel. Nothing has ever proven that fact to me like this situation has. You want me right now just as much as I want you, and it's killing me."

As was usual around Bianca, my body was beginning to betray me. My erection grew harder with every second that her eyes remained fixed on my body. I couldn't even be certain whether I could have stopped myself if Bianca told me she didn't care about the repercussions. If she told me to fuck her then and there, I honestly didn't know how I would have reacted. That was how desperate I felt.

I led her over to the couch. As I lay back, she reached out and hesitantly placed her hand on my abs. Even though she looked reluctant, it was clear that she'd been dying to do it.

"It's okay. Touch me. We won't take it any further. Just touch me."

She ran her hand along every inch of my chest as I closed my eyes and relished her touch. She then lowered her head and lay down on my heaving chest. I was sure she could feel my heart beating right into her eardrum.

"I don't want to give you up," she whispered over my skin.

Running my fingers through her beautiful dark hair, I said, "Can I tell you a secret?"

Her voice was barely audible. "Yes."

"I have to tell this to you now because the way I see it... anything I say now could be construed as okay since we don't know the truth yet."

She lifted her head and sat up to look at me. I was glad she did because this was important.

I took the opportunity to return that focused attention as I stared deeply into her eyes. "I won't ever stop loving you. Even if it turns out we're blood-related, I will *still* love you. I may not be able to admit it to you anymore then, and I may not be able to express it to you physically, but I won't stop loving you. I need you to know that. You will move on eventually. You will meet someone new, but I will still *never* stop loving you. I might meet someone and marry eventually, but when she's walking down the aisle, make no mistake, I'm going to be thinking of *you* and wishing things were different. Because I will never stop loving you. And whether you're my lover or my sister...you will still be the most amazing woman I have ever met. No matter what, Bianca, you *are* the love of my life. No one will ever replace you."

Her face was covered in tears. "I love you so much, Dex."

The need to feel her mouth on mine was unbearable. "I really need to kiss you right now."

"Kiss me. Please...kiss me," she breathed.

And so I did. With the same intensity with which she'd begged for it, I kissed her harder and with more passion than I ever had before. If it was wrong, I didn't want it to be right. Like Jelani said, ignorance was bliss. My compromise was that I wouldn't sleep with her, but I was going to damn well kiss her. Maybe it would have seemed more salacious if we hadn't done it countless times before. But it felt so natural, so familiar. Like breathing. If I was going to hell for continuing to do what felt natural, then so be it.

In fact, I'd turn myself in.

I hated that Bianca had to leave.

The next afternoon, she'd flown out for an assignment down in Virginia. I'd lightly suggested that she reschedule the interview, but Bianca had said she needed to work to make the time pass or she'd go crazy. I could understand that, but I hated that she would be sitting in a hotel room hundreds of miles away for two nights, thinking the worst was going to happen. Not to mention that two nights away from her seemed like an eternity. And while we spoke on the phone every morning and evening, I felt her slipping away from me again. Physical distance made her overthink things. Her voice was sad when I called to check in on her that afternoon.

"How did your interview go? Did you get everything you needed?" I asked.

"I think so." She sighed. "To be honest, I don't have any idea. Thankfully, I grabbed my recorder at the last minute before I left—something I never really use—because I'm pretty sure everything he said went in one ear and out the other."

"It's to be expected. You're under a lot of stress."

"You want to know something funny?"

"I could use funny right about now, yes." I leaned back into my office chair.

"I woke up in the middle of the night with a mini panic attack. I couldn't fall back asleep right away, so I got out my

Baoding balls while my mind was racing over everything from the last week."

"I might have laid in bed last night playing with my own stress balls and thinking of you, too. Let me ask you, have you ever tried inserting them and wiggling around? I think that might go a long way toward stress reduction."

I heard the smile in her voice. "You're such a pervert. And I wasn't done with my story, you know."

"Go on. I'm curious to see if your ball massage session finished off as well as mine did."

"Anyway," she continued, "I massaged my stress balls for a while and still couldn't go back to sleep, so I decided to turn on the television. Take a guess what was on at three in the morning?"

"What?"

"Cleopatra."

As insane as the entire situation was, I was glad the two of us could still laugh at our own expense. Although Bianca's voice was more serious when she spoke next. "My sister went to the lab you set up for us today."

"Oh yeah? How'd everything go?" I'd arranged for my father to go to the same chain lab facility in Florida the day he got back from his vacation. Bianca and her sister only had to give their case number when they went in for a quick swab. I didn't want either one of them to have to go through explaining everything at the lab.

"Brian went with her, and my mom took the kids so they could have a night alone."

"That's good," I said.

"It's the least my mother can do."

"Did you make an appointment yet?"

"Tomorrow afternoon. Three o'clock." I heard the dread in her voice.

I'd been tossing around bringing up something that was on my mind for the last two days, but now that her appointment was tomorrow, we didn't have much time left...

"What time does your flight land tonight?"

"A few minutes after eight, I think."

"I'll pick you up at the airport."

"Are you sure? I can just grab an Uber."

"I'm sure. I miss you. And I want to talk to you before tomorrow anyway."

"Oh God. The last few times you had something to talk to me about, you admitted you were Jay, told me my mother was a cheater, and then told me we could be siblings. I'm not sure I want to have any more talks with you." She was teasing. Well, sort of.

"I have no more bad news. I promise."

"Then why did you sound so serious?"

"I just think we should talk. In person. Tonight."

"Dexter Truitt. I'm going to get kicked off the plane for screaming at the top of my lungs and chiming my balls if you don't tell me what's on your mind right now. I can't travel home wondering what you're going to spring on me next."

Shit. I should've just told her that I'd missed her and left it at that.

"I just want to talk about you getting your DNA test done."

"What about my test?"

She wasn't going to stop until I said what was on my mind. I'd be making her head spin whether I told her or not. "I've been thinking...what if you didn't get the test done?"

"Tomorrow? I can go another day if you need me for something."

"No. I meant...what if we didn't find out at all?"

CHAPTER 29

Bianca

Dex was standing in baggage claim waiting when I came down the escalator. We'd locked eyes the minute my foot stepped on at the top, and my stomach did all sorts of flip-flops the entire ride down. *God I'm so crazy about this man.*

He was dressed casually, in a pair of jeans, dark t-shirt, and running sneakers. Yet there was nothing casual about the way he looked. Dex had an intensity on his face that made my skin tingle. He stayed still, except for his eyes following my every step. When I reached the bottom and walked toward him, I could actually feel my pulse quicken.

"Give a girl a ride?" I flirted.

He grumbled something I *think* might have been, "You have no fucking idea the ride I want to give you," then hooked one arm around my waist, pulled me flush against him, and kissed me with a passion that felt almost desperate. Any certainty I had that I should have the test done tomorrow and stay away from him until after we get the results, went flying out of my head faster than the jet I just took home.

"Get the thought out of your head," Dex said against my lips when our kiss broke.

I was breathless. "What thought?"

He arched an eyebrow. "The one where you question if this is a good idea. If we should be together in this way."

How did he know? "I wasn't..."

He shook his head with a knowing smirk and took my overnight bag from my hand. "Do you have any other luggage?"

"No, just this."

"Then let's get out of here."

During the short ride back to my place we made small talk—how was my flight, what was my next assignment, even a nice chat about the market fluctuation that day. Anything and everything but the elephant in the room. But that came to an abrupt end shortly after we settled into my apartment. I'd done a quick unpack while Dex poured wine and then the awkwardness set in.

Dex was sitting on the couch across from me and leaned forward, placing both of his hands on my knees. "I don't want to risk losing you by having the test done."

"Dex...I'm not sure I could function not knowing."

"Eventually we'd move past it. If we made the decision never to find out, I think after some time, we'd be okay."

"What if...we stayed together?"

"You mean if we wanted to have children someday?"

I nodded my head.

"We could agree to adopt. I'd be fine with that. There are plenty of children who need good homes." I had looked away, and Dex squeezed my hand to get my attention back. "Look at how good we did adopting Bandit."

I snorted. "I don't think deciding not to have children naturally should be based on how things have gone with Bandit."

He cupped my cheek. "Maybe not. But if the choice is possibly losing you or adopting instead of having a biological child, there is no choice."

I looked into his eyes. "Wouldn't you always wonder?"

"I'd get over it."

"Dex..."

He leaned in and kissed my lips. "Think about it. Just think about it some more."

"Okay. I will."

We snuggled on the couch for a while and then I yawned. Traveling always knocked me out to begin with, plus I wasn't sleeping well at night lately. My back was leaning against Dex's front, and he brushed some hair off of my face after my yawn. "You're tired. You should get some sleep."

"I *am* tired. That glass of wine was like a sleeping pill on top of my already sleepy head. Plus, my neck hurts from stress and lying flat always helps that, too. I think it's time for bed."

"I'll let you get some rest, then."

I turned to face him with my brow furrowed. "You're not staying over?"

"Do you want me to stay over?"

"Of course, I do."

Dex let out a sigh of relief. "I'm glad. Because it's been hell without you the last few nights."

Inside my bedroom, I changed into my usual tank and boy shorts, and Dex stripped to his boxers. While he slipped under the covers, I sat on the edge of my bed and took out some moisturizer from my nightstand to rub into my arms.

After rubbing the lotion into one arm, Dex sat up and took it from my hands. "Here, let me."

The room was quiet, and the intimacy between us blossomed as he massaged the lotion into the skin on my arms. While I had just applied it enough to seep into my skin, Dex was giving me more of a massage. When his strong fingers worked their way up to my shoulder, I closed my eyes and let him rub away some of the stress.

"God, that feels so good."

"You're very tense, and your neck hurts. Why don't I use the lotion and rub your shoulders for a bit."

"I'd love that."

Dex sat up with his back against my headboard and positioned me between his legs. He gently nudged my head forward to drop toward my chest and scooped my hair to one side. Then his hands disappeared for a moment, and seconds later a dollop of icy moisturizer hit my skin.

"That's cold."

"I could provide some warm cream if you prefer?" Dex's tone was playful, but at the same time it was also husky, and I heard the need in his voice.

"You're such a pig."

He chuckled and he massaged my neck. "As long as I'm being a pig, I might as well admit that I have a recurring fantasy about rubbing a certain warm cream into this beautiful skin."

His fingers worked on a knot at the apex of my shoulder where it met my neck. Loosening it, my head dropped down a little lower. "Oh yeah? And where exactly would you be rubbing this cream?"

Dex's fingers slowed. "You really want me to tell you?"

"Of course."

His fingers came to a complete stop, and his voice was low as he leaned forward to whisper. His warm breath tickled my neck. "Sometimes when I'm in the shower, I envision myself coming all over your tits and rubbing it in."

When I didn't immediately respond, Dex must have taken that as a sign that what he'd told me made me uncomfortable. Which it did, but not the kind of uncomfortable he was thinking. The discomfort was from the growing swell that ached between my legs.

"Should I have kept that to myself?" he asked.

I swallowed and whispered, "No. Actually. Tell me more."

"You want to hear more about how I fantasize about you?"

"I do."

Dex was quiet for a moment and then his fingers began to rub again. "I think of you lying on your back, your hands squeezing those beautiful tits together while I straddle your chest and slip my cock between them."

I wiggled between his legs and felt his hard-on up against my ass. "You want to know what I think about when I fantasize about you?"

"I'd empty my bank account and sign over my penthouse to hear you tell me your fantasies right now."

I chuckled. "Well, it starts with you opening ..." My deviant, fictional adventure was put on hold when Dex's cell phone started to ring.

"Ignore it," he said. Go on."

"But...it's sort of late. Almost ten o'clock. Don't you want to even see who it is?"

His response came so fast it made me laugh. "No." After a few more rings the cell phone quieted. Dex prompted me to continue. "So...where were you? What am I opening? The door? My pants? Your pants? A bag? Handcuffs? Don't leave me hanging here."

I giggled. "Okay. Well, I had this one sort of daydream where you open..." As if on cue, Dex's cell phone started to ring again. The damn thing was vibrating and jumping around on the end table.

"Maybe you should get that."

"No."

"At least see who it is."

Begrudgingly, Dex reached for his phone. He stared at the screen for a ring before speaking. "It's my father's wife, Myra."

"Aren't they in the Caribbean? Why would she be calling? And so late?"

Dex swiped and brought the phone to his ear with a huff. I listened to one side of the conversation. His body immediately stiffened.

"What happened?"

"When?"

"Where is he?"

My heart sank waiting to find out the details, but it was clear whatever it was, was not good. After he hung up, Dex immediately got up from the bed and started pacing back and forth. I was almost afraid to ask.

"What happened?"

"My father. He had a massive heart attack."

"Oh my God. Is he..."

"He's in CCU. He's alive but hasn't woken up yet."

"In Turks?"

"It happened on a plane. Apparently, he hadn't been feeling well, and they decided to come home early so he could see his doctor. Happened a few minutes before they were landing in Florida tonight."

"I'm so sorry."

Dex ran his fingers through his hair. "I need to go down there. First flight in the morning."

"I'll go with you."

He looked at me. "You sure?"

"I want to be there for you."

After a few heartbeats, he nodded. Then he proceeded to pick up the phone and call the airline. While he barked into the phone, I put away the moisturizer he'd been massaging me with and went to the kitchen to get a drink of water.

Standing at the kitchen counter, it dawned on me for the first time...I was about to meet my biological father.

Maybe.

I needed wine instead.

CHAPTER 30

Bianca

Dex was quiet the entire flight down to Florida. He'd spoken to Myra first thing this morning while we were headed to the airport and found out that his father needed a triple bypass, along with a valve replacement. His heart was weak after the massive heart attack, but they couldn't waste time because of the ninety-nine percent blockage. Surgery was scheduled for this afternoon.

When we arrived at Good Samaritan Medical Center, Dex already knew the room number so we breezed right past the line at the patient information desk and followed the signs for the elevator. It wasn't until the doors closed that I had really given any thought to what my showing up might do to Dex Sr. Up until then, I'd been only focusing on wanting to support Dex.

"Maybe I should wait out in the hall when you go in to see him."

Dex was normally so present, so aware of everything around him; it was odd to see him in a fog. "I'm sorry. Did you say something?"

"I said maybe it would be better if I didn't go in to see him with you. I could just wait in the hall."

"Is that what you want or what you think is best for him?"

"I don't want to upset him."

Dex took my hand and nodded as the elevator doors slid open. "You're coming in with me."

Dex Sr.'s wife was in the hall outside of CCU talking to a doctor. When we approached, they turned to us. Myra forced a smile. "Hi, Dex. Thank you for coming."

"Of course."

"Dr. Sharma, this is Dex's son, Dex Jr."

The doctor nodded. Then, Myra looked to me. I extended my hand. "Bianca George. I'm a...friend...of Dex's. I'm sorry about your husband's health."

The doctor looked at his watch. "I was just about to go in and visit with your father. You're welcome to join while I review his morning stats."

Dex nodded.

Dr. Sharma turned to me. "I'm sorry. But CCU is limited to family members, so you'll need to wait out here."

I saw Dex's face and braced for it. He pulled me close to his side. "Bianca is my girlfriend. But there's also a pretty good chance she's his daughter. So, she'll be joining us."

Not knowing how to respond to that, the doctor motioned us to follow him inside.

Even though he was paler than I imagined he normally was, and he had monitor lines and IVs hooked up all over, I would have recognized Dex Sr. anywhere. He looked just like my sister, even more so in person than he did in the pictures.

His eyes caught on Dex first. There was a moment of surprise at seeing him, and I thought it might be happiness. But the light in his eyes quickly extinguished when he looked at me standing next to him—a real-life reminder that darkness in the past always comes into the light. Frequently, at the worst times.

"Dad." Dex nodded.

His father attempted to take the oxygen mask off his face, but the doctor stopped him. "You need to leave that on, Mr. Truitt." Dr. Sharma then went on to examine the chart and immediately began talking about the risks of the heart procedure Dex's father was about to undergo. I thought all of us were listening intently until I felt Dex Sr. staring at me. As I turned to meet his eyes, he gave me a soft smile. Then he looked to the man standing next to me, who I realized was no longer listening to the doctor, either, but instead watching the interaction between the two of us. When Dex Sr. lifted his weak hand in my direction for me to take, I didn't know what to do. My eyes flitted back and forth between the two men, looking for someone to give me the answer. We hadn't talked about it since last night, but it was that moment that I knew. Taking his hand in mine, I *needed* to know if this man was my father.

We stayed at the hospital the entire time Dex Sr. was in surgery.

When Dr. Sharma finally came out to tell us that the procedure was a success, Dex and I let out a collective sigh. Dex planted a relieved kiss on my lips, the doctor looked confused; I think he'd given up on trying to figure out our relation to one another.

"Can we see him?" Dex asked.

"His wife is in there now. I would say wait a little bit, since he's still waking up. Give it about a half hour."

Myra eventually came out to let us know that it was okay to go in and said her husband had actually asked to see us.

My heart was racing as we entered the recovery room.

"How are you feeling, Dad?"

He swallowed, seeming like his mouth was parched. "I've been better."

"Well, the operation went well. I'm really glad to hear it."

Dex Sr. turned his head toward me. "I can't get over it. Before I went under, I thought you were her. You look like just your mother."

"Yes. Many people tell me that."

His voice was groggy, but he continued to force out the words. "I really did care for her. There were a lot of women who passed through my life. Most of them were forgettable. But I will never forget Eleni." He looked at Dex for a moment then said, "My son has the same look in his eyes now, the one I had whenever I was with her. Except, what you have going on here seems to be even stronger."

"Dad, don't talk too much. You'll waste your energy."

"No, I have to say this."

Dex blew out a breath. "Alright."

His father reached for my hand as he addressed both of us. "I'm sorry about this situation. I'll do whatever you need me to do. Nearly dying has put a lot into perspective. I'd really like to know the truth. Mostly for you but also for me."

Dex was quick to say, "Well, you need some time to recover before we deal with all that."

"Nonsense. All they need to do is swab my cheek. You get the guy in here today, and do it while you're still down here. No sense in stalling."

He seemed troubled by his father's insistence. "We haven't decided one hundred percent on the test."

Still holding his father's hand, I made sure I was looking Dex straight in the eyes when I said, "Yes, we have."

"We have?"

"Yes, Dex. We need to do it."

He just kept nodding and blinking, as if realizing he'd just given up on a losing battle. "Okay."

About an hour later, someone from the lab came in to take our samples. The entire time my cheek was swabbed, I was looking deeply into Dex's penetrating eyes while I silently prayed for a favorable outcome.

Dex then called the main lab where my sister's sample had been sent, and they informed him that it would take about two days for all of the results. I knew they would be the longest two days of my life.

We decided to stay in Palm Beach until the results came in. That way, in the event that it turned out Dex Sr. was my biological father, he and I could have a moment to absorb the news together. My sister opted to stay in New York since her husband couldn't take time off from work; she felt she'd need his support more than anything.

After I called Bandit's doggy day care to let them know we'd need to extend his staycation, I spent a good part of that evening on the phone with my father as he assured me that regardless of the outcome, nothing would change between us, that I would always be his little girl and the love of his life. When I'd finally gotten up the nerve to have the conversation with my dad, he had admitted that he always questioned Alexandra's paternity in particular over the years, but he'd ultimately decided not to pursue testing because he felt it wouldn't have changed anything in his mind or heart.

Dex and I ended up spending the night at his father's guesthouse, which was adjacent to the Truitt's main waterfront property. So exhausted from the long day at the hospital, I relaxed into Dex's arms. The mood was somber as we fell asleep in the king-sized bed listening to the sound of the waves crashing just outside the French doors.

The following morning, he snuck up behind me as I was looking out at the ocean from the patio.

He handed me a mug of freshly brewed coffee. "How are you feeling?"

"Sort of numb."

"I know what you mean. It feels like a shock. I went from preparing myself to possibly never find out...to now inevitably dealing with the truth as soon as tomorrow."

"We couldn't have lived like that. We would have always wondered."

"I think deep down I knew that, but I still didn't want to believe it." Dex suddenly looked panicked. "We can't waste these last hours, Bianca. I feel like we need to not let a second pass us by unnoticed."

"What do you want to do?"

"We have a huge day ahead."

"We do?"

"Fuck, yes. They said the results could potentially be in tomorrow...that means today could be the last full day that we're living in ignorant bliss. I feel like I need to give you a lifetime today."

"What does that mean?"

"It means there are certain things that I want to see and do with you while you're still my Bianca, in case I never get a chance to experience them. Although, the one thing I *really* need to do, I can't."

"What are we going to do?"

"I want to take you to a few different places."

CHAPTER 31

Dex

I'd made some phone calls to area businesses while Bianca showered and got dressed. The Truitt name was well known on the island, so I had no trouble getting people to cooperate with my plans.

Our first stop was Worth Avenue, which was Palm Beach's version of Rodeo Drive. Bianca wasn't very materialistic, but that didn't stop me from wanting to shower her with the best that money could buy.

A lifetime.

I had to give her a lifetime today—just in case.

We'd parked and were strolling along the sidewalk, looking in the windows of the upscale shops. Her face turned red when I intentionally stopped in front of Tiffany's.

Seeming to read my guilty expression, she asked, "What are you up to, Dex Truitt?"

"Wait right out here, okay?"

Once inside, I raced to the first person I saw.

"Can I help you?"

"Yes, I'm looking for Julia. She and I spoke over the phone."

Moments later, an older blonde woman approached. "Hi, Mr. Truitt. I have it right here. If for some reason it doesn't fit, just bring her back in today and we can resize it."

"Perfect. Thank you."

With the small blue gift bag in hand, I ventured back outside to find Bianca waiting for me, looking perplexed.

"What's in the bag, Dex?"

I wasted no time getting to the point.

"Okay, first off, I want you to know that this isn't a proposal. I'm hopeful if things turn out okay, I can do that the right way someday. I want to really appreciate that moment without this cloud hanging over us. But I wanted to give you something now that you will always remember me by."

I took the small box out and opened it, showcasing the nearly three-carat diamond eternity band. The bright sunlight beamed over the diamonds, causing them to really shine.

"I'm not getting down on one knee today, because I want to keep that option open for later. No matter what the outcome is tomorrow, you're going to be a Truitt. I want you to wear this and always remember me, remember the time we've had together. Whether I can complement this someday with another ring, or whether it stands alone as a symbol of what never could be, this eternity band represents my eternal love and respect for you, Bianca." I placed it on her finger. It fit perfectly. My earlier estimate of her ring size was right on the money; that was pure fate, kind of like this whole experience.

She looked down at the sparkling gems, seeming shocked as I continued.

"Today isn't our wedding day, but it's our *day*, and we're going to celebrate what we do have—today. There's going to be cake, and a pretty white dress, and some frolicking on the beach. And we're going to spend every moment together."

Overcome with emotion, she reached up and hugged me tightly. "I don't even know what to say that will do this gesture justice, except that I will proudly wear this forever."

Taking her bejeweled hand in mine, I kissed it hard. "Now, let's go have some fun."

We were right on time for the noon appointment I'd made at the posh boutique. The owner took Bianca upstairs to look at their selection of garments. I'd told the woman to pull all of the white dresses in the place before Bianca's arrival. Since this wasn't an actual wedding—just a celebration—I suggested she bring out more casual dresses as opposed to formal evening gowns. But the choice was Bianca's. My only condition was that I wanted to see her in white. You know... *just in case* this was all we would have.

Much to my dismay, they wouldn't allow me upstairs in the all-female dressing area. I waited down on the lower level, mindlessly flipping through the pages of a bridal magazine and talking to the pictures inside.

"Bianca's way prettier."

Flip.

"Dude, would you still marry her if there was a chance she could be your sister? Not an easy decision, is it?"

Flip.

"Oh, what's this? A facial is a great way to relax on the morning of your wedding? Well, I couldn't agree more."

I closed the magazine suddenly when my eyes caught Bianca slowly making her way down the winding staircase. The sight of her in the dress she'd chosen took my breath away. But what made my heart want to combust even more was the huge smile plastered all over her face. It was so full of hope and optimism, beautiful and heartbreaking at the same time.

Good idea, Dex. This was a good way to help take her mind off things.

I prayed that nothing would ever happen to take that smile away.

"You look stunning."

With a humble expression, she looked down at herself. "It's simple. I didn't want to go overboard. This one just felt right."

The dress Bianca had chosen was strapless, fitted at the waist, and flaring out at the bottom just above her knees.

"It's perfect."

"Get this..." She smiled. "Guess what the name of this design is?"

"The dresses have names?"

"Yes." She laughed. "This one is called *La Bandita.*"

A wide grin spread across my face. "Bandit Boy is here in spirit. I love that."

"Thank you for this experience. It was very *Pretty Woman.*"

"I could never repay you for what you've given me." I leaned in and planted a soft kiss on her lips.

She stretched out her arms. "So, I'm all dressed up. Where to next?"

"You'll have to wait to find out." I winked.

Driving away in our rented convertible, I felt high on life. Bianca's hair was blowing in the warm wind. Our hands were interlocked.

Pulling up in front of our destination, I had to parallel park. Whether the car would actually fit into the space was questionable, but I slid it right in.

"You have mad parking skills, Truitt."

"It was tight, but I managed to get it in. By the good grace of God, you'll find out more where that's concerned soon enough." I winked.

"Always the dirty mind," she chuckled. "And for the record, I certainly hope you're right." Bianca finally noticed that we'd parked in front of a bakery. "Is this where we have cake?"

"Yes. But not just one cake. We're gonna taste many different kinds."

"You set up a wedding cake tasting?"

"Sure, why not?"

"Don't you have to commit to ordering one in order to do that?"

"Probably. So, I'll order one and have them deliver it to my father."

"That'll be real good for his heart," she said sarcastically.

"Okay, how about this? I'll put down a deposit, and we'll order it to be made a year from now. If all goes well, we come back down and pick up our cake."

She reached for my hand. "That sounds like a plan."

Ganache Patisserie smelled like an explosion of sugar with a hint of amaretto. Multi-tiered cakes of various pastel colors were displayed in glass cases.

A woman greeted us and took Bianca and me into a back room. She poured us some tea and laid out several slices of cake on the table.

"You can sample them in any order. There's a pad of paper and a pen you can use to rate each flavor. They're all labeled. Hopefully, you can come to a unanimous decision in the end."

"Do couples actually bicker about which flavor to choose?" Bianca asked.

"Oh, yes. You'd be surprised how much bargaining goes into this. You have the option to choose different flavors for each layer, though. There are typically three. So, you can always compromise."

Bianca and I began sampling. We were having a blast feeding each other, and it brought back memories of my first date with her as Jay at the Ethiopian place. I'd dip my finger in the frosting then rub it on her nose. I think we made the woman uncomfortable. I could only imagine how awkward she would have felt if she also knew the truth about what was really going on with us. She finally got up to give us a bit of privacy.

When Bianca licked some frosting off her lips, my dick twitched.

"My mother used to bake cakes for friends' birthdays in her spare time," she said. "I used to enjoy helping her. Of course, the best part was licking the spoon."

"I bet you're fantastic at licking the spoon. Was it a wooden spoon, by any chance?"

"As a matter of fact, it was. Big piece of wood."

I grabbed the spoon I'd used to stir my tea. "Show me how you licked it."

The woman returned. "How do you like the carrot cake?"

Bianca looked at me. "It's very...moist."

"I bet it is," I muttered.

"Are you getting any closer to narrowing it down?" the woman asked.

"Well, it's...quite hard," I said.

Bianca grabbed my knee under the table. When the woman walked away again, we both broke out into laughter before vowing to try to take the process a bit more seriously.

About fifteen minutes later, the woman returned. "How are we doing?"

Bianca smiled. "We've decided on the vanilla cake with buttercream frosting for the bottom layer. For the middle layer, we're going to go with the lemon...also with the buttercream. And for the top, we'd like the vanilla with strawberry preserve...buttercream all the way."

Kissing Bianca's ear, I said, "I know you love the cream."

The lady cleared her throat. "Let me go grab the book. We'll choose a design and put the order in for you."

When she returned with a catalog of cake designs, Bianca pointed to a particular one. "Aw...look...balls. Just like our first meeting." She turned to the woman. "What about the one with the balls?"

"You like this design? This is one we do where we actually decorate around the cake with cake pops. We strategically stick the pops in various parts of the cake. And the best part is...everything is edible."

I grinned. "All I heard was strategically sticking shit in various parts and edible...I'm good."

"You two are quite the pair, definitely made for each other," the woman said.

Squeezing Bianca's thigh, I grinned proudly. "Why, thank you."

She took out her pen. "Okay...so when is the wedding date?"

There was dead silence for several seconds until I answered, "It's one year from today, actually."

"Oh, how perfect. We'll just need fifty-percent down now, and then the balance will just need to be remitted on delivery."

After I handed over my credit card, we were left alone for a bit, and I noticed that Bianca suddenly looked somber.

"What's wrong?"

"It feels real. I wish it was."

Fuck. This was backfiring.

"Maybe I took this too far."

"No. No, I just got a little emotional when she wrote down the date."

Before we could say anything further, the woman returned with my card and a receipt. "All set, Mr. Truitt. You can call us anytime with the venue location so that we can arrange for a delivery time on the morning of."

Bianca remained quiet as we walked out of the shop. I couldn't take it anymore. I pulled her into a tight embrace on the sidewalk and whispered in her ear, "We have to stay optimistic."

"It's hard not to want to prepare myself for disappointment. It just seems too good to be true that we could dodge this bullet."

"I have to believe. It's all that's getting me through today. I have to believe that this time next year....I'm gonna have my cake and eat you, too." I laughed, because the funny thing was, I hadn't even meant for it to come out that way. *Eat you, too*. It just did. Must have been subliminal.

She smacked my arm playfully. "I'm glad you're still finding humor in all of this."

"Gotta laugh so I don't cry, beautiful."

I meant that.

We spent the rest of the afternoon on the private stretch of beach off the guesthouse.

As the sun set, it felt like the curtain was slowly closing on our time together. Bianca was still wearing her white dress, which was now covered in dirt, water, and sand. I wanted to burn the image into memory.

"I don't want to sleep tonight," she said. "I feel like I just want to stay up all night."

"Who needs sleep?" I grabbed her hand. "May I have this dance?"

No music was required as we slowly swayed to the sounds of the beach. We rocked back and forth until the sun completely went down then stayed up and talked, vowing not to fall into slumber.

Sleep eventually won out, though, as we later crashed in each other's arms on the sand.

The sound of the seagulls woke us up the next morning. Looking like we'd washed ashore, we'd slept in surprisingly late; we must have both been exhausted from forcing ourselves to stay up.

As we sat up on the sand, I wrapped my arms around her body from behind.

"So, you never finished your sentence," I said.

"What?"

"You know, before we flew down here. You started telling me about your sexual fantasy. You said it started with me opening something. I need to know the rest."

"I should've known you wouldn't forget about that."

"Not a chance. I have to live vicariously through the fantasy version of myself right now. My jealousy in regards to fantasy Dex is worse than it was for that tool, Jay."

"Okay. So, anyway...it starts with you opening—"

My phone rang, interrupting her.

"Are you fucking kidding me?" I groaned.

"I think you're destined not to find out, Truitt."

"I'd better get this...in case...you know."

She sat up suddenly. "Take it."

I answered, "Dex Truitt..."

"Hi, Mr. Truitt. This is Erika Raymond from Leominster Laboratories."

My heart began to palpitate. "Okay...yes?"

"Your results are in."

CHAPTER 32

Bianca

I thought I might throw up. Or pass out. Maybe even one right before the other. *Oh God.* What if I passed out first and then vomited while I was unconscious? I stood and started pacing in the sand. My skin was clammy, and from the look on Dex's face, I must have turned pale. He spoke into the phone. "Can you please hold for a moment?" Covering the receiver, he asked, "Are you okay? You should sit down. I don't like the way you look right now."

"I don't like the way I feel right now, either."

Dex returned to the call. "Erika? Did you say your name was Erika?"

I heard the *yes* even though the phone was pressed to his ear.

"Listen. I need to go somewhere more private. Would it be possible for me to call you back in, say, five minutes?"

He was quiet for a moment, then said, "Okay, yes. The number came in on my caller ID. I'll ask for extension two eight three. It'll just be a few minutes, and I'd appreciate it if you could stand by for my call."

Silence again, then finally. "Okay. Thank you very much."

After he swiped to end the call, Dex put one hand on the small of my back. "Come on. Let's go inside. I think we should talk for a few minutes before we do this."

In a fog, I let Dex guide me inside to our room. I'd been so sure of myself, so anxious to know the truth, and now that it was within reach, I suddenly wanted to run in the other direction. *I need more time.*

Dex led me to the bed and sat me on the edge. I'd heard the term numb before, but I'd never actually experienced it. In my life, stress meant palpitations, playing with my balls and yelling at the top of my lungs. But this stress was entirely different. I couldn't feel my toes. I actually looked down and wiggled them to make sure I could still do it.

Dex kneeled before me and cupped my face in both hands. "You sure you want to do this?"

"I'm not sure of anything right at the given moment." I let out an audible sigh. "My name is Bianca, right?"

Dex smiled. "That's right. And mine is Jay."

Somehow his silly comment seemed to bring me back to reality. I smiled back and looked Dex in the eyes for a long while. What was staring back at me was absolutely beautiful. Not the man himself, but looking into his eyes, I saw love in its purest form. It was honest and open and willing to give me anything I wanted. As much as it took my breath away, it also reminded me that I needed to know. I wanted that love unconditionally and not knowing would always have that question mark out there.

I didn't even feel the tears start to fall until Dex used his thumbs to wipe them away. He closed his eyes and accepted the decision I'd made without me having to say it out loud.

"Tell me how you want to do this. Do you want to know

about yourself first, or your sister?"

I pondered it for a minute. "It's Saturday and Alexandra and the girls are probably at ballet. Why don't we find out about my results first and then take some time to absorb that before we find out about Alex. I don't think I can handle both at the same time."

"Alright, then that's what we'll do." He squeezed my hand. "You sure you're okay? You're not going to pass out on me, are you?"

"I think I'm good." I took a deep, cleansing breath, then nodded. "Go ahead. I'm ready to make the call now."

"I will. In a minute. There's something I need to do first."

"What's that?"

"This." His mouth crashed down on mine. He kissed me with so much passion, so much intense feeling that when it finally broke, I was crying again. *God, I'm a disaster.*

Laughing through my tears as I wiped them away, I said, "I'm sorry. These are happy tears."

"You don't look very happy at the moment."

I leaned my forehead against Dex's. "Oddly, I am. I love you, Dexter Truitt."

"I love you, too, Bianca. More than I can even understand."

I didn't ask what Dex was doing over the next minute, but I closed my eyes and said a prayer. When I opened mine, his were still closed and his lips were moving a little. I was pretty sure we were making the same request of the big guy in the sky. Eventually, he squeezed my hand one more time and then picked up his phone.

I took a deep breath and held it while he dialed.

"May I have extension two eight three, please?"

I heard the woman through the receiver but couldn't make out what she was saying on the other end this time.

"Yes, Erika? This is Dex Truitt calling back for the results. Only, we'd like to have the results from the paternity test between Dexter Truitt and Bianca Georgakopolous at this time. We'd like to call back for the results between Alexandra Fiore and Dexter Truitt a little later."

I got up from the bed and started pacing.

Dex read the security code we were given by the technician and again confirmed he would only be hearing one result at this time. When he was done, Dex looked up at me as he spoke into the phone. "Yes, I'm ready."

After what seemed like forever but was probably only thirty seconds of quiet, Dex's eyes closed. He cleared his throat. "And what is the accuracy of those results?"

"I see. Thank you very much. We'll call back for the other results soon."

My heart clenched in my chest when I saw the look on Dex's face. It was his turn to lose it. Tears were streaming down his face as he walked toward me.

"Say it," I whispered. "Just say it."

The next thing I knew, I was lifted into the air and being cradled in Dex's arms. "The odds of you being my sister are exactly 0.00%."

"What?" *Did he just say what I think he said?*

"You heard me right. We're not related, Bianca."

"Oh my God! Oh my God!" My hand flew to my chest. My poor heart was beating so fast, it felt like it could explode. "Are you serious? Are you sure?"

"I've never been more serious in my life. And I'd say that 0.00% chance is pretty fucking certain. Thank Christ!"

Leaning in, I pressed my lips to Dex's. "We're not related. We're really not related." I kept repeating it over and over like some sort of mantra, but in truth I needed to keep hearing it to let the enormity of it sink in. Dex's face was damp with tears when he set me down on the bed.

While I was completely overwhelmed with relief, Dex suddenly seemed to have the opposite feeling. An intense look of need and determination washed over his face. He began to strip out of his clothes with urgency. When he was down to his boxers, I stopped him.

"Wait."

"I don't think I'm capable of waiting any longer. I need to be inside of you, Bianca. Call me an asshole if you want, but I have the urge to mark you. Sink my teeth into your skin to brand you as mine and then come so hard inside of you that parts of me will never find their way out again."

I swallowed. "Jesus, Dex."

"Too much truth?"

"Not at all, it's the sexiest thing I've ever heard in my life. It's just that...I want to do something for you."

"Can it wait until after I do something for you?" He'd set me in the middle of the bed, but reached for my legs and yanked me to the edge where he was standing. "Multiple times. Can it wait until after I do something for you, multiple times?"

I giggled. But climbed off the bed. "Sit. Dexter, not my brother, Truitt. Sit down."

He pouted but complied. Sitting on the edge of the bed, his huge erection was straining through his boxer briefs.

I began to unbutton my blouse slowly. "We haven't talked about it before, but I'm on the pill."

"Thank fuck. Because I need to feel you skin to skin, and I'll never be able to pull out once I bury myself inside. We might be sleeping with my cock still inside of you tonight."

After I slipped off my shirt, I shimmied out of my pants and stood before Dex, letting him take his time looking at me. His patience was dwindling when he reached for me, and I took a step back. "Not yet."

He groaned in frustration, but gripped the sides of the bed.

I reached behind my back and unhooked my bra. A few shakes of my shoulders, and it slipped to the floor.

Dex swallowed. His chest was rising and falling in deep heaves. "You're fucking beautiful."

"Thank you."

I left my panties on and stepped closer to him before dropping to my knees.

"Bianca...I can't. I mean...you can't. I'll not last ten seconds with your mouth on me."

"Good. Because I wasn't going to use my mouth on you."

With a devious smile, I squeezed my breasts together, giving him a hint what my plans were. "Take off your boxers, Mr. Truitt."

"I won't last like that either, Bianca. I've been dreaming about slipping my cock between those beautiful tits for too long. I want to come all over them, but the next time I come, it's going to be inside of you."

With one swift motion, somehow Dex lifted me from kneeling, swung me up and onto the bed, and was hovering over me. "Thank you for wanting to give me my fantasy. It means a lot to me that you would offer that before even finding your own release."

"I want nothing more than to play out every deviant fantasy that is in your head. I plan to spend lots of time exploring the depths of your pervyness, Mr. Truitt."

Dex maneuvered out of his underwear without breaking contact, and his rigid cock was hot against my skin. I could actually feel it throbbing against my stomach. We'd been waiting so long, I couldn't take it another second. Spreading my legs underneath him, he shifted into position, and then held my eyes as he slowly pushed inside. Every inch he eased in, my heart opened wider. This was it. It felt so unbelievably incredible to finally have the last part of him inside me. He'd been in my heart since the first time I met him, now it was the physical connection at last. I realized that this was what it truly felt like to consummate a relationship.

Dex moved in and out gently, taking his time to stretch my body to accept his girth. It was beautiful and sweet, but I could tell he was holding back. Encouraging him to let go, I wrapped my arms around him and dug my fingernails into his ass.

His pupils dilated. "*Fuck.*"

That did the trick. His head lowered and he bit down on my right breast hard as he sped up his pace. It was definitely going to leave a mark, and I wanted that...to be marked by him in every way.

"*Fuck. Fuck*," he groaned as his mouth moved to my neck where he sucked and bit while winding fistfuls of my hair in his hands. I moaned when he tugged at it.

Everything else in the background faded away except the sound of our jagged breathing and wet bodies slapping together as he thrust deeper and deeper inside of me.

"I'm gonna fill up this tight pussy, Bianca." He pulled his head back to look at me, and that was all it took. My body had already been humming along, but my orgasm hit me head on. I called out his name over and over as my muscles pulsated around his thick cock. Just when I thought my pleasure had crested, Dex drove into me faster and deeper, letting out a sexy groan as he released inside of me which, in turn, sent my body riding a new wave of pulses as we came simultaneously together.

Catching our breath, Dex kissed me gently on the lips. He was still semi-hard inside of me as he leisurely glided in and out. "I love you, Bianca."

"I love you, too."

"We took some crazy path to get here, but it's made me realize just how much I'd do to keep you in my life. For what it's worth, I had no plans to let you go even if it turned out you were my sister."

"Oh, really? And what exactly were you going to do to get me to stay?"

"Let's just say, I've been doing my research."

I squinted. "What are you talking about?"

"Full siblings share fifty percent of their DNA. Half siblings only share an average of twenty-five percent of their DNA. It's not technically inbreeding, it's called line breeding."

"You were going to try to sell me on the scientific aspects of sleeping with my brother?"

"Of course not."

"Oh."

"I set up an appointment with a genetics counselor to do that."

"Are you joking?"

"And maybe a psychologist, too." He laughed, but I knew he was telling the truth.

"You're crazy."

"Crazy in love with you, Georgy Girl. Crazy in love with you."

EPILOGUE

Dex

"Everything turned out the way it was supposed to, didn't it? And we didn't even have to move to Europe."

My driver called out, "Did you say something, Mr. Truitt?"

"Uh...no, Sam. I'm talking to Bandit."

I rubbed behind my dog's ears. "So, anyway...as I was saying...everything worked out. You didn't end up at that farm upstate. Neither one of us is screwing our sister, although whatever happened with you in the past is in the past, eh? Your secrets are safe with me."

"Ruff!"

"And now...there's so much more to look forward to."

We finally pulled up to our destination. I knew it was a little strange to be bringing a dog to a ribbon cutting ceremony, but he was an important part of the family; I wouldn't have had it any other way.

Holding onto Bandit's leash, I breathed in the not-so-fresh Brooklyn air and looked up at the sign that read, *The Jelani Okiro Arts and Cultural Center.*

Filled with pride, I couldn't wait to show Bianca what we'd done to this place.

Bandit and I took the elevator up to the second floor to find Alexandra standing in the foyer. She was holding a clipboard and grinning at us.

"How's my sister from the same mister?" I smiled.

"Great, brother from another mother. No one from the press has arrived yet, by the way."

"Good." I clapped my hands together. "That gives us some extra time to make sure everything is in place."

"Yes. We need all the time we can get."

After I set Bandit up with some water in one of the spare rooms, I returned to where my sister was standing and could sense that she was tense. "You okay?"

"I'm a little nervous to see him again."

I nodded sympathetically. "I know you are."

Alex would be seeing our father today. He and Myra were in town and planned to stop by the center. Even though it had been a few years since we'd found out the results of the test, Alex had only spent a minimal amount of time with Dexter Sr. It was never comfortable or easy for her. And in all the ways that mattered, she still considered Taso her true father.

About a year ago, I hired Alex as a special projects manager at Montague. One of her more recent assignments had been to oversee the development of the arts center that was built in honor of Jelani. He'd passed away about six months after Bianca and I returned from that fateful trip to Palm Beach. His colon cancer had metastasized despite all of his treatments. When things took a turn for the worse, Bianca and I visited him every day. I think my friend even had a little crush on my Greek goddess—not that I could blame him.

Shortly before he died, I'd told him of my plans to continue his legacy. Even though he was resistant to the attention, he'd allowed me to bring a photographer in to document our final whittling sessions. Large, framed black and white images of Jelani's hands in action were now placed in various spots around the center along with Kenyan-themed artwork.

Jelani left me all of the wooden sculptures he'd ever made. We had them displayed in glass cases throughout the place. The center featured a woodshop for whittling in addition to other art and music rooms. The non-profit would welcome children and teenagers from all over the borough. All staff would be funded and employed by Montague Enterprises while some supplies and other expenses would be funded through charitable sponsors.

Alex tapped her pencil against the clipboard. "Oh, I forgot to tell you. I got that Clement kid to agree to fly here one weekend and do a whittling workshop like you asked."

"No shit? I'll get to meet my little YouTube nemesis in person. Although, he's not so little anymore. Finally going through puberty. Makes it a bit more appropriate to be in competition with him now."

She laughed. "Where's Bianca?"

"Sam went back to get them. She was running late."

"Understandable."

Alex and I spent the next fifteen minutes making sure all of the rooms were in pristine shape.

Back out in the foyer, I asked, "Are Hope and Faith coming?"

"Yeah, Brian's bringing them."

"Good. They'll love it here."

She looked beyond my shoulders. "There's Bianca now."

It was amazing what the mere mention of my wife's name did to me. The second the word "Bianca" exited Alex's mouth, the moment brightened for me. That feeling pretty much summed up my entire life now.

I turned around to find my gorgeous woman all dressed up. She looked nothing like someone who'd been up last night with a sick two-year-old. I knelt down, prompting my daughter to come to me. My heart melted every time she'd eagerly run toward me with excitement in her eyes like there was nothing more she needed in the world than to be in her daddy's arms.

Lifting her up, I kissed her cheek and whispered in her ear, "I wasn't sure you'd make it, Georgina Bina."

"The Motrin is kicking in." Bianca smiled. "I didn't want her to miss this. I know you have the photographer coming."

"I'm glad she's here."

"Are Mom and Dad going to make it?" Alex asked.

Bianca shook her head. "No. Dex and I invited them, but neither was comfortable confronting Dexter Sr."

Even though Bianca's parents' relationship was strained over the years, in recent months, they'd been on better terms. In fact, we'd just had them both over to our house for breakfast the previous weekend. So while dealing with my father was another story, I was happy that things with Taso and Eleni were now cordial, especially for our daughter's sake.

I turned to Alex. "Do you mind watching Georgina for a few minutes so I can show Bianca around before people arrive?"

"Of course, I don't mind."

I handed my daughter to her aunt. Georgina looked just like her mother, and I couldn't have been happier about that. She was conceived some time before Bianca and I were married. We'd had a lavish ceremony in the city a couple of years ago. At the time, we didn't know that Bianca was already pregnant.

The weekend after our wedding, we'd flown down to Palm Beach to pick up our wedding cake one year to the day from when we'd ordered it at the cake testing. The bakery delivered it to our private spot on the beach. We took pictures, fed each other a couple of slices, then transported the rest to a senior center down the road.

Taking Bianca's hand, I led her down the hall to the music room.

She jumped the second she saw it. "Are you serious?"

"Perfect, right?"

The Liza Minnelli statue finally had a permanent home, as did the Elvis painting from Jay's apartment. I'd picked up other similar pop culture memorabilia to finish off the space. A baby grand piano sat in the corner along with other musical instruments.

"Finally, a place that makes sense for her." Bianca laughed.

"Right? It's like all this time she's been wandering around, looking for a more meaningful place to sneak up on you for the very last time." I pointed to the giant painting on the wall. "Elvis is here, too. Did you notice him?"

"This is amazing, what you've done with this entire place."

Pulling her close, I spoke over her lips, "I'm glad I can still impress you, Mrs. Truitt." I stepped back to take her in. Her nipples were protruding through the black material of her dress. "God, your tits look amazing right now. I feel like I need to suck on them."

"You compliment my tits every day. What's any different today?"

"They're saluting me especially nicely. Not to mention, we're in that in-between time when you're not breastfeeding. I get them all to myself for a while." I bent down to gently kiss over her nipple and spoke into her chest. "Have I mentioned I love your body pregnant?"

"A few times an hour, yes."

"Can we just keep having babies forever?"

"Who exactly is going to birth these children?"

"Well, I was hoping you would, my Greek goddess."

She rubbed her four-months pregnant belly. "I think I'm done after this one. Two is good."

I wrapped my hands around her ass and squeezed. "You said you were done after one."

"I know...then after I wasn't pregnant anymore and the heartburn was gone, I changed my mind."

"Well, then, I'll just keep hoping that you change your mind ten times over."

Her eyes widened. "Ten?"

"The truth? If you'd let me...yes. Ten."

"You're crazy, but honestly I don't trust myself not to let that happen, either. There are two main things working against me. One, as soon as I go off the pill, you just look at me and I get pregnant. Two, I can't resist you. You bat those blue eyes at me, and all I want to do is make you happy."

"And the problem with this is?" I joked, nuzzling her neck. I had to stop myself before I ended up with a raging hard-on in front of the New York media.

Speaking of the media, Bianca still freelanced part-time for *Finance Times* but only took local assignments now. Between Georgina and my needy ass, she didn't have time for much else. She knew I fully supported her going back to work full-time if that was what she really wanted. But what seemed to be making her the happiest as of late was being a wife and mother. I certainly couldn't complain about having her there when I got home from work. I rarely worked late anymore, too eager to get home to my girls.

I reluctantly gave her one last kiss. "We should get back outside. People will be arriving soon."

We emerged to find Alex following closely behind our daughter, who was racing around.

"What's Georgina playing with?" Bianca asked.

"I thought we'd put all of the wooden figures in the display cases," Alex said. "But it looks like she found one."

Bianca rushed toward her. "Those aren't toys. She's putting it in her mouth."

"It's okay. Uncle Jelani wouldn't mind," I said. When I took the drool-covered figurine from my daughter, I smiled upon realizing it was the giraffe. The more I thought about it, the more perplexing it was that she even had it. We'd definitely put *all* of Jelani's pieces into the glass cases. I'd overseen that process myself. I looked up at the recessed lights on the ceiling for a moment. *Hmm.* I'd chalk it up to an insoluble mystery even though, deep down, I really wanted to believe that he was here, sending me his blessing.

The local news reporters were beginning to arrive. I eventually took my spot outside, smiling for the cameras alongside my family as we cut the ribbon, marking the grand opening.

Back inside, my father and Myra had just arrived, and I noticed them talking with Alexandra, who looked like she wanted to be anywhere else in the world but there. I made it a point to go over and break the ice until I was dragged away for some interviews.

The camera light stung my eyes as it shown over my face. Three reporters shoved their microphones in front of me. I heard one ask, "Tell us why you decided to open up the center, Mr. Truitt."

I cleared my throat and spoke from the heart.

"I wanted to give back to the community some of what Jelani had given me: a safe place to come and vent my frustrations and where I could also discover my creative potential. When I first came to him for help, it was for the wrong reasons. I was trying to use the *idea* of honing an obscure, artistic skill in order to woo a woman." I chuckled. "Over time, I realized that the art in and of itself was so much more important than I ever realized. It was saving me— saving me from my own mind and allowing me to express my feelings in other ways besides words. It was, in a sense, a spiritual experience. The wood whittling had started out as a joke, but it was Jelani's entire life, and I was beginning to see why. Some people express love through words. Others... through actions. And some...we express it through art. In essence, art is love. I wanted to share some of the love that my friend had given me, because I've been blessed with an abundance of love in my life right now." I smiled. "And I've become a damn good whittler, if I do say so myself. Let's just say, one or two of the animals displayed might be mine."

A camera flash nearly blinded me.

"Did you get the girl in the end, Mr. Truitt?"

I winked. "I did."

After my press obligations were finished, I rounded up Bandit to look for my girls. Noticing that Bianca had taken a seat in the corner with Georgina, I took a moment to stare at them.

"Look at them, Bandit. Look how beautiful. Can you believe they belong to us?"

I couldn't have possibly loved them more.

If there was one word to describe how I felt about my life now, it was gratitude. I was just so damn lucky to have this beautiful family. And I knew, without a shadow of a doubt, I would never take it for granted. The scare we had only made us stronger. There was nothing that made you appreciate someone more than almost losing them.

Bianca looked exhausted, and Georgina, whose cheeks looked like they were burning up, was coughing with a runny nose. I needed to get them home. If I was being honest, there was nothing I wanted more than to get out of here and spend a lazy Saturday lounging on the couch with my family.

I lifted Georgina out of Bianca's arms. "Let's go home."

Bandit took the opportunity to place his head in Bianca's lap. Between the three of us, she had her hands full.

"You can't just leave, can you?"

"I own the joint. I can do whatever I want. Things are winding down anyway."

After saying our goodbyes to my father and Myra, the four of us quietly snuck out and ventured down the hall.

As we entered the elevator, Georgina started to cry. Her medicine had worn off, and she was done, so ready for a nap. Bandit was barking as he often did whenever she cried, which clearly demonstrated why we weren't getting much sleep lately.

Right after the elevator doors closed, something unusual happened. The lights went out for about three seconds then came back on again before we finally began to descend.

Bianca chuckled. "Well, that wouldn't have been good."

"No, it wouldn't have. As much as I appreciate the reminder of how we met, I'm not sure I could handle two babies screaming at the top of their lungs at once."

She smacked me playfully. "You loved my balls and my screaming that day."

"I did. I loved your balls from the moment I first met you, and I especially loved your—"

"Be careful. She understands more than you think."

"Ruff!"

"So does he," I added.

We all packed into the waiting Town Car. After Bianca fastened Georgina into her car seat, our daughter was finally falling asleep.

Halfway into the ride home, it was actually quiet. A thought occurred to me as I turned to Bianca.

"You never told me what I was opening."

"What?"

"That fantasy from years back. You kept getting interrupted whenever you'd go to tell me about it." I rubbed her thigh. "What was it?"

"My fantasy at this very moment would be more along the lines of you *opening* a carton of ice cream and feeding it to me in bed while rubbing my feet. That sounds divine."

I bent my head back in laughter. "We can do that."

She ran her fingers through my hair. "Okay, you really want to know what it was?"

Leaning in, I growled, "Fuck yes."

"Okay, so it started with you opening my...shit!"

The Town Car came to a screeching halt. My arm instinctively reached out across Bianca's chest to protect her.

"Sorry about that, folks. Guy cut in front of me, so I had to slam on the brakes," Sam said.

And that was the end of our peaceful quiet time.

Georgina woke up and began crying hysterically.

I bent down to kiss her head. "Shh...it's okay." Taking out my phone, I quickly logged onto YouTube and pulled up the Chance Bateman channel. I scrolled down to the video of his baby girl laughing hysterically at the goat's noises, hoping it would help calm Georgina down.

She took my phone in her tiny hand, but it didn't help. She started to cry even harder.

"Ruff!"

Bianca chuckled, "That backfired. Now, we have a barking dog, a goat saying 'baa,' a baby laughing, and a baby crying."

The truth was, I couldn't imagine my life without chaos. Couldn't imagine my life without her, without them—without *this*.

"These are the sounds of life, Bianca." I beamed. "Music to my ears, Georgy Girls."

ACKNOWLEDGEMENTS

First and foremost, thank you to all of the bloggers who work so hard to help spread the word about our books. In an age where reach is tougher than ever, we are eternally grateful for all that you do.

To Julie – Thank you for your friendship and for always being just one click away when we need you. We look forward to the next journey your amazing writing will take us on this year.

To Elaine – Your edits undoubtedly made this project a better one. Thank you for your attention to detail and for your encouragement along the way.

To Luna – Your creativity and passion is a gift. We're so lucky that you have chosen to bestow it upon us through your gorgeous interpretations of our stories. Thank you for everything.

To Eda – Thank you for being such a great final set of eyes.

To Dani – Your help in organizing our releases and keeping everything in line is invaluable. We appreciate you very much!

To Letitia – Thank you for working your magic on yet another beautiful *Cocky Bastard* cover.

To our agent, Kimberly Brower – We are so lucky to know that you always have our backs. Thank you for working tirelessly for us and for being our liaison to the world.

Last but not least, to our readers – We keep writing because of your hunger for our stories. Thank you for your excitement, your love and support, and for the many goats posted on our Facebook walls. We adore you!

Much love,
Vi and Penelope

OTHER BOOKS BY
VI KEELAND & PENELOPE WARD

Playboy Pilot

Stuck-Up Suit

Cocky Bastard

OTHER BOOKS BY VI KEELAND